Fiona Leitch is a novelist and screenwriter with a chequered past. She's written for footballing and motoring magazines, childbirth videos and mail order catalogues; DJ'ed at illegal raves in London, been told off by a children's TV presenter during a studio debate; and was the Australasian face of a series of TV commercials for a cleaning product. All of which has given her a thorough grounding in the ridiculous, and helped her to write funny stuff.

facebook.com/fionakleitch

instagram.com/fionaleitchauthor

Also by Fiona Leitch

The Nosey Parker Cozy Mysteries

The Cornish Wedding Murder

The Cornish Village Murder

The Perfect Cornish Murder

A Cornish Christmas Murder

A Cornish Recipe for Murder

A Cornish Seaside Murder

The Cornish Campsite Murder

THE CORNISH CASTLE MURDER

A Nosey Parker Cozy Mystery

FIONA LEITCH

One More Chapter

a division of HarperCollins*Publishers* Ltd

1 London Bridge Street

London SE1 9GF

www.harpercollins.co.uk

HarperCollinsPublishers

Macken House, 39/40 Mayor Street Upper,

Dublin 1, Ireland, D01 C9W8

This paperback edition 2025

1

First published in Great Britain in ebook format
by HarperCollinsPublishers 2025

Copyright © Fiona Leitch 2025

Fiona Leitch asserts the moral right to be identified
as the author of this work

A catalogue record of this book is available from the British Library

ISBN: 978-0-00-864728-5

This novel is entirely a work of fiction. The names, characters and incidents portrayed in it are the work of the author's imagination. Any resemblance to actual persons, living or dead, events or localities is entirely coincidental.

Printed and bound in the UK using 100% Renewable Electricity
by CPI Group (UK) Ltd

All rights reserved. No part of this publication may be reproduced, stored in a retrieval system, or transmitted, in any form or by any means, electronic, mechanical, photocopying, recording or otherwise, without the prior permission of the publishers.

Without limiting the author's and publisher's exclusive rights, any unauthorised use of this publication to train generative artificial intelligence (AI) technologies is expressly prohibited. HarperCollins also exercise their rights under Article 4(3) of the Digital Single Market Directive 2019/790 and expressly reserve this publication from the text and data mining exception.

This book is dedicated to the love of my life, Dominic.
The day I married you was one of the best days of my life.
Not THE best, but definitely up there, near the top.

Top 5, at least.

Chapter One

'You know how I said we should just elope?' I asked, slipping my arm into Nathan's. 'I'm glad we didn't. I think...'

We were standing outside the venue for our imminent nuptials, gazing up at the stoney exterior in awe. Kervoy Castle was, well, not an actual castle, for starters – more like a massive country house with castle pretensions. It *did* have a crenellated tower, and a massive wooden front door big enough to drive a bus through, but it also had an Art Deco inspired brasserie, a swimming pool and luxury spa, and a golf course, the lush greens stretching down to the banks of a gently flowing river, stocked with trout for guests to catch. And it had enough bedrooms to accommodate all of our family and friends for a long weekend of pre-nuptial shenanigans, post-shenanigan relaxation and recuperation, and (finally) the small matter of the wedding itself.

My handsome fiancé smiled at me and leant in for a kiss.

'My mum and yours would never let us hear the end of it if we eloped,' he said. 'Mine was vocal enough when I told her we only wanted a registry office.'

'Yeah, I know,' I said, remembering the (somewhat passive-aggressive) Zoom 'discussion' with my mum-in-law-to-be, Liz, which had started with us telling her about our plans for a small, intimate wedding, and somehow ended with us booking a bloody castle instead. I *thought* I was glad we'd gone big, after all, but there was a large part of me that was absolutely terrified. Not at the thought of being married to Nathan – we'd been living together for a few years by then, and although Sensible Jodie kept telling herself if was just a piece of paper and would make no difference, Romantic Jodie kept going *squeee!* at the thought of being Mrs Nathan Withers. Not that I was taking his surname, partly for feminist reasons but mostly because it was awful. No, I was terrified of walking down the aisle in my fancy frock, tripping over my own feet, and ending up face first in the massive floral arrangement at the end. Probably with my skirt rucked up and my bottom, clad in big knickers to avoid VPL (visible panty line), on show to the congregation. Not that I'd lain in bed worst-case-scenario-ising and imagining everything that could go wrong.

I took a deep breath to steady my nerves. Nathan squeezed my hand.

'You okay? No last-minute nerves?'

'Plenty of those,' I said, 'but no regrets or changing my mind.'

'Thank god for that, because I don't think we'd get our deposit back now.' Nathan laughed as I nudged him indignantly. 'Oh alright, I'm relieved because I can't wait to marry you.' I sighed happily and snuggled into him. 'Although we could've used that money to buy a new car...'

'You're such a romantic,' I said, rolling my eyes.

'Who's a romantic?' asked Mum, popping up next to us. Daisy arrived next, panting slightly as she pulled a massive wheelie suitcase along behind her.

'Blimey, Nana, what have you got in this case?' she puffed, hoisting her own overnight bag over her shoulder.

'I'm Mother of the Bride, I am,' said Mum. 'I gotta look me best. I'm hoping the best man's a looker.'

'Mother!'

'Nana!'

'Sorry, Shirley,' said Nathan. 'I've ended up with two best men, and they're both taken.' Nathan's right-hand man, DS Matt Turner, had taken on most of the best man duties, helping to organise the stag do that would be taking place that night, and helping Nathan choose his wedding suit. He would be joined by one of Nathan's older friends, Craig, who was flying over specially from New York. He and Nathan had worked together back in Liverpool. He'd been part of an exchange programme with NYC's finest, but after falling for a local woman he'd decided to stay there. Matt had been like an excited, eager puppy when Nathan had asked him to help organise things, but a bit put out when he heard that he was only *a* best man, not *the* best man, and I got the feeling he was ready to be unimpressed with Craig, when he finally turned up. Talking of whom...

Nathan glanced at his phone as a text message arrived on it with a *ping!* 'Craig's through Customs and is on his way,' he said, relief evident on his face. 'I thought he was winding me up when he said he'd missed his flight.'

'He'll be here in time,' I said, giving him a squeeze. 'It's what, five hours to get here from Gatwick? He's just lucky he got on another flight.'

'He's lucky he got an invite,' grumbled Mum. 'Your Aunty Wendy would love this place, and your cousin Kevin—'

'Mother, when was the last time you saw Aunty Wendy?' I said, exasperated. We'd gone over this several times already. 'You've never got on with her, not even when Uncle Bob was still alive.' Bob had been Mum's big brother. He'd moved away from Cornwall as soon as he'd been old enough, and although they'd still been on friendly terms, he and my mum hadn't really stayed in touch other than the odd phone call and getting together at Christmas. Aunty Wendy was alright but she wasn't very affectionate or demonstrative, which couldn't be more different to my mum, who enjoyed a good cuddle and who wouldn't let us leave the house (even to nip down the corner shop) without a kiss goodbye.

'Well, alright, but Kevin...'

'Is Kevin the one with the stinky breath?' asked Daisy, innocently.

'That's him,' I said. 'We couldn't invite him, we've got

floral arrangements for the wedding and his halitosis would knock 'em over from twenty paces.'

Nathan struggled to suppress a laugh, but Mum managed to look affronted. 'Poor Kevin, he can't help it. Do you remember his wedding? Proper posh, that was. And there was Wendy dressed up like a dog's dinner, all fur coat and no knickers.'

'Is *that* what you've got in this bloody case?' asked Daisy.

'Might be,' said Mum, sniffily. 'Although I'll be wearing *my* knickers.'

'They must be what weighs so much,' I said. 'Come on, let's check in!'

Stepping inside the hotel was like entering Camelot. The glass entrance doors opened onto a grand, somewhat cavernous medieval-style hall. Above us was a high, galleried ceiling, with enormous wooden beams crisscrossing the room. What looked to me like the biggest chandelier in the world hung from a beam, a sparkling mass of crystal droplets cascading down towards the floor, the flagstones polished and worn by thousands of pairs of shoes over the years. Thick rugs made it feel warm, the rich colours contrasting with the grey stone of the floor. In front of us, a row of tall but narrow arched windows overlooked the grounds, each tiny leaded pane twinkling in the sunlight but not actually letting much of it in. To one side, taking up most of one wall, was a massive stone fireplace. There were still plenty of old cottages in Penstowan that had inglenook fireplaces, but none on even half this scale; this one was so big, had it been in London an estate agent would be sticking a bed and a kettle in there and trying to rent it to someone as a studio flat for £1,200 per calendar month. Above it rose a tall stone chimney breast, decorated with pennants bearing heraldic crests. Large iron candle sconces stood on the wall either side of the fireplace, although they were clearly for show rather than use. An occasional table stood underneath each one, with a couple of intricate stained-glass Tiffany lamps throwing out a warm glow that transformed the otherwise dim room into a cosy haven. As cosy as a space that big could feel, anyway.

On a day like today, of course, with the temperature being in the high twenties, there was no fire lit, but I could just imagine being cuddled up with Nathan on one of the deep, sumptuous velvet sofas in front of it on a winter's night, the shadow of the flames dancing across the hearth, preferably with a selection of classy nibbles and a bone china pot of tea on the mahogany coffee table in front of it, with a butler on hand to cater to our every whim. I am a woman of simple pleasures; most of them involve food, drink, and Nathan.

When we'd first come to look at the hotel, I'd been expecting a pastiche, almost a Disneyfied version of an English castle. The rich landowner and industrialist, Sir Humphrey Compton, had built it around two hundred years ago, having spent his boyhood reading about knights and kings and wanting to live in a castle. Not having the wherewithal to buy a genuine one, he'd damn well gone and built his own, and over the years – most noticeably in the 1920s, when it had been sold by his impoverished descendants to another rich industrialist, this time a local newspaper magnate – all the mod cons demanded by early twentieth-century toffs had been added. But it had been done sympathetically and, it was obvious, with no expense spared. It might have central heating – not something found in most medieval castles – but it still had character, and charm, and elegance. Put simply, it was one of the most beautiful buildings I'd ever been in, and certainly the most expensive hotel I'd ever stayed in.

We were met in the wood-panelled reception area by Arabella, the hotel's wedding planner. She was lovely, if a little over-enthusiastic, and I made a mental note not to get too drunk at my hen party that night, because dealing with her the next day whilst hungover and physically fragile would be a nightmare.

'Welcome to Kervoy Castle!' she cried, flinging her arms open wide. I thought for a moment she was going to attempt to encompass all of us in one massive hug, but she settled for giving me a quick squeeze and then Nathan a much longer one. Nathan looked at me over her shoulder, eyebrows raised and a 'save me' expression on his face. She released him and stood back to look at us. 'Lovely to see the happy couple again. And, of course, the mother of the bride. And this is…?'

'Daughter of the bride,' said Daisy, stepping back in case Arabella tried to hug her, too.

'Oh yes, that's right.' Arabella nodded, smiling brightly. 'Let's get you all checked into your rooms, and then we can go over the arrangements for the weekend again.'

We were happy to escape her well-meaning ministrations, but before we could, Nathan and I were accosted by the hotel manager, Mr Robbins.

'Miss Parker, Mr Withers,' he said, with a smile that was probably meant to be ingratiating but was bordering on smug. 'Welcome to Kervoy Castle. We're so looking forward to hosting your wedding. Do please let me know if there's anything you require to make the weekend extra special.' He clicked his fingers at the smartly dressed young man standing by the door. 'Clive, cases please.' Clive obediently stepped forward and relieved Daisy of my mother's heavy suitcase, his pleasant smile faltering for a second under the unexpected strain.

'Thank you,' said Nathan. 'That's very kind.' *Not THAT kind*, I thought, bearing in mind the eye-watering sum we'd forked out. I smiled and turned away, but Mr Robbins was not letting us go that easily.

'I wondered… I believe that you and several of your party are involved in law enforcement, yes?' he asked. Nathan and I exchanged a 'here we go' look.

'We're off duty,' said Nathan politely. 'We're getting married.'

'Oh yes, yes, absolutely, and I wouldn't want anything

to get in the way of that,' said Robbins. 'I was just wondering if I could pick your brains about something?'

Nathan plastered on a smile. 'Well, I can certainly try to give you some advice...'

'Thank you. If we could just...?' Robbins gestured for us to move to a discreet corner, where a highly polished round table sat, surrounded by four richly upholstered chairs. He pulled a chair out for me, and then one for Nathan, and then sat down himself. Daisy looked quite put out at being so obviously dismissed. I shrugged.

'Go on, sweetheart, we'll follow you up.'

There was a large crystal vase on the table, holding an impressive floral display of lilies, and they almost completely blocked the manager from view. 'Before I start,' the vase of lilies said, 'can I count on you to keep this to yourselves?'

'Of course,' said Nathan, reaching out to move the flowers so we could see him. I snorted back a laugh.

'Soul of discretion, me,' said Mum. I rolled my eyes at her until she got the message and left, grumbling to herself. 'I'll just go then, shall I? Never mind me...'

I turned to Mr Robbins with an apologetic smile. 'Sorry about that. What were you going to say?'

'It's rather embarrassing,' said Robbins. 'I've always prided myself on my ability to hire only the highest-calibre staff for this hotel.' The truth of this statement was rather called into question by the appearance of a second young male concierge entering through the front door, sniffing and wiping his nose on the sleeve of his uniform. He was lucky he hadn't been around to give poor Clive a hand, because my mum would've had something to say about his unsanitary habits. 'But we appear to have a thief, or thieves, amongst us.'

'Really?' said Nathan. 'What's been taken? Guests' belongings?'

'No no, nothing like that, otherwise, of course, I would've informed the police officially. No, hotel property.'

'Such as?' Nathan prompted.

'Toilet rolls, soap, cleaning products, that kind of thing,' said Robbins, looking horrified at the thought of someone making off with his stash of Andrex.

'Right…' said Nathan, attempting to sound sympathetic. After all, it *was* still theft, even if the swag wasn't exactly the Crown Jewels, and as a police officer he was supposed to take this stuff seriously. I, however, wasn't a police officer anymore.

'Isn't petty pilfering pretty much a part of running a hotel?' I asked. 'I know it's annoying, and it's stealing, but more or less every business that hires minimum-wage staff has this kind of thing going on. If it's not loo roll it's printer paper or tea bags or pens or whatever.'

'So I'm supposed to just turn a blind eye to it?' Robbins looked even more horrified.

'Well – yeah. Or pay your staff enough that they don't feel the need to nick the essentials from you,' I said, which in retrospect wasn't the most diplomatic thing to say. Nathan groaned and held up a hand before I or Mr Robbins could say anything else.

'I would just like to point out that Jodie isn't a police officer anymore, and that her views do not represent those of the Devon and Cornwall Constabulary,' he said, giving me a look which meant *Behave yourself!* I recognised it because it was the same look I'd just given my mother. 'I do, however, think she has a point – about it being a widespread problem that's not easy to solve. Do you have CCTV cameras around the building? Can you see who's behind the thefts, or do you have any idea?'

Robbins shook his head. 'We do have some cameras, but not many, as we need to respect our guests' privacy. It's a fine line between making them feel safe, and making them feel like they're being spied on. As for who's doing it...' He shook his head. 'Housekeeping are the ones who have the most opportunity, of course, but they're not the only members of staff to have access to supplies.'

'Okay...' Nathan looked thoughtful. 'And of course you don't want to call the police in and come across as heavy handed, or risk it getting out and ruining the hotel's reputation?' Robbins shook his head again. 'Then really all I can suggest is limiting the number of people who have access to the supply cupboard.'

'Can I make a suggestion?' I asked. Robbins looked at me, a little hostile, while Nathan gave me another *Behave yourself!* 'Have you spoken to your staff about this?'

'No, I haven't.'

'Then maybe you should. Hold a staff meeting and tell everyone that you know the cost of living is really high at the moment, and that if anyone is struggling to make ends meet they should come and talk to you. Tell them that you're aware that certain things are regularly going missing, and that it needs to stop. But you are going to turn a blind eye to what's already been taken, and your staff are always welcome to ask for help if they need it.'

'And that's it?' he asked.

'Not quite. Tell them how much you appreciate them and their hard work. Maybe give them a little bonus at the end of the season, or a gift or something – a few drinks and some nice food – just to show them that you care about them.' I smiled. 'A cash bonus is always better, of course.'

'You want me to pay people to stop stealing from me?' He looked incredulous.

'Look at it this way: it probably wouldn't cost you much more to give them a bonus at the end of the summer season – or even a little pay rise – than it's costing you now through the thefts. But you'll end up with happier staff. Happier staff work better, have fewer sick days, and are less likely to leave you in the lurch.' I stood up. 'Business Management 101. Now if you don't mind, we've got a wedding to prepare for.'

Nathan grinned at me and stood up too. Robbins stayed in his seat, looking a little dazed.

'That sounds like a good plan to me, Mr Robbins,' said Nathan. He took my hand and we headed towards the foyer's grand staircase.

'Don't you want to use the lift?' I asked. He shook his head.

'No, I want him to watch you sweep up the stairs

majestically, like an absolute queen.' I laughed and pulled him towards me for a kiss, and we fled to our respective hotel rooms before Mr Robbins could ask us to solve any more crimes. The cheek of it! On our wedding weekend!

When we'd been working out what to book, Nathan and I had fully intended to share a room for the whole weekend, but everyone (apart from Daisy but including Arabella and even *Debbie*, who I'd thought would be far too sensible for such superstitious nonsense) had had kittens at the thought of the bride and groom seeing each other the night before the wedding, never mind that we'd seen each other every night for the last couple of years. Mum wanted a room on her own, although all of the rooms were twin or double. I'd persuaded her that she should share with Daisy, but then my daughter had kicked up a stink about Mum's snoring, which to be fair was very loud and bore a marked similarity to a rusty chainsaw. It wasn't fair to inflict that particular nocturnal treat on anyone, so Mum was going to spend the whole weekend in solitary splendour, while I shared an ordinary twin-bedded room with Daisy on the Friday and Saturday nights. Nathan had somehow managed to bag the honeymoon suite all to himself until Sunday night, although it was on the same floor as mine and Daisy's room, so I envisaged myself sneaking along the corridor to him when everyone was asleep…

Our room was lovely, with a beautiful view out of the window across the manicured lawn and down to the stream. Daisy plopped herself onto one of the beds and nodded approvingly, bouncing up and down on her bottom and smoothing the crisp Egyptian cotton bed linen with her hand.

'Nice…' She looked around the room. 'It's proper posh, innit?' She shuddered. 'Oh my God, I sounded like Nana then. I'm turning Cornish.'

I laughed. 'You've still got a London accent, but I have noticed a few West Countryisms sneaking in…' I reached out and picked up an expensive-looking vase from the white marble mantlepiece over the open fire, turning it over in my hands. It shone like highly polished stone and was cool and tactile, and while I knew nothing at all about art, it felt expensive, much like everything else in this room. 'No wonder they wouldn't let us bring Germaine. Look at that rug! Persian. She'd have pooped on that in no time. She's no good with rugs.'

'Poor Germaine, locked up in doggy prison,' said Daisy.

'I don't think the Tiddys' B&B counts as doggy prison,' I said. 'Maggie Tiddy loves Germaine, she'll be spoilt rotten and won't want to leave.' I put the vase back and picked up the bag which contained my wedding dress. I hung it over a hook on the back of the door and unzipped it, shaking the dress free so any creases would fall out of it by Sunday. I felt Daisy join me and stand there in quiet contemplation of what had to be the most beautiful gown I'd ever owned. I still couldn't quite believe I was going to wear it in a couple of days.

'You're going to look amazing,' said Daisy, sighing. I reached out and put my arm round her.

'Thank you. Aunty Wendy would have a thing or two to say about the colour, though.' We both laughed.

'Aunty Wendy can get stuffed,' said Daisy.

'Language!' I said. 'That's *Great*-Aunty Wendy, not Aunty… Come on,' I said, 'let's go and see the honeymoon suite…'

The honeymoon suite was (fittingly) even more luxurious than our room. Nathan opened the door to us with a big grin on his face and stood aside to let us in.

'Welcome to the marital boudoir,' he said, with a sweeping gesture to the ornately carved four-poster bed in the middle of the room. It was huge, three pillows wide in fact, although there were at least eight of them on the bed along with a gold velvet throw and a pair of kissing swans formed out of bath towels. On the floor, another glorious Persian rug lay in luxurious contrast against the dark mahogany-stained floorboards, which shone like the highly polished timbers of an expensive yacht. Yeah, I was impressed.

Daisy shuddered. 'Don't *ever* use that word again,' she said.

'What, welcome?'

'No… *boudoir*. It gives me these… mental images…'

I skipped over to the grand bay window (I'm not making this up, I actually skipped, I was that excited), which was framed on either side by rich, damask drapes. Below us was a terrace, set with wrought-iron tables and chairs. On each table was a small terracotta pot, planted with lavender. Dotted all around the terrace were much larger planters, all moss-covered stone and terracotta, potted up with more lavender and rosemary. It would smell as wonderful as it looked, sitting at one of those tables in the sunshine. Beyond the terrace was a classical, formal garden; flower beds full of jewel-coloured blooms bisected by pathways lined with topiary, box plants cut into the shapes of chess pieces, which met at a stone circle in the centre. A tall statue of a mythical creature playing a pipe or flute stood at its core.

'I want that in our garden,' I said, as Nathan joined me and slipped an arm around my waist.

'You don't want much, do you? I can't promise I can recreate it *exactly*,' said Nathan, grinning, 'but we can pop down to B&Q after the honeymoon…'

'What honeymoon?' I said, pointedly.

'I know, I know. We will go away, I promise.'

'It doesn't matter,' I said. 'The important thing is we're getting married! Once I've got a ring on my finger I can officially let myself go.'

'I didn't realise you were waiting,' murmured Daisy.

'Cheeky! It's not too late for me to find a new bridesmaid, you know…'

But Daisy's demotion from bridesmaid (as if I would!) would have to wait, as our guests had started to arrive.

Chapter Two

'I hope I'm not going to end up as referee,' said Nathan. We were back in the honeymoon suite, having sneaked off to spend a bit of time together before our respective hen and stag parties took place.

Nathan's parents, Liz and Roger, had arrived from Crosby, Roger dragging a suitcase that was even heavier than Mum's. I'd been relieved to discover that (passive-aggressive Zoom discussions about wedding arrangements notwithstanding) I got on well with both of them – my mother-in-law from my first marriage had been an absolute harridan – and I could see where Nathan got his sense of humour, his pragmatic approach to life and his kindness from. After that came two of his friends and ex-colleagues from his old nick in Liverpool, Ben and Danny. Nathan had warned me they were both real 'scallies', and going by the (almost incomprehensible to me) Scouse banter that they greeted Nathan with, I could see what he meant. I thought they were probably nice enough and a lot of fun, but after twenty minutes in their presence I started to get a headache. When Tony, my oldest friend in the world, arrived (we'd sat together on our first day at primary school and had been in each other's lives ever since), he'd said hello to the two men and they'd briefly chatted about football, which amused me because I knew Tony wasn't really into it and only watched the England team playing in World Cup games, and then he'd made an excuse and wandered off to talk to Debbie, who had turned up not long after we had. She was taking her duties as Matron of Honour very seriously, even though I hadn't asked her to be one; it all felt a bit too formal to me, although I supposed we *were* getting married in a flipping massive country house, so she was probably right to assume the mantle of chief bridesmaid.

Craig had finally arrived not long after Matt, who had been manning the police fort back in Penstowan all day. To say the two best men had not immediately hit it off would be an understatement. Craig had been exhausted, which was understandable after a long flight followed by a long drive, but also irritable in a slightly aggressive kind of way which took me by surprise. His mood seemed to infect the whole group. Even Debbie's husband Callum, who was the sort of person who got on with everybody, had kept his distance from the incomers.

'Referee?' I said. 'What do you mean?', but I knew what he was getting at. I'd half-expected Matt to be a bit resentful of his co-best man, but it wasn't just him and Craig; it was all of them.

'The great North–South divide,' said Nathan. 'Is it just me, or do all of my Liverpudlian friends hate all of my Cornish ones?'

'I think hate's a bit strong. Despise, maybe…'

Nathan laughed. 'And that's better, is it?'

'No, not really.' I sighed. 'I think maybe they think we're country bumpkins, and to be fair some of us are, a bit. Penstowan's not exactly cosmopolitan, is it? And Matt and Tony have lived here all their lives.'

'Yeah, but Danny and Ben have lived in Liverpool or thereabouts all *their* lives, so they can't really judge.'

'No, but… They're just different, that's all.'

'Yeah. Ben's a good bloke, he's easy to get on with. Danny's alright too if you give him a chance, he just goes on sometimes like he's "The Man". They've both had my back on more than one occasion in the past.'

'Yeah, I know.'

'And I couldn't really invite one without inviting the other. The four of us all went through police college at the same time, went our different ways for a few years and then ended up at the same nick. They're all good blokes. I only hope that Matt gets over himself and tries to get on with Craig.'

'Hmm…' I said, trying to sound noncommittal, because I was thinking *The problem ain't with Matt…* Nathan looked at me.

'What's "hmm" mean?'

'Well… Matt's got a point. How hard is it to get to the airport on time?' Nathan opened his mouth to defend Craig, but then closed it again. 'And then the business with the clothes. We purposely made your groomsmen's outfits generic grey suits, so they didn't have to go out and buy anything fancy or try to co-ordinate with each other. It's not like we wanted him to wear a morning suit and a top hat or anything.' Nathan shuddered at the thought; although he looked good (or great) in a suit, he drew the line at anything *that* formal, and I agreed with him. 'And then Craig turns up looking like he hasn't had a wash in about a week and he tells me he hasn't even brought a shirt with him.' Nathan opened his mouth again, but I spoke again before he could. 'And *then* he tries to make it sound like I'm some kind of Bridezilla, even though all I did was say he'd have time to pop into Truro and buy one before the ceremony on Sunday.'

'I know,' Nathan admitted. 'I told him he was out of order, and he apologised.'

'Not to me, he didn't.'

'He will. No one upsets my bird.' I laughed as he pulled me into his arms. 'I'm sorry, I don't know what's going on with him. He's never been rude to you before, has he? Whenever we've FaceTimed him the two of you have got on really well.'

'Do you think it's got anything to do with Nicky?' I asked, thoughtfully. Nicky was Craig's fiancée, a native New Yorker who none of us had met yet, and we'd been looking forward to finally meeting her. 'Only we did invite her as well, and of course she's not come…'

'She doesn't know us,' Nathan pointed out. 'It's a long

way to come for a long weekend, to watch two people you don't really know get married.'

'Yeah, I suppose so.' I looked up at him and gave him a peck on the lips. 'Anyway, my hens will be waiting in the cocktail bar for me. Do you know what your stags have got planned for you?'

'We're just having a few drinks in Ben and Danny's room,' said Nathan. 'I told Matt I didn't want anything too mad, because we've got loads of activities planned for tomorrow and I don't want a massive hangover.'

'Quiet night in with the lads?'

'Yeah.' We both paused for a moment and then laughed. 'Yeah, I don't think it'll be *that* quiet, but hopefully having it here means I won't end up naked and chained to a lamp post on the high street.'

'Never mind,' I said. 'I'll pop along afterwards and see if we can rectify that.'

'There aren't any lamp posts in here,' said Nathan, giving me a cheeky grin that made me go all hot and wonder if we could cancel our respective parties and just celebrate on our own.

'We'll just have to work with what we've got…'

So I wandered down to the cocktail bar, where Mum, Daisy, Debbie and Liz were waiting. I had more friends coming – I wasn't a complete saddo, with all the guests being relatives… Carmen, Tony's partner, was coming for the party but not staying overnight, as she had another wedding to officiate the next day, before coming back to do ours on Sunday. She was sharing a minibus with three of my old school friends, Nina, Lily and Louise, who again weren't staying but would be back on Sunday for the ceremony.

'Here she is!' cried Mum, waving a brightly coloured drink in my honour and swaying to the music playing on the sound system – a mix of 70s and 80s disco classics, which felt a bit incongruous in the glamorous Art Deco bar, which was all shiny chrome, opaline glass globe lamps, and geometric patterns. Daisy ducked as a cocktail stick bearing a glacé cherry and a small paper umbrella veered dangerously close to her eye. Debbie reached for the bottle of bubbly on the bar, poured some into a crystal champagne coupe glass and passed it to me.

'Get that down you and let's get this party started before your mother ends up in hospital with alcohol poisoning,' she said. Daisy rolled her eyes.

'God, old people are *so* embarrassing,' she said. 'I had to persuade Nana not to climb up on the table when they started playing "I Will Survive".'

'Don't be a spoilsport,' I said, sipping what turned out to be a rather nice champagne. 'Let her have her fun.'

'It's alright for you, I'm having to do this sober,' she said, eyeing the bottle on the bar hopefully. I laughed.

'Alright, just a small glass,' I said, pouring her some. 'If we were at home you could have more, but you're still under the legal drinking age…'

'Only just,' she said, but she didn't complain too much in case I took the glass away from her again.

By the time the rest of the party had turned up, Mum had been warned by the barman about standing on the table (twice), Daisy had had two small glasses of champagne and was giggling to herself (*No more for her*, I thought), and Liz had flirted shamelessly with a group of extremely drunk and rather younger golfers (who were there for a lads' weekend celebrating someone's birthday) while Debbie and I watched in awe. Liz sat down, gave a discreet little burp and said, 'And *that's* how we did it in my day.'

Carmen looked at Liz, then at me, then laughed. 'And we were worried on the way here that you'd get bored waiting for us.'

From there, of course, there was only one way the party was going, and that was downhill. The barman cut us off at midnight; the bar staff had started to put the chairs up on the tables, and they obviously wanted us out of there. The golfers put up a spirited argument about why we should all be allowed to stay in the bar for another hour (their mate Stuart would only be fifty-five once, after all), but eventually they accepted defeat and left. Daisy had lost interest an hour or so earlier, after I'd put my foot down about her drinking; she'd gone up to our room to FaceTime with her boyfriend, Joe, who was coming to the wedding but who (for some reason…) had chosen not to spend his Friday night getting drunk with a load of old people. I'd managed to rustle up some bar food and had been stuffing my face with chicken wings (alcohol makes me ravenous), so I was relatively sober, as was Carmen, because no one wants a hungover vicar officiating on their big day. The minibus home was booked for midnight, so she, Nina, Lily and Louise drove off, and I suggested that we call it a night too.

'We've only just got started!' protested Debbie, even though I pointed out that we'd been drinking since seven and 'just got started' was completely inaccurate.

'I bet that husband-to-be of yours is still having fun,' said Mum, slyly. 'You know what I think we should do?'

'Gatecrash the stag do!' cried everyone else. Mum looked a bit put out.

'Well, yeah,' she said. 'That was my idea.'

'What room are they in?' asked Debbie.

'Ben and Danny's,' I said before I could stop myself, because I didn't really want to gatecrash Nathan's stag do. What happens on the stag do, stays on the stag do…

Luckily no one knew what number room they were in, but unluckily, as we headed upstairs, it became immediately apparent by the noise. Debbie whooped and led us down the wood-panelled corridor to the room at the end, where the sound of loud music came pumping out. I hoped they weren't disturbing the other guests, but then we had booked most of the other rooms on the same floor, and the golfers were probably drunk enough not to care if Nathan and his mates got a bit rowdy.

Debbie slipped off her high heels and rapped on the door, while the others pushed me forward as it was my hen do, after all. Mum giggled.

'Are all Nathan's friends coppers?' she asked.

'Yes, why?'

As the door started to open, Mum took a deep breath and said loudly, "Ello, 'ello, 'ello, what's going on 'ere, then?' And then stopped, shocked.

'Who are you?' asked the scantily clad young woman in the open doorway.

Chapter Three

We all stood in shocked silence for a moment, until I recovered enough to splutter, 'Never mind who I am, who the bloody hell are you?'

Behind the young woman, over the sound of loud music, I heard male laughter and a Scouse accent saying, 'Uh-oh, youse in trouble now, lad!'

Tony and Nathan appeared at the door. Tony bundled the girl away, somehow managing to touch as little of her exposed skin as possible in the process, while Nathan gave me a guilty smile.

'What the—' I started.

'Jodie, babe…' Nathan stepped out into the hallway and tried to shut the door behind him, but Debbie was already there, sticking her foot in the gap and shoving it hard.

'Callum Roberts, you'd better not have your grubby hands on some half-dressed floozy!' she called, storming in. Nathan winced.

'It's not what it looks like,' he said.

'Good, because it looks bad,' I said.

'I know. The lads organised it…' He looked at me helplessly as I pushed past him – gently, because as bad as it looked having a semi-naked woman answering the door, I couldn't imagine him and his mates having an orgy or anything.

Inside, there were two more scantily dressed young ladies, serving drinks and canapés. Matt was chatting excitedly to one of them as she poured him a drink – obviously not his first or even his fifth, by the state of him. He looked over and saw me, and his face dropped.

'Don't tell Chrissie!' he said quickly, and I laughed.

'Mate, you're lucky she was on duty tonight and couldn't come,' I said. I turned to look at Nathan. 'Semi-naked waitresses? Classy.'

'They were meant to be topless,' blurted Matt. Nathan groaned.

'Yeah, thanks for that,' he said. 'I'm sorry, babe, the lads organised it for a laugh, but to be honest it made everyone feel a bit uncomfortable, so I told them to put their bras back on.'

'Like heck you did,' I said.

'He had to,' said Tony. 'We thought Roger was going to have a heart attack when that blonde one picked up the cocktail shaker and started making a martini.'

'I was shaken *and* stirred,' said my future father-in-law, who'd obviously recovered his equilibrium.

Meanwhile, Mum and Liz had bustled their way in, Liz

shaking her head at her husband (although to be fair, she had been chatting up the golfers earlier) and Mum staring at one of the girls' underwear.

'Mother!' I hissed. 'Show a bit of decorum!'

'Don't mind me,' she said to the young lady. 'I were just admiring your knickers. I bet you didn't get undies like *that* at Marks and Sparks.'

'Ann Summers,' said the girl. Mum nodded wisely.

'Yeah, that used to be my shop of choice whenever I, you know, wanted to put on a bit of a show for my hubby.'

'Oh my God,' I said. Thank goodness Daisy had gone to bed, she was far too young to be imagining her grandmother in red satin French knickers. So was I. Nathan took me to one side.

'I'm actually really glad you're here,' he said. 'It was a laugh when they first turned up, but it's all gone a bit—'

'Seedy?'

'Well, I wouldn't have gone *that* far, but I have to admit you're the only woman I want to see prancing about in her underwear, serving me drinks…'

'In your dreams,' I scoffed. 'The serving you drinks bit, anyway. The rest sounds fine to me…' He laughed and pulled me in for a kiss.

'Am I off the hook, then?' he asked. I nodded.

'Yeah… I trust you.'

'Good.'

'And I'd be a total hypocrite if I didn't, because you should've seen the male stripper Debbie booked for me.'

Debbie looked up from where she was sitting next to

Callum, who was quite red in the face – I wasn't sure if it was from embarrassment, over-excitement, or because she'd just given him an earful.

'Phwoar, yeah! Those tight trousers with the quick-release Velcro were the absolute *business*. He looked like Thor, after dance lessons from Magic Mike,' she said, giggling. Nathan raised an eyebrow.

'Yeah alright, there was no male stripper, although I reckon if we'd left your mum alone with the other guests for much longer she'd have had someone's shirt off,' I said. 'And I thought *my* mum was bad.'

'Oh God, there were other guests? Are they likely to sue her for sexual harassment?'

'Oh no, the main one she was targeting thought it was his birthday.' I frowned. 'Actually I think it *was* his birthday because he kept talking about unwrapping her. I think he thought his mates had booked her as a Cougar-a-Gram.'

Nathan shuddered. 'Now you know why Shirley's antics don't throw me. My mum honed her flirting skills over all those years of running a pub. She said they sold more alcohol that way.'

There was a loud knock on the door.

'I'll get it,' said Matt. 'Have a drink, Jodie, enjoy yourself.'

'I am going to have to ask you to keep the noise down,' said a voice at the door. I looked over. Another young woman – fully dressed this time, in a smart hotel uniform – stood in the doorway. 'Please be considerate of the other guests, as it's now past midnight.'

'Of course, yes, sorry,' said Matt.

'What can I get you?' asked one of the waitresses politely, approaching us. 'There's beer or whisky.' The woman at the door, who I assumed must be the night manager or something, peered around Matt and saw the waitress. Her eyebrows shot up so high in surprise that they almost flew off her head and went into orbit. She set her mouth in a thin, disapproving line, and I had to admit I didn't entirely blame her.

'You are aware that there are rules about having non-hotel "staff" in your room?' she asked icily, in a tone that made it quite clear exactly what type of working girls she thought these were.

'What? Oh no, sorry, they're just serving drinks. It's my mate's stag do. I did clear it with the manager,' said Matt, although it looked like a drunken bluff to me.

'Right, well... Please just keep the noise down, then.' With a last look at the waitress, the woman left. Matt shut the door.

'We need to turn the music dow—' he started, but Danny stood up waving his beer and roared, 'Send in the strippers!'

Nathan facepalmed while Matt tried to shush Danny, but Ben and everyone else started laughing, and after a while Nathan did, too. He turned to the girl who was still waiting to take my order, who hadn't found that remark funny at all.

'Sorry about that,' he said. 'He doesn't come this far

south very often, I think the change in altitude affects his IQ. Jodie, did you want anything?'

'No, I'm good, thank you,' I said. The girl smiled at me and wandered off. I looked around the room. 'How's the North-South divide been?' I asked, lowering my voice. 'Broken up any fights?'

'Not amongst the lads, no…'

'Not amongst the lads? Amongst who, then?' I lowered my voice even further. 'Not the girls? They didn't have a bitch fight about who'd get to make Roger his cocktail?'

'Ha! Of course not. No, it was Craig…' Nathan looked uncomfortable. I looked around the room again, but there was no sign of Nathan's other best man.

'Where is he? What did he do?'

'Made a bloody nuisance of himself with one of the girls,' said Matt, who might have been drunk but was still sober enough to complain about the behaviour of his perceived rival for Nathan's best-friend status. 'The redhead one, over there.' He nodded towards the girl who had previously poured him a drink. 'Proper shook up, she was.'

'So you've been comforting her? You're very noble.'

'I am.' Matt burped. Nathan rolled his eyes.

'I don't know about being shaken up – I reckon she's probably used to it. But he was out of order. He basically asked her if drinks were the only thing on the menu tonight.'

'Eww…' I grimaced. 'What *is* up with him? Or is this what he's normally like? I only know him from our Zoom conversations, and he's obviously not going to talk to me like that, not in front of you.'

'It's been a long time since I've actually been out with him, or any of the lads, but no, this is not what he's normally like.' Nathan glanced over at Ben and Danny, who were dancing with one of the waitresses and getting pretty close to her. He bent down to murmur in my ear. 'I think it was a show of bravado in front of those two.'

'Why would he do that?'

'They were winding him up, saying he'll be next...' Nathan noticed my confused expression. 'The next one to get married. The next one to be a henpecked husband.'

'Is that what they think you are? Henpecked?'

'Probably.' He smiled as my expression turned from confusion into outrage. 'Ben's forty years old and never had a serious relationship in his life, and Danny's got kids with two different women, neither of whom want anything to do with him, so I'm not exactly taking their advice to heart.'

'Fair enough. I'm just surprised Craig would take any notice of them, in that case. Where is he?'

'Sleeping it off in his room, with any luck. He was absolutely steaming when he propositioned her, so even if she had been up for any "extras" he wouldn't have been capable.'

'Right,' said Debbie, coming up behind me and making me jump. 'Party in your room.'

'Daisy's in there,' I said.

'Okay, party in your mum's room. I've put the fear of God into Callum, so we can go now.'

There was a loud knock on the door, although it was less of a knock and more of a furious banging.

'Probably that concierge woman coming back to tell us to turn the music down again,' said Nathan. He walked over and opened the door. 'Sorry, I'll get them to—'

'Where is she?' shouted the man in the doorway. Nathan involuntarily took a step backwards in surprise.

'What? Who?'

'Don't play innocent with me, you—' The man swore at Nathan and pushed his way into the room aggressively. The redhead, who had been about to pour Mum a whisky (although heaven only knew why, because Mum hated it), gasped and dropped the bottle. It didn't smash, but lay on its side on the thick carpet, glugging quietly.

'Frankie!' she said, looking around wildly as if searching for a way out without having to go near him.

'You f—!' The man – Frankie – swore again, calling her a really horrible name. A gasp of shock rang through the room, and Nathan and Ben immediately stepped forward to place themselves in front of him. The rest of us gathered around the poor girl.

'Alright, mate, that's enough of that,' said Ben. Frankie ignored him.

'Kel, get your clothes on. NOW,' he ordered. Mum put a protective hand out in front of the girl.

'You don't have to do anything you don't want to,' she said, and I felt an immense rush of pride for her. She was getting on a bit and this girl and her boyfriend/brother/whoever he was had nothing to do with her, but she would never stand by and let someone be bullied.

'I'm working, babe,' said the girl, moving closer to Mum, and to Debbie, who was right next to her.

'I said NOW, Kelly.' Frankie pushed his way past Nathan and Ben and reached out to grab her arm, but Matt stepped in and blocked him.

'Kelly, is it?' I said, not taking my gaze off Frankie. I could see out of the corner of my eye the girl nodding. 'I take it you know this person?'

'He's my boyfriend,' she said.

'Do you want to go with him?'

'I'm working. They've paid me up to two o'clock.'

'But do you *want* to go with him?'

'What the bloody hell has it got to do with you?' snarled Frankie. Nathan laughed.

'You've just gatecrashed a stag party full of coppers, mate. If you wanted a roomful of people who'd be happy to turn a blind eye, you've come to the wrong place.'

Frankie immediately stepped back and held up his hands. 'I ain't done nothing wrong. I just don't like seeing my bird poncing around in her underwear, acting like a sl—'

'No one's acting like that,' I said. 'She's pouring drinks, that's all.'

'That's *all*? You can see everything in that outfit!' I had to admit he did have a point, but what Kelly chose to do was her own business.

'It's no worse than wearing a bikini on the beach,' said Debbie.

'I won't have people laughing at me because my girlfriend's a prostitute!'

'Frank, lad, people *are* laughing at you but it's got nowt to do with your bird,' said Danny, which was funny but not particularly helpful. Frankie lunged at him, but it was one man against Danny, Ben, Nathan, Tony and Matt – with Callum and Roger staying out of it after warning looks from their respective other halves. The angry young man flailed around ineffectually, trying to get a punch in, but none of them landed; the others just held him back, not hurting him but not being overly gentle either. Eventually it dawned on him that he was on a hiding to nothing, and he stopped. He stepped back and adjusted his clothing, then pointed at Kelly, locking eyes with her.

'I'll see you at home. You've got some explaining to do, you f—' He swore again. I shook my head.

'Do you kiss your mother with that mouth?' I asked, but he ignored me and carried on glaring at his girlfriend.

'You hear me? This ain't over.' He started to back away, all the better to keep glaring threateningly at her, but he'd forgotten about the small table next to the door and walked into it. A few of us sniggered – not exactly mature, I'll admit, but it broke the tension – and he whirled around and stormed out, one hand flung out behind him to give us a one-fingered salute. Nathan followed him out, making sure to see him leave, then came back and shut the door.

'Well, I don't think much of your entertainment,' I said.

'I thought my imaginary male stripper was bad enough, but this guy…'

Behind me, Kelly burst into tears and was immediately engulfed in a group hug with her two fellow waitresses. Debbie and I gathered around too, while Mum fumbled in her pocket, brought out some crumpled tissues and handed them to the weeping girl.

'They're clean,' she said. 'Ish.'

Kelly blew her nose and declared herself fit to carry on working. But the fun had gone out of it. The three young women found their clothes and went into the bathroom to get dressed, although it seemed odd that they were feeling modest now, having spent the last few hours in their undies.

'That's us done,' declared Liz, hauling Roger to his feet.

'Great floor show, son,' said Roger, grinning. 'See you in the morning.' He allowed himself to be led away.

'Bed time for us, too,' said Debbie. Callum looked at her hopefully, but she snorted and his face fell. 'In your dreams, sunshine.' She winked at me and whispered loudly, 'He's going to get lucky but I'm going to make him beg first.' Callum cheered up and practically carried his wife out of the room.

The three now-dressed waitresses left the bathroom, Kelly smiling bravely but (to me) unconvincingly when Ben asked her if she was okay.

'I'm fine,' she said.

'He's got a bit of a temper, that boyfriend of yours,' said Mum, and she nodded.

'Yeah…'

'Do you live together?' I asked. 'Is he going to be home when you get there?'

'Yes.'

'Hmm,' I said, looking round at the others. When I'd been in Uniform, we'd been told that we couldn't interfere in domestic disputes, unless we actually caught someone in the act of physically assaulting their partner, or if the abused person reported them and asked for our help. Sod that. I wasn't in Uniform anymore, but I was still in the Sisterhood. 'Is it safe for you to go home? Can you stay somewhere else until he's cooled down?'

'That's what we said!' said one of the other girls. 'Kelly, you know what he's like—'

'He's never hit me,' she said quickly – a bit *too* quickly for my liking, as if he hadn't done it yet but there was always that possibility, the threat of violence lurking under the surface.

'There's always a first time,' said Matt.

'Come and stay at mine,' urged the other waitress. 'My flatmate's away for the weekend, you can have her room.'

'I don't want to put anyone to any trouble…' Kelly sounded hesitant, but we all made encouraging noises and eventually she capitulated and agreed to stay with her sister instead. Tony did a massive yawn and a stretch, and smiled at the three girls.

'Come on, I'll walk you to your cars and then I'm off to bed,' he said.

'You can trust Tony,' said Matt. 'He goes out with a vicar.'

So Tony chaperoned the girls out of the hotel, Matt wandered (or staggered) down the corridor to his room, and I led Mum off to hers. At the door she stopped and looked at me with a grin. 'I take it you're off to the honeymoon suite now?'

I gave an exaggerated gasp of horror. 'What? But Nathan's in there, and we're not married yet…'

'Get on with yer.' She flapped her hands at me. 'You chose a good one this time. Better than the last one.'

'The last one did give us Daisy, though,' I said.

'That he did, and I'm very grateful for that. He was still an idiot, though.'

I laughed. 'I wish you'd told me that before I married him…'

'Well, this one isn't. Dad would've loved him.' We looked at each other with sudden tears in our eyes. Mum did a big sniff. 'Look at me, daft old baggage…' I reached out and hugged her fiercely, sniffing furiously myself. She kissed me on the cheek. 'Love you, sweetheart.'

'I love you too, Mum.' We both laughed as we wiped at our streaming eyes. 'Oh God, how much have we had to drink?'

'Not enough. Night-night, darling.' She stepped into her room, then paused before shutting the door. 'Say good night to Nathan for me.'

Chapter Four

'Look at him, cocky little bugger,' murmured Nathan affectionately, watching as Matt took aim at the target with a slightly self-conscious but confident air, aware that everyone was watching him. 'He's loving all this, isn't he?'

It was the afternoon after the (drunken) night before, and our guests – those of them who weren't still tucked up in bed, suffering from alcohol poisoning and groaning – were enjoying a selection of country pursuits, which all seemed to be aimed at killing things. We'd already had axe-throwing (which had been fun but much harder than it looked – a few of us had been lucky not to cut our own legs off), and clay-pigeon shooting was scheduled for later on. But after a delicious buffet lunch we were on to activity number two, archery.

I'd always fancied having a go at archery, ever since watching *Robin Hood* as a child and, later, *Lord of the Rings*, but to my dismay I was as terrible with a bow and arrow as

I was with axes. Maybe I'd be better with a gun, but I somehow doubted it. Still, I wasn't the worst; watching Debbie flailing around with the axe had been entertaining but scary, and Tony, who had been necking paracetamol and water as if his life depended on it, wasn't much better. The painkillers and the food he'd forced himself to eat at lunch seemed to have helped, though, and he'd redeemed himself a little at the archery.

No one, however, could hold a candle to Matt's prowess, even with a hangover. He unleashed his arrow and it flew (as expected) straight into the bullseye. Everyone clapped and cheered apart from, I noticed, Danny, who rolled his eyes and muttered something to Ben. Ben ignored him and called out, 'Well done, mate! Nath, you'll have to get this one here on a firearms course.'

Tony laughed. 'Firearms training? Nathan, you better tell your mates they're in Cornwall now, not Toxteth...' He turned to Matt and slapped him on the back. 'Nice work making the rest of us look rubbish.'

Matt shrugged and tried to look modest, but bearing in mind that so far he'd beaten all of us in axe throwing as well as archery, I thought he deserved to feel pleased with himself, particularly as that made it Cornwall 2, Liverpool 0. 'I grew up on a farm, I'm used to shooting rabbits with me dad's old shotgun, which handles about as well as one of these.' He waggled his bow. So he was probably a safe bet to beat us all at the shooting, as well.

'You're lucky Craig's hungover,' said Danny. 'He'd be a crack-shot by now, I reckon, all that time in the States.'

'How come *you're* not hungover?' said Nathan. 'You were matching him shot for shot up until we threw him out, and then you carried on drinking even more.'

'Sound as a pound, me. I can take it, unlike some people.'

Debbie stepped forward, grimacing and holding her own bow like it was a month-old dead fish. 'I'm so glad I get to follow you, Matt. No pressure for the rest of us or anything...' *Oh dear God*, I thought. The archery targets were set out on a wide strip of grass that ran along the top of one of the golf tees, well away from the hotel terrace and the formal garden it overlooked – and therefore also well away from any other guests, who might otherwise get caught in the crossfire. The layout of the course meant that any golfers would be aiming away from us, down to the stream that ran through the grounds, over the water, and onto the green, so we should be quite safe from flying balls, and in theory they should in turn be safe from our arrows; but if I were on the golf course, I wouldn't fancy my chances against Debbie and her dodgy aim. Luckily it appeared that the only people on the course today were Nathan's parents, and they'd set out earlier that morning and should be nowhere near us by now.

Matt smiled and took Debbie's arm. 'You'll do fine. Just hold it like this... watch your fingers or you'll get them caught when you fire the arrow. Like this.' He stood behind her, carefully adjusting her stance and the position of her fingers. He helped her insert the arrow and gently nudged it upwards, so she was actually aiming at the target now and not down at her own feet.

'Ooh, this is just like that bit out of *Robin Hood, Prince of Thieves*,' said Mum, suddenly appearing behind us and making us all jump. She'd cried off the axe-throwing earlier, although she'd denied it was because she was feeling the after-effects of too much Prosecco the night before. 'Where Maid Marian blows a lucky kiss along his shaft.' Several members of the group made strangled snorting noises, unused to my mother's habit of innocently saying things that sounded like *double entendres*. 'Only with Debbie as Kevin Costner. Proper romantic, that bit.'

Matt abruptly dropped Debbie's arm at that, glancing warily at Callum (who wasn't looking the least bit jealous) at the exact moment Debbie took her shot. The arrow veered wildly – but impressively strongly – off course, flying way past the target and disappearing down a slight incline and out of view.

'Kevin Costner had better aim, of course,' said Mum, sniffily.

'Kevin Costner didn't have you turning up and distracting him,' I pointed out. 'That might've been off-target, Deb—'

'*Might've* been?' said Tony, and everyone laughed, including Debbie.

'Alright, it *was* way off target, but look how far it went! Much further than mine. You could get a job shooting flaming arrows into Viking longboats at funerals.'

'Much call for that round here, is there?' asked Danny. 'I

thought it was all druids and New Age hippies in Cornwall, not Vikings…'

The instructor, who was actually called Kevin and by rights should've been the one showing Debbie how to use her bow, but who seemed a little bit intimidated by Matt being so good at everything, stepped forward with a hand raised.

'Okay, let's break for a minute while we collect the arrows, then we'll have round two,' he said. He headed towards the row of targets. Nathan and Ben followed to help.

'I'm glad Germaine isn't here,' I said. 'She'd have been running around like a maniac, chasing after the arrows and getting in everyone's way.'

'I'd probably have shot her,' said Debbie, and then added as an afterthought, 'by accident, of course.'

'Of course.'

'But then you could've given her a Viking send-off down at the harbour, and I could've had a go with the flaming arrow…' She sounded almost wistful.

'Do you mind? That's my baby you're talking about!'

My indignation was interrupted by a loud scream.

Kevin, who had gone in search of Debbie's stray arrow while Nathan and Ben collected those that had been more on target, staggered up the incline shrieking at the top of his lungs, before he abruptly stopped and vomited behind a small, neatly pruned bush. *Kevin Costner wouldn't have done that*, I thought. Everyone rushed towards him, which must've been a frightening enough sight in itself, but Nathan and Ben got there first.

'You alright, mate?' asked Ben, which was a daft question – he clearly wasn't – but it was obviously meant to be soothing. The distressed young man shook his head and pointed behind him.

'Down there,' he said, the tremor in his voice evident. His hand shook. 'There's someone in the water. They're—' He shuddered and retched, but managed not to throw up again. Debbie reached out and gently led him over to a nearby stone bench, persuading him to sit down.

'It's okay, you're fine,' said Debbie, although again, it was obvious that he wasn't. Nathan made his way down the slight hill and stopped; we could just see his head and shoulders, looking down at something. And then he disappeared. Matt and I exchanged looks and went to follow, but Tony stopped me.

'This is your wedding party, Jodie. Whatever's going on, I don't think you want to get involved.'

'Blow that!' I said, shaking his hand off my arm. 'You're my oldest friend and it's like you don't even know me...' Matt grinned at me and gestured 'ladies first', following close behind me. And then we both stopped in shock.

The slope led down to an ornamental pond. A red Japanese-style wooden bridge led over the tumble of boulders which dammed and separated it from the river. Rushes lined the edge of the pond, and dragonflies and damselflies darted in and out, their iridescent wings glittering. In the open water in the centre of the pond water lilies floated, their flower petals open to bask in the glorious sunshine. Floating next to a particularly large and beautiful lily was a body, face down, long red hair spread out like undulating seaweed around the head. An arrow – presumably Debbie's – stuck out of the unfortunate mermaid's back. Nathan had already waded into the water and was attempting to reach the body, but the water was deeper than it looked, and the thick reeds around the edge hindered him.

'Holy crap,' I said.

Next to me, Matt gasped. 'Shit. That's Debbie's arrow, isn't it? She hit them.'

'Looks like it,' I said. 'No one else's arrow came this way.'

'Oh God,' said Matt. 'Then it's my fault.'

'What's your fault?'

'I jogged Debbie's arm right as she was letting her arrow go.' He looked absolutely stricken with guilt, and I thought, *Oh no, how's Debbie going to feel?*

Nathan looked back at the two of us and shook his head. 'I don't suppose either of you actually want to help get her out before you start conducting a post-mortem?'

Matt slipped off his shoes and reluctantly tiptoed into the water. 'Should we be touching her? Shouldn't we leave it to Forensics?'

Nathan shook his head. 'She's in the water, there's going to be precious little forensic evidence left on her already. And it's a hot day, she's in water, and *someone's* got to get her out before things get nasty…'

Very gently he and Matt pulled the body clear of the reeds and out of the water, and even more gently laid it – her – out on the grass, on her belly because of the arrow.

'What's going on?' asked Ben, stepping forward. He stopped abruptly. 'Oh bloody hell, that's her from last night, innit? The one with the no-mark boyfriend?'

'Who? What's happened?' said Mum, trying to peer round Ben. I held my hand out to stop her.

'No, Mum, you don't want to see this,' I said, because a body that's been in the water for a few hours is not a pretty sight. Nathan straightened up.

'Mate, get everyone back, will you?' he said to Ben, who nodded.

'Sure thing.' Ben put his arm around my mum. 'Come on, Shirley, let's get everyone back to the hotel…?' He raised an eyebrow at Nathan.

'Yeah, good idea.'

Ben led Mum away, stopping briefly to say to Danny in an undertone, 'Floater.'

'Shit,' said Danny. He cleared his throat. 'Okay everyone, last one back to the bar's getting the round in.'

'Handy when there's an incident, having a guest list full of coppers,' I said, and Nathan smiled thinly.

'Handy, or tempting Fate.' He turned to Matt. 'Can you call this in? We need CSI here, not that there's going to be much for them to work with.' He squatted down next to the body, gently moving the tangle of hair out of the way to look at her face. 'She was at my stag do, wasn't she? What was her name again?'

'Kelly,' said Matt, taking out his phone, his eyes on the arrow again. Nathan noticed and shook his head.

'Look closely, Matt. It wasn't the arrow that killed her,' he said. 'There's no blood around the wound. And she's obviously been dead a while.'

'Probably overnight,' I said. 'Nothing to do with you or Debbie. In fact, if it wasn't for you accidentally nudging Debbie's arm, we wouldn't have found her.'

'S'pose not,' said Matt glumly, but he looked a little less guilty. He pulled himself together as his call was answered. 'Hey, Sunil? You are not going to believe what's happened...' He wandered away as he filled DC Sunil Bakshi in. Nathan stood up and reached out to touch my arm.

'You okay?'

'Better than her.' I nodded to the corpse. 'I feel terrible that we were all here, and this still happened. Because this wasn't an accident, was it?'

'We can't say that yet.'

'I think we can. It's not like she could've fallen in, is it? There's a gentle slope down to the water – it doesn't really get deep until you get out to the middle, and even then you managed to stand up quite easily. If you fell in, surely you'd just get up? There's no rocks to bang your head on or anything.'

'There are by the bridge.' Nathan pointed across the pond.

'*Under* the bridge, yes,' I said. 'I think you'd be unlikely to bang your head on those, though.'

'Yeah, I'm just playing Devil's advocate, but you're probably right...' Nathan looked around. 'And why would she be going over the bridge anyway? It doesn't lead anywhere.'

'So you know what this looks like? Or rather, *who* this looks like?' I asked.

'The boyfriend. I know.' He sighed. 'We saw what he was like last night.'

'A hotel full of coppers, and she still wasn't safe.' I crouched down next to Kelly's body and put my hand on her back. She was cold. 'I'm so sorry, sweetheart.'

Nathan took my arm and gently pulled me to my feet. He leaned in to kiss me on the forehead, and then pulled me close. 'Not what we want in the run-up to our wedding, is it?'

'Nope.' I sighed. 'Right, let's get back to the hotel and start fending off everyone's questions...'

'Well *that's* put a bit of a dampener on things,' said Mum, after most of us had traipsed back to the hotel – Matt and Nathan were waiting with the body for the authorities to arrive. We were sitting in the bar, attempting to recover our spirits with, well, spirits, but it wasn't really working. The hotel manager, Mr Robbins, was fussing around in the background, probably, I thought, trying to get hold of his lawyer to make sure Nathan and I couldn't sue the hotel for ruining our wedding weekend.

'So what's the rest of the serious crime unit like down here?' asked Ben. I laughed mirthlessly.

'The local "serious crime unit" is basically Nathan and

Matt,' I said. 'There's a very keen DC, Sunil, and Matt's girlfriend Chrissie helps out, but she's technically Uniform.'

'Is that it?'

'That's usually enough, to be honest,' I said. 'Cornwall as a county has got the second-lowest crime rate in the country, especially outside of the summer tourist season. We average two or three suspicious deaths a year around here, maximum. That doesn't include drug-related deaths or drowning, but it doesn't always mean it's murder, either.'

'Not like our patch, then,' grinned Danny. The grin could've been construed as a bit heartless, but to be honest most police officers – career-orientated ones, anyway – preferred working in areas with a high crime rate, because at worst it gave them something to do, and at best it provided more opportunities to make a name for themselves. I'd been guilty of it myself back in the day, when I'd first started in the job; why else had I moved to London and joined the Met, rather than staying in sleepy Cornwall? 'So who's gonna be sorting this one out, then?'

'Well, Nathan,' I said, surprised that he was even asking, but Ben shook his head.

'Doubt it,' he said. 'It's a conflict of interest, like, innit? The last place anyone saw her was at his stag party.'

'Well, technically the last person who saw her was Tony, when he walked her and the others to their cars,' said Debbie, leaning across the bar to flag down the barman. Tony, hearing his name, looked up. 'Tone, I was just saying—'

'Yes, thank you, Deb,' he said, rolling his eyes. 'Thanks

for putting my name out there as a suspect. She was fine when I left her. And I *wasn't* the last person to see her. You lot were.' He gestured to Ben and Danny.

'What?' I looked at Tony, confused. 'But I saw them leave with you.'

'Yeah, but when we got down to Reception she realised she'd left part of her costume behind and went back for it.'

'She had a costume?' asked Mum. 'I thought they was just dancing about in their drawers…'

'They had these little frilly aprons,' said Ben. 'She came back up to the room in case she'd left hers in the bathroom when she got changed. I had a look but it wasn't there. I asked if she wanted to have a look for it herself but she said it didn't matter. She didn't even come in.'

'So *you* were the last person to see her alive,' said Debbie. Danny shook his head.

'No, the last person to see her alive was the killer,' he said firmly, and we all went quiet, thinking about the poor girl.

'Oh man, my hangover is *wicked*,' said Craig, appearing beside us. 'Wicked as in, it feels like someone dropped a house on me 'ead and stole me shoes.' He looked round at us, faint surprise slowly registering on his face. 'What are youse lot all doing in here? I thought you were shooting stuff this afternoon?' He settled onto a bar stool and waved the barman over. 'Just some water please, mate.'

'There's been a murder!' said Mum, dramatically, but Craig was too hungover to take it in straightaway.

'I could murder a fry-up,' he said. 'Best cure for a

hangover.' He took a long swig of water and then suddenly stopped and looked at her. 'Hang on, *what?*' He looked around, almost panicking. 'Where's Nathan?'

'Not Nathan, soft lad, one of the waitresses from last night,' said Danny.

'Oh no, really?' Craig looked shocked, but was there something else underneath it? Guilt? Or fear?

'Yeah,' said Ben. 'That girl you were out of order with last night.'

There was no mistaking the shame and embarrassment that crossed his face now. 'Oh shit, no.' He ran a shaking hand through his hair. 'Poor girl...' He gazed down at the bar for a moment, and then looked back up at his friends. 'What exactly... what did I do last night?'

'You don't remember?' I asked.

'No, I don't. I was bladdered. I just remember...' He smiled ruefully. 'I just remember going back to my room after everyone had a go at me.' He rubbed his cheek. 'I remember her slapping me round the face, too. I'm assuming I deserved it?'

'Yep,' said Danny. 'And you know me, if *I* say you've gone too far, then you've really gone too far.'

'You asked if she were a young lady of negotiable affection,' said Mum. I made a mental note to stop her watching too much *Bridgerton* in future. Craig looked befuddled.

'Eh? Pretty sure I've never asked *anyone* that, I don't even know what it means.'

'You wanted to know if she was a prozzy,' said Ben.

'Oh God, I didn't…'

'Yeah, you did. You really don't remember?' Ben was scrutinising his face closely, but Craig still looked blank.

'I don't remember anything much until I woke up this morning with you banging on my door, telling me to come and join in with the axe throwing,' said Craig. He grinned. 'I remember what I told you to do, though. It ended with "off"…'

'Well that's just bloody marvellous.' Nathan plopped himself down on the bar stool next to me and looked at Craig. 'Afternoon, sunshine. You heard the news?'

'Yeah, poor girl…'

'What's bloody marvellous?' I asked.

'They're sending that new DI over from Exeter,' said Nathan. Matt joined us.

'DI Mackintosh. I've heard all sorts about *her*,' he said, darkly. 'Right stickler for the rules, she is—'

'Which is good,' I pointed out.

'Yeah, but it means we're out of it,' said Nathan. 'Apparently we're "personally involved", even though neither of us knew the victim and didn't even know she existed until last night.'

'Told you,' said Ben. 'Conflict of interest.'

'Sunil's holding the fort until she turns up,' said Nathan. 'She's bringing a team over with her.'

'At least you've still got a man on the inside,' said Craig.

'Yeah,' I said. 'Sunil can keep us posted about the investigation.'

Tony placed a bottle of beer in front of Nathan. 'Or you

could both just let them get on with it and enjoy your wedding celebrations instead.'

Nathan and I looked at each other.

'He's got a point, babe,' said Nathan. I smiled.

'He has. You're right, Tone. Let DI Mackintosh do her worst.' I raised my glass in a toast, and Nathan followed suit with his beer bottle. 'Bugger the investigation, I'm going to celebrate our upcoming nuptials. Let's do this!'

But of course that was never *really* likely to happen…

Chapter Five

'I always miss all the fun,' grumbled Daisy. She'd spent most of the day in the spa and swimming pool with her boyfriend, Joe, who had come along mid-morning to make use of the hotel facilities. I didn't mind as they were costing us enough. Only now we'd all been corralled into the private dining room to wait for the police to interview us, even those of us who hadn't been anywhere near the victim, so he was probably wishing he'd avoided today's events as well.

Joe laughed. 'You do realise your idea of "fun" is a bit weird, don't you?'

'Yeah, but that's why you love me,' said Daisy, and then she stopped talking abruptly, probably mortified that she'd used the 'L' word. Joe didn't look mortified at all, though, and I thought that she was probably right. They'd been together for almost a year by now, and so far they'd survived GCSEs (Daisy had just finished hers, and it had been a stressful time), UK tours (Joe had a burgeoning music career), and embarrassing parents (me and Nathan, and Joe's mum and dad, Flo and Lawrence, an artist and a lawyer originally from North London).

'I know what you mean, sweetheart,' I said, because the apple doesn't fall far from the tree and, like me, she always liked to know what was going on, 'but it was pretty horrible, finding her like that.'

'I still can't believe you had topless waitresses at your stag do,' she said to Nathan, with a sly smile on her face. Nathan rolled his eyes.

'They weren't topless, they were – oh I get it, wind up your stepdad…'

'I felt sorry for her, when her nasty boyfriend came up and had a go at her,' said Mum, soothingly. 'That wasn't nice to watch, either.'

'No,' said Daisy, but she sounded unconvinced.

'Do you reckon that was who did it?' asked Joe. 'Her boyfriend?'

'I don't know,' said Nathan, ever the diplomat, just as I said, 'Yeah, definitely.'

'It's too early in the investigation to speculate about that,' said a female voice behind us – a voice that I was sure I recognised.

We all turned to see a smartly dressed woman of around my age (mid-forties) standing in the doorway, with Nathan's DC Sunil and a couple of other plain-clothes police officers. Mr Robbins stood behind her, looking anxious, and I felt a momentary pang of sympathy for him, because nobody expects to find a fully dressed topless waitress floating in their ornamental pond. But my sympathy was swiftly replaced with a feeling of surprise.

'This is DI Mackintosh—' began Nathan, but I interrupted him.

'Di?'

'What? No, *DI* – Detective Inspector—' Nathan was looking at me like I was mad, but DI Mackintosh – or Di, as I knew her – was staring at me in bemusement.

'Jodie Parker, as I live and breathe!' she said, stepping forward. I felt a bit awkward and went to hug her but she stepped back, and I thought, *Of course, she's on duty...* 'I knew you'd moved down here but I didn't expect to find you at one of my crime scenes.'

'You'd be surprised,' murmured Matt and Sunil together.

'You know each other?' asked Nathan.

'Yeah, we were both at Stockwell, what, ten years ago? Only she was DS Haslemere at the time.' I looked her up and down. 'Married *and* promoted? You've been busy.' In the intervening years, of course, I'd been equally busy, getting divorced and quitting, but I wasn't going to bring that up.

She shrugged. 'You know me, I don't like to stand still.' She looked around at the rest of the gathered guests and pulled out her warrant card. 'My name is Detective Inspector Diana Mackintosh. I normally work out of Exeter, but as most of the Penstowan constabulary are already here, I've been called in to take charge of this investigation.'

'What's happened?' asked Roger. He and Liz hadn't taken part in the morning's activities, preferring instead to play a leisurely round of golf on the hotel course. They'd only just finished their game and had been ushered in to join us with no idea what was going on.

'For those of you who are unaware, the body of a young woman was found this afternoon in a pond behind the archery targets. The cause of death has yet to be established, but we are treating it as suspicious.' She turned and looked at Debbie. 'I understand you shot her with an arrow?'

Debbie turned pale. 'It was a mistake!' she said, looking absolutely stricken. Callum put an arm round her. I bit my tongue. Diana hadn't been known for her tact and diplomacy when we'd been at Stockwell – it had actually been one of the things I'd liked about her at the time, as long as I wasn't on the receiving end – and it seemed she hadn't got any better at it.

'I know, and I can confirm that it did not contribute to her death.' Mackintosh gave a tight smile. 'In fact, in other circumstances it would have been an impressive shot.'

'Who was the victim?' asked Liz. 'Do you know?'

'One Kelly Lawson. I believe she had been hired as entertainment for the stag party last night.'

Mr Robbins gave a sanctimonious shake of his head. 'Which is totally against hotel rules – hiring in outside staff without our consent.'

'Entertainment?' asked Roger, confused. 'Oh right, you mean the topless waitresses.' Behind him, Robbins managed to look even more sanctimonious. Daisy smirked and mouthed, *See? Topless!* at Nathan. 'Oh no, which one?'

'The redhead,' said Matt. 'Kelly.'

'The one with the nasty boyfriend,' said Ben.

'Oh, *him*,' said Liz, managing to load that one word with enough contempt to get the man convicted and sent down without even facing trial. Not that Di Mackintosh was having any of that.

'As I said before, it's too early to speculate, but we will of course be interviewing Ms Lawson's family and friends.' She smiled, but it was all business rather than friendly, designed to put us at ease, but not *too* much. 'Now my colleagues and I will be conducting interviews of everyone in this room. I'm assuming this is everyone in your party who was here last night, DCI Withers, Miss Parker?'

'Yes,' I said quickly, because no, it wasn't strictly everyone – Carmen, Nina, Lily and Louise had been here, but they hadn't gone up to the stag party or interacted with the waitresses at all, and I didn't see the point in dragging them into it. 'Although Daisy – you remember my daughter? – she *was* here but she didn't go anywhere near the stag party, and Joe there only arrived this morning.'

'They may still have seen something,' insisted Mackintosh, calmly but firmly. 'So please, everyone take a seat and we will get round you all as quickly as possible.'

I half expected her to make a beeline for me. We hadn't been friends, exactly, but we'd got on okay, and as only a handful of female officers (and an even smaller handful of female sergeants) we'd had each other's backs at work on almost a daily basis. But instead she murmured instructions to her officers and headed out the door, the hotel manager following quickly (but ignored) in her wake.

Nathan beckoned Sunil over.

'How you finding her?' he asked his detective sergeant. Sunil glanced around before answering.

'She's alright, Guv, but I have to admit I feel a bit out of place with all these high-flyers from Exeter.'

'Don't,' said Nathan. 'You're a good copper, this lot are lucky to have you.'

'Mackintosh is fine,' I agreed. 'She knows what she's doing.'

'Everyone says she does everything by the book,' said Sunil. 'Is that good?'

'Ha! Yes, it is,' I said. 'Although she wasn't always like that...' I could almost see Nathan's and Sunil's ears prick up. I laughed. 'Yeah, forget I said anything.'

'Just keep us posted on what's going on, okay?' said Nathan. Sunil nodded.

'Of course, Guv.'

It took almost three hours for the team to interview all of us. Daisy, Joe and Mum were the first to be called forward, which was a relief because it meant I wouldn't have Mum pacing up and down, muttering about being bored. They were let go afterwards, with instructions (from me, rather than the police) to take Mum off and feed her, which was bound to keep her in a good mood and out of trouble. Possibly.

Nathan, Matt and I were left until the end, but I don't think any of us minded because it gave us a lot of opportunity to speculate over the investigation.

'Go on,' said Nathan, as we huddled together in a corner of the room, away from the interviews. 'What were you going to say about Mackintosh?'

'Ooh, have you got dirt on our new DI?' asked Matt. 'Spill.'

'Honestly, you're worse than my mum,' I said.

'I have a lot of time for your mother,' said Nathan. 'If she'd joined the Force she'd have made Chief Superintendent just by keeping her ear to the ground.'

'By being nosey, you mean,' I scoffed, noticing the way they exchanged grins. 'Yeah alright, I am too, but the irony of you two suggesting that while you're hanging on my every word… You want this dirt or not?'

'Yes!'

'Okay. So when she first came to Stockwell, she was obviously trying to make a name for herself – which I don't think has changed – and she decided to go and interview this drug dealer on one of the estates in the area. He supposedly had information on some big new supplier who'd moved in. Anyway, I got wind of it because she asked one of my uniforms where the estate was, and he was like, "Hell no, we don't go onto Gresham Park estate unless something's literally on fire." We'd all been told to run any calls about Gresham past our superior officers first, Uniform *and* CID. But she was insistent, so he told her and then came to find me.' Matt was looking at me, wide-eyed, and I had to remind myself that he didn't have a clue what policing was like in London. 'We'd had calls to the estate in the past, someone reporting a mugging in progress or whatever, but they were basically ambushes – we'd get there and there'd be a row of kids looking down on at us from a walkway, chucking bottles and jeering. There was a lot of tension between certain residents and the police, and at any given moment it could all just go off, so we only went on there when we had really good reason to.'

'But she didn't know that?'

'Not at first, but my PC told her, and then I found her and told her, but she just shrugged it off. Like, "I'm not in uniform so they won't even know I'm police."'

Nathan laughed. 'Yeah, that's not how it works. They might not know you're police, but they'll know you're an outsider, and that's good enough.'

'Yep. So anyway, she drags this poor DC along with her, and what do you know, there's a whole gang waiting to welcome her to the estate.'

'Damn!' Matt shook his head, but I could see he secretly thought it was all very exciting. Bless him.

'Luckily for her, I'd sent a couple of squad cars along to lurk discreetly outside the estate, ready to descend not so discreetly if it all kicked off, so they swooped in and escorted her back to her unmarked but still obviously police car. And when she got back to the station we both got an almighty rollocking for not clearing it with her SO.'

'Wow!' said Matt. 'Not fair that you got into trouble as well, though, when you were just covering her back.'

'No,' I said. 'I told them that I'd warned her against going there, and I'd only sent the cars as back-up when I realised she wasn't taking any notice of me, so I did get off lighter than her – I wasn't going to suffer because of her pig-headedness. I should've gone straight to her boss and told him what she was planning, but you don't want to drop a fellow officer in it, do you?'

'But she learnt her lesson after that,' said Nathan, and I nodded.

'Yep. She had to at first, because the brass were waiting for her to take a step out of line, and then it just seemed to become second nature.' I smiled thinly, watching the interviewing officers dismiss the last lot of interviewees and turn to us. 'Almost to the point where she wouldn't even go for a wee without filling in the relevant forms in triplicate first, if some of the gossip I heard is true.'

Sunil joined us. 'Your turn,' he said.

'You can interview me,' said Nathan. 'I can pick your brains about the investigation so far.'

'No can do, Guv,' said Sunil, apologetically. 'DI Mackintosh told me I'm not allowed to interview anyone who's a serving member of the local police.' He grinned. 'But I'm assuming Jodie will be up for hearing about our progress.'

I sighed. 'Well, if it's down to me to carry the torch for the Penstowan constabulary, it's a cross I'm willing to bear.'

We sat down at a table as Nathan and Matt crossed the room to talk to some of Mackintosh's officers. Sunil took out his notepad and looked at me expectantly.

'You know what I'm going to say,' I said. 'The same as everyone else. None of us knew the victim, the first we knew of her was when she turned up at the stag party as one of Nathan's topless waitresses—' Sunil grimaced. 'Yeah, that's how I feel about it, too.'

'We don't really go in for stag and hen parties in my culture,' said Sunil. 'There certainly wouldn't be strippers or topless women involved. My *nani* would have had a seizure if there'd been anything like that at my wedding.'

'I'm with your *nani*, to be honest,' I said. 'And I don't think Nathan really enjoyed having them there, either. I think he felt a bit uncomfortable.'

'Yes, I expect he did,' said Sunil, sounding relieved. I hid a smile. Nathan was well respected at Penstowan nick, but it was quite touching just how much both Matt and Sunil looked up to him.

'So yeah, none of us knew her. She seemed happy enough until her horrible boyfriend turned up—'

'Frankie Lewis.'

'Yeah. Has Mackintosh looked into him yet? Does he have form?'

Sunil looked around, then lowered his voice. 'Yes. Two previous convictions, one for being drunk and disorderly, another for actual bodily harm. There was a fight about three years ago, outside the King's Arms.'

'When *isn't* there a fight outside there?'

'This wasn't the usual Saturday night fisticuffs, though. There was an argument inside the pub, the other man walked away but Lewis completely lost it and followed him outside. He only just avoided a charge of GBH.'

'What about domestic assault?' I asked. 'Kelly was frightened of him, that was obvious, and I got the impression it wasn't the first time he'd shouted at her like that.'

Sunil shook his head. 'No convictions, but I spoke to Chrissie because I knew she was due to join your wedding party today, and she knew the name. There'd been reports.'

'Poor Kelly,' I said. 'It's so frustrating. You know this stuff's going on, but you can't do anything unless the victim reports it. And they're too scared or too stuck to report it, because it could just make it so much worse.'

'Yes,' said Sunil sombrely, and we both paused for a moment, thinking about what Kelly's life must've been like. The poor girl deserved justice, even if it was too late to save her.

'So from all of this—' I waved my arm around, encompassing the other officers interviewing Nathan and Matt, 'can I assume that it's definitely being seen as a murder?'

'Yes,' said Sunil. 'Mackintosh hasn't officially ruled out an accident, but at the same time she's not seriously considering it could be.'

'With Lewis in the frame?'

'Yep. Particularly as he's not at home and not answering his phone.'

'He's done a runner.' I shook my head. 'That doesn't make him look guilty at all, does it? Evil *and* stupid. Who else have you interviewed? I don't know how many staff were on duty last night, but there was the night concierge – she knocked on the door to tell Nathan to keep the noise down, and she was *not* impressed when she saw the waitresses there. Oh, and there was a group of golfers in the bar with us, but they didn't have anything to do with the stag party.'

Sunil consulted his pad. 'Yeah, your mum mentioned the golfers too, although it sounds like they were pretty drunk. I haven't seen them yet, they must be out on the course—'

He was interrupted by a commotion outside in the hotel's reception area; shouting, and the sounds of a scuffle. We all leapt up and rushed outside, to find none other than Frankie Lewis himself pinned to the floor under the weight of a couple of Penstowan's uniformed finest, Brett and the longest-serving copper in Penstowan history, 'Old' Davey Trelawney, who (after being nicknamed Old Davey at birth – long story) was finally starting to live up to his sobriquet, although he was still strong as an ox.

'I ain't done nothing!' howled Frankie.

'You done something, then,' said Davey, struggling to clap some handcuffs on him.

'What?'

'You 'aven't done *nothing*, so you 'ave done *something*. Two negatives make a positive, dunnit?'

Frankie stopped struggling, puzzled, long enough for Davey to snap the handcuffs shut and haul him to his feet.

'Nice work, Davey,' I murmured, and he grinned.

'If in doubt, confuse 'em,' he said.

'Right, you going to calm down now, sonny Jim?' asked Brett. Mackintosh appeared from the manager's office.

'What the he— Who's this?' she asked, looking at the now-defeated Frankie.

'Frankie Lewis, ma'am,' said Davey.

'Frankie Lewis? We've been looking for you,' she said, smiling grimly. 'Thank you for making my job easier and coming to find us instead. If only all my suspects were that courteous.'

'What's going on?' Frankie wailed, limply. 'I only come back to find me girlfriend, she didn't come home last night.' We all stared at him. 'What?'

'Where were you between the hours of one thirty and five thirty this morning?' asked Mackintosh. So she already had a time of death; an approximate one, anyway. There was no way of knowing for sure (or almost sure) until the post-mortem.

'I was driving around, and then I parked up on the cliffs and fell asleep,' said Frankie, which of course sounded very suspicious.

'You spent the night in your car?' asked Mackintosh, not bothering to hide the disbelief in her voice.

'Yeah,' said Frankie. 'I'd had a bit to drink…' He looked around at all of us again, and I could see panic starting to rise in his eyes, panic and confusion. 'What's going on? Where's Kelly?'

I looked over at Nathan, and I could tell from his

expression that he was thinking the same thing as me. *Where's Kelly?* Frankie Lewis was either trying to be clever and pretend that he didn't know what was going on, or he genuinely had no idea his girlfriend was dead. But which was it?

Chapter Six

Mackintosh and one of her plain-clothes officers led Frankie off to the manager's office, which she had commandeered, and left the rest of us – the two uniforms, me, Nathan and Matt, who had also finished being interviewed – looking at each other.

'What happened?' I asked Davey. 'Did he just turn up?'

'Yeah,' he said. 'We were outside, keeping an eye on people coming in and out, when he drove into the car park. When he saw us lot he tried to drive off again, but I recognised his car – there was a call out with the make and the car reg – so I stood in his way and made him get out.'

'I thought he was going to keep on driving,' said Brett. 'I was getting ready to drag Davey out the way.' *Good luck with that*, I thought. Moving an unwilling Davey would be like trying to move a wardrobe full of bricks.

'He says he's looking for Kelly,' said Nathan, thoughtfully.

'Of course that's what he *says*,' I pointed out. 'He wouldn't be the first murderer to come back to the scene of the crime. It would've been dark when he dumped her body, so maybe he came back to check he'd left her somewhere she wasn't likely to be discovered, and move her if necessary.'

'We wouldn't have found her today if Debbie hadn't been so bad at archery,' said Matt.

'True,' said Nathan. 'And it sounds like he doesn't have an alibi, either.'

'Sleeping in his car?' I scoffed. 'He obviously didn't think anyone would've found her yet, so he hadn't even bothered to come up with anything plausible.'

'No,' said Nathan. 'Hmm…' Matt and I exchanged exasperated looks.

'Oh come on!' said Matt. 'It's normally *her* going "hmm" at this point in an investigation.'

'I would resent that, but you've got a point,' I admitted. 'What is there to "hmm" about?'

'I don't know about you, but I would've given at least *some* thought to what I would say if someone asked me where I was. Even saying you were at home in bed is preferable to "I was sleeping in my car in a deserted place like a hobo."'

'Yeah, but that's because you're intelligent and he isn't,' I said, but I couldn't deny he had a point. If you were guilty of your girlfriend's murder, you'd obviously be the first person police would look at. It didn't take brains to realise that you'd need to get your story straight as soon as you could, especially if you were going to go back to the scene of the crime and look around. But then being deliberately vague could potentially work *for* you, just as much as it could work against you; in fact, if you couldn't find or trust someone to lie and give you an alibi, then saying you were somewhere on your own was probably your best bet. No one could back you up, but no one could say for certain that you weren't there. And coming back today – that could be a double bluff, to make it look like he didn't know she was dead. Maybe he wasn't as stupid as we – okay, I – had thought he was.

'He's certainly got a temper on him,' said Davey. 'I've seen him outside the pub, arguing with a girl, shouting right in her face. Nasty bit of work.'

'Which girl? Kelly?' asked Nathan. Davey shrugged.

'I dunno. They all dress the same these days, don't they? All got the same hairstyle – long, blonde, dead straight.'

'Kelly was a redhead,' said Matt.

'Weren't her, then.'

'When was this? Was this recently?' asked Nathan. Davey shook his head.

'Not *that* recent. Couple of months ago? I dunno. She wouldn't press charges so I just stayed with her until he calmed down and buggered off home.' He scoffed. 'Cheeky sod tried to blame *her*. Said she wouldn't leave him alone. Like he's a proper catch or something.'

'How long had he and Kelly been together?' I asked Nathan. 'Maybe he was cheating on her.'

'I don't know.' Nathan shrugged. 'But being a cheat doesn't automatically mean he's a murderer as well.'

'Makes him a garbage boyfriend, though,' I said stubbornly. Nathan laughed and pulled me in for a hug.

'I won't argue with that. But not *everyone* can be perfect husband material like me, you know…'

'Eww, get a room,' said Daisy, reappearing next to me.

'We've got one,' I said. 'But I think people might notice if we disappeared for an hour.'

'An hour?' said Nathan. 'You're optimistic, after the amount I had to drink last night.'

'Ewww, again!'

I laughed. 'Sorry, sweetheart. Anyway, where's Nana? You haven't left poor Joe looking after her, have you?'

'Nah, she's with your lot,' said Daisy, gesturing to Nathan. 'Your mum and her are swapping gossip on eligible bachelors amongst the hotel staff. I keep telling Nana they're all too young for her, and she just says—'

'"Just because I'm on a diet, it doesn't mean I can't look at the menu."' Nathan and I spoke together. My mother was nothing if not predictable.

'Yeah, like she always says. But anyway, we all want to know what the plans for this afternoon are now,' said Daisy. 'Because I don't know if anyone feels like shooting stuff with all the fuzz around.' She looked at Nathan. 'No offence.'

'None taken.'

'If the axe throwing and archery were anything to go by,

I think it might be safer for the crime scene guys if we're not allowed guns,' I admitted. 'Especially Debbie.' I turned to Nathan. 'Is it poor taste to carry on at all, after there's been a murder?'

'You don't mean cancel the wedding?' He looked aghast.

'No, of course not! But I mean half the people staying here live in Penstowan, less than an hour away. Maybe we should send everyone who lives nearby home, and then just get together tomorrow for the ceremony. Keep it all low key. It feels a bit wrong to have a weekend of debauchery with that poor girl meeting a grisly end a few feet away.'

'Yeah, I know what you mean. Although I didn't realise there was any debauchery planned...' He looked thoughtful. 'If we did send people home, that would still leave my parents, Craig, Ben and Danny. Your mum will probably refuse to leave, and we can hardly leave either, can we? We invited all these people down here to spend time with us, so we can't go home. So that means Daisy has to stay as well. Debbie and Callum are using this as a mini-break from the kids—' Their children, Matilda and George, were staying with Callum's parents for the weekend. We had invited them as well, but Debbie had decided it was going to be an 'adults only' weekend, with almost indecent haste. '—so they won't want to leave either. Callum's already told me he's got plans for the hot tub.'

Daisy put her fingers in her ears. 'La la la, I'm not listening!' She grimaced. 'Adults are all sex mad.'

'They're married, they're allowed to be,' I said. I lowered

my voice as Matt wandered away to answer a phone call. 'And if *they* stay, Tony will too, and Matt, because he won't want to be outdone by Craig in your time of need.'

'Who does that leave?'

'No one. Except Carmen and Chrissie, who were due to show up today after work,' I said. Matt rejoined us.

'Chrissie said she'll be here for the dinner tonight,' he said.

I sighed. 'So I think there's our answer.'

'Life goes on, and so does the wedding,' said Nathan, simply. 'We've seen enough death in our time to know that.'

'Okay,' I said. 'But let's cancel the clay-pigeon shooting this afternoon, otherwise we might see some more…'

It was a subdued group that reconvened in the hotel bar, but there was at least some relief that the perpetrator had been caught. There was no doubt in anyone's mind that Frankie Lewis had hung around the hotel and caught up with his girlfriend as she'd left, killing her and then dumping her body in the pond.

There was no doubt in anyone's mind… except Nathan's, and he'd planted a seed of it in mine, too.

Perhaps mindful of the fact that he now had a hotel full of people with nothing to do except spend the afternoon drinking, the hotel manager brought out a selection of board games for us to play, although, to be fair, sipping cocktails and playing Snakes and Ladders were hardly mutually exclusive (and, one could argue, more fun to do at the same time). Daisy took one look at the Monopoly board Mum had started to set out, shook her head with an emphatic 'Nope', and led Joe out by the hand.

'Where are you going?' I called after her.

'Anywhere but here,' she said, and looking at the determined expression on Mum's face as she picked up the Monopoly dog (*everyone* wants to be the dog, or the racing car), I couldn't blame her. Whatever she did would be safe enough, I thought, as the grounds were crawling with Cornwall's finest.

Nathan reached for the racing car with a resigned sigh. 'This should be interesting,' he said, as Ben and Craig joined us. Tony plonked himself down at the table next to them and selected the battleship.

'That's one way of looking at it,' he said. 'I remember my mum and dad playing this one Christmas at Jodie's house when we were kids. Shirley takes it proper serious…'

'No point playing if you're not going to take it seriously,' said Mum. 'In another life I could've been Gordon the Gecko.' Ben and Craig both looked at me with expressions of such complete befuddlement that I would've laughed, had the mood not been quite so sombre.

'Gordon Gekko, from *Wall Street*,' I said. 'Greed is good and all that rubbish.'

'Ah, right…' Ben nodded and then grinned at me. 'Your ma cracks me up.'

'She has that effect on most people.' I reached out to take a player token and stopped. There was only one left. 'The old boot? You have *got* to be kidding me…'

We played for about an hour, by which time Mum had

cornered the market in luxury hotels and bankrupted everyone except Craig, who was down to his last twenty quid but refused to concede victory. At the beginning of the game Craig had been pale and withdrawn, and I had the feeling he was avoiding talking to me; maybe he was feeling a bit embarrassed about the way he'd spoken to me the day before, or maybe his hangover was still giving him grief. Either way, he seemed to relax as Mum fleeced us all and managed (suspiciously, to my mind) to avoid jail. Matt had gone off to rehearse his best man speech for the next day (not that he'd told us that; he'd confided in Debbie, who had immediately told me and we'd both *aah*ed at how sweet his loyalty to Nathan was). Tony went off to his room to call Carmen; we still didn't know whether she was going to join us for the evening meal, or if she was steering clear until the ceremony the next day. Ben crossed the room to where Danny, Liz and Roger were playing cards and talking quietly. Debbie and Callum had gone off to soak in the hot tub and make the most of being child free, so that just left me and Nathan.

'Well, that was a lesson in not underestimating your mother-in-law,' said Nathan, signalling to the barman. 'She could give Alan Sugar a run for his money. They'll be getting her to host the next season of *The Apprentice*.' I laughed.

'My mum? You're kidding. She cheats. ALL THE TIME. You must've noticed that whenever we play Monopoly, she's always the bank? I reckon she slips herself a couple of extra fifties when nobody's watching.'

'That would explain a lot. You want a drink?'

'Only if I can have a cup of tea. I don't want any more alcohol, my liver's not used to it.' The barman nodded and went off to make some tea. I sighed. 'This is not quite how I envisaged this weekend.'

'Nor me. But at least they've got Lewis now and we can start getting back to normal.'

'I thought you were "hmm" about Frankie Lewis?' I asked. 'I thought you had doubts?'

'I did, but as we all know, nine times out of ten, it's the partner. And we already know he's got a temper.' Nathan shrugged. 'It's okay to have doubts – they make you double check you really have got the guilty party – but they can also make you ignore the most obvious answer. And the most obvious one in this case is that Lewis did it.'

'Yes.' He was right, and I did think it was Lewis, but… it still surprised me that he'd made no attempt to come up with an alibi overnight.

'Psst!' We looked up to see Sunil in the doorway, looking around cautiously.

'What's he being all Secret Squirrel about?' I wondered. Nathan laughed.

'Bless him, I think he's scared of your friend Di…' He beckoned the DC over to us. 'Sunil, everything alright?'

'Yes, Guv—'

'Nathan,' corrected Nathan, gently. 'I'm not on duty.'

'Nathan,' said Sunil hesitantly, and I felt sorry for him; there was no way he was ever going to feel comfortable using his first name. 'Yes, it's all fine.' He stopped. So obviously everything *wasn't* fine.

'How's the investigation going? I know you can't tell us anything—' I started, but Sunil interrupted.

'I don't know what to do, Gu— Nathan. I am on the horns of a moral dilemma.'

'What's happened?'

'The DI's taken Frankie Lewis back to the station and she's getting ready to charge him,' said Sunil. 'There's CCTV footage of his car entering the hotel grounds last night at ten past twelve – there's a camera at the entrance to the drive, on the wall of the gatehouse.'

'What about cameras outside the hotel?' asked Nathan.

'There is one at the hotel entrance, but it only covers an area of about four metres in front of the door.' Sunil pulled out his notebook. 'He's caught on that camera at twelve twenty-five, entering the hotel.'

'That's about the time he came up to the room and confronted her,' said Nathan. 'What then?'

'He's seen leaving the hotel at just after twelve thirty, but his car doesn't pass the camera on the drive until one fifty.'

'By which time Kelly and her friends had got changed and left,' I said. 'And that's within Mackintosh's time of death, isn't it?'

'Just,' said Sunil. 'Mackintosh says that he hung around outside after the argument at the stag party, then killed her when she came out.'

'Okay, that makes sense,' said Nathan. 'The time of

death is a bit tight, but it's do-able.' He smiled gently at Sunil. 'So what's this dilemma that's worrying you?'

'One of the groundskeepers found this.' Sunil held up a mobile phone in a plastic evidence bag and handed it over to Nathan. The screen was cracked, and the pink glittery protective cover was scuffed. 'It's Kelly's. Lewis described it to us, and when you move it you can see where she's missed messages from him.' Nathan rolled the phone around in his hand until the screen lit up. *8 missed calls from Frankie* flashed up, along with the first few words of a text message: *Babe I sorry your worrying me now—*

'Definitely hers,' I said, looking at the message over Nathan's arm. I frowned. 'He sent that text this morning at eleven thirty,' I said. 'I know it could be a bluff, to make it look like he didn't know she was dead, but…' I thought for a moment. 'If I'd done you in, I'd maybe send a few messages, but then I'd report you missing, like I was expecting you to come home but you didn't.'

'Should I be worried that you worked out that scenario so quickly?' asked Nathan.

'He didn't report her missing, but he did spend the morning and early afternoon driving round to her friends' houses and making a nuisance of himself,' said Sunil. 'He says he thought she'd stayed with her sister or a friend, but when he realised no one had seen her, he came back here, saw her car, and saw Old Davey hanging around looking scary, and he panicked and tried to drive away.'

'Right… Where did they find the phone?'

'On the edge of the golf course, not far from her car,'

said Sunil. 'I saw the text message when they handed the phone over, and I thought the same as you, Jodie. But what I was really wondering, Guv, is should I look at the health data on her phone?'

'Health data?'

'Yes. She was wearing a smart watch, same as this one.' He held up his arm to show us the very expensive and fancy-looking smart watch on his wrist. 'It links up to an app on your phone.' He smiled hesitantly. 'I read up on one of your first cases here, Gu— Nathan, and you worked out the time of death by getting the victim's heart rate off her watch. We could do that here.' He looked around uneasily, as if expecting Mackintosh to leap out from the woodwork and go "AH HA!" – but of course she didn't. 'I already know her passcode. It's her birthday. Lewis told us.'

'Does Mackintosh know you've got this?'

'No, she left before the receptionist thought to mention they'd had a phone handed in. And I thought...'

'You thought if you could unlock the phone and crack the case, you'd end up showing those high-flyers from Exeter, right?' said Nathan, sternly.

'Well, yes...'

Nathan gave his DC a huge smile. 'Too bloody right. Let's do it. If Mackintosh has a problem with it, you can tell her I said it was okay. I'm still your DCI, after all.' He looked serious again. 'She needs to narrow down that murder window if she wants to prove Frankie Lewis managed to murder his girlfriend and hide her body in just twenty minutes, so I think that's grounds enough for us to check her vitals.' He handed the phone back to Sunil. 'You can do the honours.'

Sunil took the phone from the plastic bag. He looked up at Nathan. 'I'd normally use gloves, but it won't work with them on. Plus the groundskeeper found it this morning and handed it into Reception, before you found the victim's body, so it's been handled by several other members of staff already.'

'That's alright, can't be helped,' said Nathan. Sunil nodded and entered the passcode – 210702.

'21st July 2002?' I said. 'She didn't even make it to her twenty-third birthday. God, she really *was* young.'

'Yes,' said Nathan. 'Far too young.'

'Do you want to see the text messages from Lewis first?' asked Sunil. 'There's thirteen unread ones.' He began to read them out. '"Sorry about tonight but I told you not to go" – that one was at two thirty. "You giving me silent treatment" – that was half an hour later...' He held the phone out to Nathan. 'There's a gap after that one until eight o'clock this morning, just saying "stayed at Ian's, on my way"—'

'Who's Ian?' I asked. Sunil shook his head.

'No idea. Maybe a friend?'

'Are you talking about Ian Lewis?' We all turned to look at Tony, who had come up to the bar with Ben to get a round of drinks in.

'You know an Ian Lewis?' asked Nathan.

'Yeah, he works at the store.' Tony's family owned and ran Penhaligon's, the town's long-running department store, and over the years they'd probably employed just about everyone in Penstowan in some capacity. 'I didn't realise Frankie Lewis was his brother. That's what this is about, yeah?'

'Yeah. Frankie texted Kelly that he spent the night with this Ian,' I said. 'You sure they're brothers?'

'No, I'm not sure, but I've heard him talk about his idiot little brother, and how many Lewises are there in Penstowan?'

'Yes,' said Sunil, 'but if Ian's his brother, and he *did* stay the night with him, why didn't he tell us that? Why isn't Ian Lewis his alibi?'

'Maybe he actually spent the night with someone he shouldn't have, to get back at Kelly,' I said. 'Davey said he saw him arguing with another woman. Frankie might have been cheating on Kelly.'

'Or maybe he really did get legless and fall asleep in his car, but he didn't want her to know that,' said Nathan.

'But if he knew she was dead, he would have known that she wasn't at home and wouldn't have missed him anyway,' said Sunil. 'So why send that text?' We all looked at each other.

'Yeah, but he didn't strike me as the sharpest tool in the box,' said Ben, reaching out to take two bottles of beer from the bar. 'Murderers don't always make sense, do they? Especially when it's unplanned. They panic. He's probably sent these text messages as a bluff, trying to be clever, like, and then when youse lot asked him where he was last night he forgot what he'd texted her.' He shook his head. 'We all saw him last night – well, not you, mate—' He nodded at Sunil. 'But the rest of us did, and I don't think any of us would think it was out of character for someone like that to do in his bird in a fit of jealousy.' Ben raised the bottles in a toast to us and headed back to the others. Tony shrugged.

'He's got a point. And Ian Lewis would be the first to tell you his brother's a dick.' He picked up the other drinks and wandered off.

'Well,' said Nathan. 'What do you make of that?'

'It's one thing to get your brother to cover for you if you're cheating on your girlfriend,' I said, 'or if you really did fall asleep in your car and you're embarrassed about it, and quite another to ask him to lie to the police. So I don't think we can necessarily read guilt into that. But equally Ben could be right. We've all dealt with people who think they're criminal masterminds but are actually just criminally stupid and forget what lies they've told.'

'I know.' Nathan sighed. 'Or he could genuinely be telling the truth and didn't do it.'

'Yes,' agreed Sunil. Nathan and I exchanged glances and then both looked at him.

'You really don't think he's guilty, do you?' I said. 'Even before this. What makes you think that?'

'I don't know really, it's just a feeling…' Sunil looked embarrassed. 'I remember you saying once, Guv, that a good copper doesn't ignore their instincts. That we should always follow the rules and conduct a thorough investigation, but that at the same time if we get that little voice niggling at us, we shouldn't ignore it.'

'And that voice is niggling at you now?' asked Nathan.

'Yes. I know some people are good liars, I know that some really evil people have managed to convince others they're innocent, but Frankie Lewis... I don't get that feeling from him. He looked completely bewildered when DI Mackintosh told him what had happened, like he really didn't know she was dead.' He smiled apologetically. 'Sorry, I know that's not a good enough reason, but...'

'If the evidence against him was strong enough, then no, it wouldn't be a good enough reason to dismiss him as a suspect,' said Nathan. 'But at the moment it *isn't* strong enough. Don't ever apologise for questioning someone's guilt *or* innocence. That's what makes you a good copper.'

'And we haven't even looked at the health data yet,' I pointed out. 'That might back up your hunch.'

'Or destroy it,' said Sunil, but he looked gratified that Nathan was taking him seriously. Nathan handed back the phone to him.

'Okay, you know more about these health apps than I do,' he said. Sunil hit the icon, opened the app and started scrolling through the data.

'Right... here's the heart rate monitor,' he said, holding up the phone to show us. 'You can customise how often it records all your health data, but it looks like Kelly's just left it on the default setting, where it makes a note of your average heart rate every hour.' Nathan and I peered at the phone screen. 'So up to one o'clock this morning, she was averaging between sixty-four and sixty-seven beats per minute.'

'Is that good?' I asked.

'Yes, it shows she was quite fit and healthy.' Sunil scrolled further. 'Now this is during the presumed murder window…'

'This is where it gets interesting,' said Nathan, and Sunil nodded.

'Between one and two, her average heart rate was ninety-eight bpm.'

'That's quite an increase,' I said. 'But what caused it? Your heart rate goes up when you're scared, doesn't it?'

'Yes, and during exercise,' said Nathan. 'And if you're injured or in pain, I think. All of which could apply here. Frankie Lewis—'

'Or someone else,' pointed out Sunil.

'Let's just say it's Lewis, for the sake of argument,' said Nathan, 'but we'll keep an open mind. Lewis confronts her in the car park after she leaves the hotel, she gets scared—'

'Maybe she runs away?' I suggested. 'We've assumed that the killer dumped her in the pond, but she might've run away and ended up there.' I looked at Nathan. 'If we're covering all bases, we have to include the possibility of her falling in, even though I think it's unlikely.'

'Yes, on both counts,' said Nathan, 'depending on the cause of death. Did she drown, or was she already dead when she ended up in the water?'

'It looks like drowning,' said Sunil, 'but that doesn't mean it was an accident. There is also a minor head injury, but we won't know anything more about that until the ME's had a look at her.'

'And this heart rate reading is an average, right?' I said.

'Yes,' said Sunil. 'The watch records your heart rate every ten minutes, so that's an average from six readings. And it was still registering a heartbeat between two and three.'

'So she was still alive?'

'Yes.' Sunil showed us the phone screen. 'Thirty-six bpm. But remember that's an average. That could be one massive spike caused by fear or by the actual attack, followed by immediate death, so no heartbeat at all, or it could be her heart slowing down as she dies…' He pulled himself together – I could see that it took a real physical effort for him. 'So we can say that she died between two and three a.m., but we can't narrow it down exactly, and we can't say when the attack took place because if she drowned it would've taken some time to happen.'

Nathan discreetly reached out and took the phone from his DC. 'Good work, Sunil,' he said softly. 'I think DI Mackintosh needs to know about this now, don't you?'

'Yes, Guv.'

'This app,' I said. 'The company that make it, would they be able to give you all this in greater detail? Like, rather than just give you an average, would they be able to tell you what each reading was? So you can narrow down the time she actually died, and maybe even when she was attacked?'

'Yes, probably,' said Sunil. 'I'll get on to them. We've got enough here for an information request, haven't we? It'll probably take a few days, though.'

'Good man.' Nathan put the phone back in the plastic evidence bag. 'Get back to the station and log this in, then get on to the software company. And if Mackintosh has a problem with any of this, tell her to call me.'

'Will do.' Sunil smiled gratefully at him and left.

'That was nice of you, backing him up like that,' I said.

'Of course. She might be in charge of the case, but Sunil's still one of mine, and this is still my manor…'

Chapter Seven

By now it was quite late in the day, and there were mutterings about dinner. We hadn't planned to eat until around eight, but cancelling the shooting and swapping it for board games had thrown everything off schedule, and I thought that boredom and being indoors had made everyone hungry. After finally persuading Craig to accept defeat at Monopoly so Mum could crow in victory and we could all move on with our lives, I decided to ask the manager if we could eat a bit earlier. I left Nathan packing up the board (and pretending not to have found Mum's secret stash of Monopoly money) and wandered out to Reception, where a delivery driver was dropping off a parcel. The receptionist was looking something up on her computer, so I waited.

'Yes, he's a guest here,' she said, smiling at the driver. 'In fact I think he's one of this lady's party.'

'Who's that?' I asked.

'Craig Carter,' said the delivery driver.

'Oh yeah, he's one of mine,' I said, eyeing the parcel. It was from Next, so I was hoping it was a shirt to go with the rest of his best man's outfit, although I had to admit I was rather less excited about the ceremony now. I just wanted it to be over so I could be Mrs Nathan Withers (although I thought it would be better all round if Nathan became Mr Jodie Parker...) and we could go home and put that poor girl's death behind us. 'Do you want me to sign for it? Or leave it with the receptionist and I'll tell him it's here?'

'Nah, all good,' said the driver, leaving the parcel on the reception desk and tapping something into his phone. 'I've told him it's here.'

I smiled at the receptionist, noticing the name tag on her jacket, as the delivery driver left us. 'Hi, Chelsea. Was it you on duty last night?' Davey Trelawney had said all the young women these days looked the same, and he wasn't wrong here – certainly the receptionists all looked the same: young, blonde and pretty. Apart from one spotty bloke with a runny nose.

'No, that was my colleague, Marissa,' she said, smiling warily. 'She's not on again until tonight. Is everything okay?'

'Oh yes, I just wasn't sure if it was you or not. She came up and told my husband-to-be off for being too noisy,' I said lightly. 'Don't worry, I'm not complaining, he probably needed to be told off.'

She smiled again but looked a little bit uneasy, obviously expecting me to go full Karen and ask to see the manager. 'Yes, sorry about that but we have a strict no-noise policy after midnight.'

'Oh no, I get it,' I reassured her. 'People need their sleep. No, I just wondered how she was faring after the events of last night.'

Chelsea turned pale, as another receptionist joined her. 'You mean that poor girl they found? Terrible, isn't it? We were all talking about it at lunchtime.'

'We've always felt so safe working here, even though we're in the middle of nowhere,' said the other receptionist. 'But I thought it happened after she'd clocked off?'

'That's when they found her, but it looks like she was killed last night.'

'Oh my goodness, you mean she could've been sitting here while all that was going on?' Chelsea shook her head. 'That's horrible. I hope she doesn't get too freaked out when she hears that.'

'Not Marissa,' said the other receptionist, dryly, and I got the impression there was no love lost there. I raised an eyebrow and the young woman hurried to cover up her remark. 'She's made of sterner stuff than us,' she said. 'She's very career orientated, very focused.'

'I'm sure the police will have spoken to her about it by now,' I said. 'I hope it won't put her off working here overnight.'

'No,' said Chelsea. 'It's been bad enough being here

during the day with everyone around, knowing that poor girl's body was out there. Do they think someone…? Could it have been an accident?'

'Too early to say yet,' I said, feeling a bit bad for bringing it up; I tended to forget that not everyone was used to dealing with murder, and the staff, many of whom I realised were probably about the same age as Kelly, must be pretty disturbed by the whole thing. 'Statistically speaking, this is now an even safer place to work than it was before, because the police are still keeping an eye out. And as they say, lightning doesn't strike twice.' Although of course that was rubbish; lightning struck in the same place all the time. 'Anyway, sorry to bring that up, I shouldn't have mentioned it. I actually just came out to ask about moving our dinner booking…'

Chelsea agreed to speak to the restaurant manager about an earlier dinner sitting for us, and I was just about to turn around to go back into the bar when I felt someone appear behind me; Craig.

'Oh – Jodie.' He looked awkward. 'I just had a text about a parcel.'

'Yeah, it's here,' I said, nodding at the two receptionists.

'Great.' Craig reached out and took the parcel. I turned away and went to head into the bar, but he reached out to stop me. 'Er, it's a shirt. For tomorrow. After I forgot to pack one.'

'Good,' I said, going to leave again, but he stopped me again.

'Sorry, Jodie, can I have a word?'

Oh God, what now? I thought, but I didn't say that. 'Of course.'

'Not in there. Just the two of us?'

'Alright...' This wasn't going to be awkward or anything, was it? But I followed him over to the same discreet corner we'd sat in with the manager the day before – it seemed to have been made especially for awkward conversations – and plopped myself down on a chair opposite him.

'Look, I just wanted to apologise for being a dickhead,' he said, and I shrugged.

'No, it's fine—'

'I can see by your face it wasn't fine. I'm a bit of a mess at the moment, and I've been taking it out on, well, everyone really. I was rude to you yesterday, I didn't mean to be but I was, and I knew I was the moment I said it. You are so far from being a Bridezilla—'

I laughed. 'Yeah, that did sting, I have to admit.'

'I just felt like an idiot already, missing me flight and that, and then getting here and realising I hadn't packed half me stuff.' He threw his hands up in a gesture of frustration at himself. 'I'm a bloody mess, but that ain't your fault. The last thing I wanna do is ruin your wedding.'

'I wouldn't bloody let you, don't you worry about that,' I said, but in a light-hearted way to let him know he was forgiven.

'Good. If I'm being a dickhead again, tell me, will ya?'

'You can count on it.' I smiled, and he returned it with the first genuine (but small) smile I'd seen on his face so far that weekend. 'You don't have to tell me, but… You said you're a mess. What's going on? What's the matter?'

'Oh, you know… just stuff.'

'Well it must be important "stuff", because you're not the cheeky Scouser Nathan and I know and love. If you want to talk about it, Nathan or I are happy to listen. He's so glad you're here, and I am too.'

'Thanks, Jodie,' he said, and to my alarm his eyes filled with tears. I reached out to take his hand.

'Come on, whatever's happened can't be that bad, can it?' I asked, but of course things could be that bad, what did I know?

'They couldn't be much worse,' he said. 'I am such a—'

'Dickhead, yes, we all know that,' I said, smiling at him. 'Oh wait, you mean you've been more of a dickhead than usual? Bloody hell, you better tell me.' He smiled weakly and I thought, *Damn, it really IS bad.* 'What is it? Is it Nicky?' He nodded, miserably. 'Is that why she hasn't come?'

'Yeah. I've really mucked it up, Jodie. We had a massive argument before I left. I think it might be over. It *should* be over. I was an idiot.'

'You don't think it's something that can be forgiven, maybe? Lots of couples argue.'

'Do you and Nathan?'

'Well, not really, no. We have "heated debates" occasionally, but I think we've only ever really had one big argument, and making up afterwards meant it was almost worth it.'

Craig smiled sadly. 'Yeah, I'm not sure we'll be making up any time soon.'

'It can't have been that bad, surely? There are very few things that can't be sorted out and put right.'

'Yeah… not sure this can.' He sat for a moment, looking absolutely heartbroken. I squeezed his hand, but I didn't push him to speak; if he wanted to tell me, or maybe Nathan later on, then he would. He sniffed and pulled his hand away, reaching for his phone. 'Did I ever show you a picture of her?'

'No, I don't think so…'

Craig held out his phone. The lock screen showed a photograph of a happy, smiling couple: him and Nicky. Nicky was tall and slender, with long brunette hair. She was gorgeous, done up to the nines with dark-plum lipstick and a well-tailored, silky emerald-green trouser suit. Craig stood next to her, gazing at her with an adoring expression on his face.

'Wow,' I said, and I meant it. 'She's beautiful. You look really good together.'

'Yeah, that was a good night. She does PR for an art gallery and that was the opening night of this big exhibition.' He smiled again. 'Bit different to the nights out I was used to having back home. I grew up in Kirkdale, the only art we 'ad round there was scallies tagging the wall behind the Co-op.' He put his phone down on the coffee table. 'She was one of the first people I met when I went over there, apart from other cops, of course. I'd been there about three weeks, and I decided to go out on me own one night to this bar down the road from where I was staying. She was in there with some friends, and they saw me sitting there on me own like Norman No Mates and took pity on me. Never met anyone like her before in my life.'

'She sounds great,' I said. 'So what happened?'

Craig fiddled with his phone, making the screen light up again. He stared at the photo of the happy couple. 'She found out she was invited to the wedding.'

'"Found out"? What do you mean? You hadn't told her?' He shook his head. 'Why not?'

'She accused me of being ashamed of her. She said I was embarrassed to be seen with her.'

'What? Why on earth would you be ashamed? She's bloody gorgeous!' I looked at the photo again, but for the life of me I couldn't see anything that would make any man in their right mind embarrassed to be seen with her. Craig sighed.

'Did Nathan tell you I'm bi?'

'Bi? You mean bisexual? No, of course not. Why would he?'

'He's the only one here who knows. I dated lads when I was younger, but since I've been a copper, I've only had girlfriends. Not on purpose, like, it's just turned out that way.' He paused. 'At least, I didn't think it was on purpose. Now I'm not so sure.'

'Okay. So why would you bringing Nicky be embarrassing…?' I stopped, not sure if I'd suddenly worked it out. 'Are you saying Nicky isn't a girl?' I asked carefully. 'Or maybe she wasn't always one?'

'Can you tell?'

'That's she's transgender? Because that's what you're saying, isn't it?' He nodded. 'No, I can't tell. I just guessed by what you were saying.' I picked up the phone and studied it, and then stopped, faintly appalled at what I was doing; looking for tell-tale signs. *You can always tell.* That's what people on the Internet always said, but I'd come across enough transgender people in my days in the Met – usually (sadly) victims, rather than perpetrators – to know that was rubbish. 'I would never in a million years have thought that. It wouldn't even occur to me.'

'She does have this deep, throaty laugh,' he said, and I shrugged.

'So what? Have you heard my mum? Someone told her a dirty joke earlier, and I thought Brian Blessed had gatecrashed the wedding.' Craig laughed softly and I reached over and put a hand on his arm. 'But none of that matters anyway, does it, if you really love someone. And you *do* love her, don't you?'

'More than anything else in the world.'

'Then who cares what anyone thinks? Even if they *do* think anything nasty, which I can't believe any of this lot would. Sod 'em.'

Craig looked at me thoughtfully. 'You're right, of course. But she was right, too. Not that I'm ashamed of her, not for one minute, she's brilliant. She's funny, and sharp, and kind… I think maybe I was embarrassed about what people would say about me if they knew I was with a trans woman.' He gave what I thought was the saddest, longest, most depressed sigh I'd ever heard. 'The whole thing's made me take a look at myself, and I don't really like what I see.'

'Oh, sweetheart…'

'I'm an idiot. I was more concerned about what Ben and Danny would say – not Nathan, not so much anyway, because he's always been pretty sound. But the other two… There was this gay fella when we were all working together out of Smithdown nick, he was a bit of a prat if I'm being honest, but it had nothing to do with his sexuality, ya know? But Danny in particular was always 'aving a go at him, taking the mickey out of him, mincing up and down and saying stuff like—' He put on a high-pitched, mocking voice and adopted a 'weak wrist' pose, '"What a gay day!" – rubbish like that. And that was very mild compared to some of the others.'

'I can imagine,' I said, because the same kind of thing had happened back at my old nick in Stockwell, certainly in the early days. It probably still happened now, only less blatantly.

'So yeah, I was more worried about how I'd look in front of me mates than how the woman I love might feel. Idiot or what?'

'Idiot,' I agreed. 'But it's understandable.'

'And I was worried about them saying stuff to her too,' he said, a tad defensively, I thought. 'I wanted to shield her from any transphobic comments they might make.'

'Which is gallant, but ultimately not down to you,' I said. 'Avoiding situations where things like that might happen is not really your decision, is it? She's probably dealt with a lot of stuff like that. Do you think she hides away and doesn't meet new people, just in case they say something nasty?'

'No,' he said. 'She's the bravest person I know.'

'She must be,' I said. 'She was prepared to marry you.'

'Oh, ha ha,' said Craig, but he wasn't really offended. 'You're right. I told her I was trying to protect her, and she basically said the same as you. It's her choice. I was just using it as an excuse.'

'Again, it's understandable,' I said, 'but it's a shame, because honestly, I don't think any of my lot would've said anything. Well, my mum might've, but it wouldn't have been any more inappropriate or offensive than the stuff she says to everyone else. And that's supposing any of them even guessed, because I'm assuming you weren't planning to out her in front of everybody?'

'Oh God, no. It's down to her to tell people if she wants them to know.'

'So what it boils down to is, who matters most to you? Nicky, or Ben and Danny?'

Craig shook his head. 'Mad, isn't it? Of course it's Nicky. I realised that the moment I set foot on the plane, when it was too late. I shouldn't care what people think—'

'You're still assuming people will think *anything*. In my experience, most people are too busy dealing with their own stuff to be that bothered about other people's. And anyone who is bothered, well, they can bugger off and mind their own business. Nobody can tell you who to love.'

'Yeah, you're probably right.' He gave me a grateful smile. 'Thanks, Jodie.'

'What for?'

'For listening and not judging.'

'No worries. I've never understood why people get so het up about what's in other people's pants anyway. I mean, I love absolutely everything about Nathan, including his bits and pieces, but they're not the most attractive thing about him.'

'My gran used to say they look like the last plucked chicken hanging up in the butcher's window,' said Craig. We looked at each other for a moment and then both burst out laughing.

'Oh my God, your granny was right,' I gasped. Nathan came into the foyer and saw us in the corner. He walked over to us, looking a bit puzzled.

'Everything alright, is it?' he asked. 'What are you two gassing about?'

'Your chicken,' said Craig, and I started laughing again.

'Or more accurately, your giblets,' I said. Craig howled.

'The parson's nose and two nuggets!' he burst out. I wiped my eyes as Nathan shook his head, smiling but bemused.

'I can't take you two anywhere,' he said. 'Did you get dinner changed?' I nodded and opened my mouth to speak, but he interrupted me. 'Please tell me chicken's not on the menu.'

We sat down to eat about half an hour later and of course, chicken *was* on the menu but for some reason (ahem) I didn't really fancy it and went for the vegetarian option instead, which was *lush*. The wait staff were professional to a fault, friendly but also discreet; I almost didn't notice them put the plates down, and it was as if the food just politely materialised in front of us. It felt weird sitting down to eat with such a large group, as normally in that kind of situation I'd be out in the kitchen, doing the catering. I have to admit I did pretty much deconstruct my spiralised vegetable tart to see what ingredients they'd used and to admire the work that had gone into it. It was a crisp buttery pastry tartlet case, with a filling of whipped feta, into which were set spirals of carrot, beetroot, courgette and yellow squash, making rings of vibrant colour that looked beautiful against the bed of green salad it was served next to. It looked and tasted fabulous, but I did have to wonder just how long it must've taken to spiralise all the veg, as I wasn't the only one having it. Far too much faff for me to make, I thought. Nathan had the chicken – a massive, juicy burger with avocado and bacon – and despite our earlier conversation I did suffer momentarily from a case of 'Oh no, I wish I'd ordered *that* instead', especially as it came with proper, big fat chunky chips. But I nicked a few off his plate, and that made me feel better.

Dessert was *heavenly*, a proper chocolate fondant cake with an oozy middle, served with clotted-cream ice cream. I hesitated before ordering it (for about two seconds) because that beautiful wedding dress hanging over the back of the door upstairs was already very fitted, but... Come on, it was a *chocolate fondant cake* for heaven's sake, who turns their nose up at that?! I'm not made of stone.

Any boredom or ill humour was completely banished as we all tucked in, everyone chatting away and getting on – even Matt and Craig, which was nice to see. Matt's girlfriend Chrissie had finally clocked off from the station and joined us, and the three of them were laughing and swapping stories about their days on the beat. As Craig finished a story, Matt laughed and raised his glass to him.

'Mate, that is *gold*!' he said. Nathan turned to look at me with his eyebrows raised.

'I don't know what you and Craig were talking about earlier,' he said in a low voice, 'but whatever you said to him seems to have worked wonders. He's still not quite his usual self, but he's making an effort. Even *Matt's* getting on with him now.'

'Yeah, it does your heart good to see your kids making new friends, doesn't it?' I said, and Nathan laughed.

'Yeah, bless him...' He looked at me expectantly.

'What?'

'You're being uncharacteristically discreet and not telling me what you and Craig were talking about.'

'Am I?' I pretended to think about it. 'Yeah, I s'pose I am...'

'I'm practically your husband, you know. No secrets between man and wife.'

'Okay, I'll tell you tomorrow when we *are* man and

wife.' I grinned at him. 'No, seriously, it's kind of what we suspected—'

'Nicky?'

'Yeah, big argument, he's worried it's all over.' I looked over at them, to make sure Craig didn't realise we were discussing him. 'It's not down to me to tell you what it was all about, though. I'm sure he'll tell you, he just needs to find the right moment.'

'That bad?'

'Not bad, no. Just… surprising.'

'Come on, everyone!' cried Mum, pushing her empty plate away and standing up. 'No more lollygagging and sitting around, it's karaoke time!' She grabbed Liz's arm. 'You and me, "Sisters Doing it for Themselves", what about it?'

'Count me in!' said Liz, jumping up. Behind her, one of the waiters' professionalism slipped for a moment and they gave a broad grin. Daisy looked across the table at me, horrified.

'Oh my God, there's two of them,' she said. 'As if Nana needs an enabler…' Joe, sitting next to her, watched wide-eyed as the two pensioners (who were both much more spritely than that word makes them sound) headed out to the bar, corralling the other participants (some more willing than others) along with them.

'Just be thankful my nana's not here, there'd be three of them,' he said.

Nathan reached out to hold my hands as the room emptied.

'So, soon-to-be Mrs Withers,' he said.

'Yes, soon-to-be Mr Parker?'

He laughed. 'I can't deny you've got a better surname than me, but I'm not changing mine. Maybe we should double barrel, for the sake of the children?'

'You mean almost-adult child, because I'm afraid that ship has long sailed, buster. So Nathan Withers Parker?'

'I don't know, do I?' We both laughed, and then he pulled me into a proper hug. 'Anyway... I was just going to ask if you'll be sneaking along the corridor to join me again tonight?'

'Why, you had a better offer?'

'There is no better offer than you, Mrs Withers Parker.'

'Smoothy. But no, I'm not.' I grinned at his surprised face. 'I'm not going to be sneaking, I'm planning to stride along purposefully to join my husband-to-be. Blow all that superstitious nonsense about not seeing each other before the wedding. The ceremony's not until three, am I supposed to avoid you all day until then as well? Not happening.'

'I love that you're a rebel.'

'I love *you*.'

'Oh my *God*,' said an exasperated Daisy behind us. 'Can't you two ever leave each other alone? We need you in the karaoke room, *now*. They didn't have Annie Lennox and Aretha Franklin so Nana's asked if she can do The Prodigy instead.'

'Not—'

'No, "Firestarter", thank God.'

Nathan looked at me, puzzled. 'You remember that

fourteenth birthday party I did back in February?' I explained. 'They asked us to leave because Mum made the kid's seven-year-old sister cry.'

'What's that got to do with The Prodigy?'

'She insisted on singing "Smack My B— Up".' I turned to Daisy. 'If the worst comes to the worst, we can set off the fire alarm. It'll probably be more in tune than Nana.'

Chapter Eight

I woke the next morning to the sound of a text message arriving. I wouldn't normally have left my phone on overnight (Daisy tells me that's because I'm old), but I'd set an alarm so that I could get up and go back to my own room before the rest of the guests emerged. There was no way I was going to spend the whole morning avoiding Nathan, but I could at least lie and say we hadn't spent the night together in an effort to placate the traditionalists. I wasn't *that* much of a rebel…

I picked up my phone just as the alarm went off, and read the text message.

'Everything okay?' asked Nathan, sleepily throwing an arm around me.

'Yes, except Maggie Tiddy's going to drop Germaine off here in about an hour,' I said. He groaned.

'What? I thought she had her for the whole weekend?'

'She did, but her son – the one who lives up in Bristol – had an accident last night, so she's going up to make sure he's alright.'

'Fuss over him, more like,' grumbled Nathan.

'Well, yeah, but that's what mums do, isn't it? I'm sure she told me once he lives on his own, so the hospital might not send him home unless he's got someone there to help him. And Brian's away this weekend—' Maggie's husband was a lorry driver, who was often away for several nights at a time with work '—which is why she was so happy to take Germaine in, for a bit of company. But obviously she can't take our little princess to Bristol.'

Nathan sat up, a bit more awake and alert. 'Is she okay? Is her son badly hurt?'

'Broken leg and a lot of bruises. Do you think I should ring her?'

'Only if you want to spend the next two hours on the phone,' said Nathan mildly. Maggie was a big talker.

'Yeah… I'll just text her back and then I'll have a chat with her when she gets here,' I said. 'She won't hang around if she's on her way up to Bristol.'

I left Nathan to shower and dress and headed back to my room. I stopped at the door, suddenly hesitant. I'd told Daisy I'd be spending the night with Nathan, and had left her saying goodnight to Joe, who was waiting for a taxi to pick him up; he was coming back later today for the actual wedding. But what if he hadn't gone home? What if he'd stayed the night with Daisy? They'd been together for a year now, they were both of legal age for, you know, *that* kind of thing, and they genuinely cared for each other. And my daughter was sensible, and so was Joe, and it was surely better that if they *were* getting up to, you know, *that*, that they were doing it somewhere nice and safe, rather than in the back of a car or upstairs at a house party or somewhere equally seedy. And I couldn't exactly judge if they had, you know, done *that*, because I hadn't been much older when I'd first done it, and it wasn't with someone I'd been going out with for a year either, *and* my track record since then (until I'd met Nathan) hadn't been particularly good. But…

Oh for goodness sake! I had a word with myself sternly. I gave the door a gentle rap with my knuckles and waited for thirty seconds before going in.

Daisy was sitting up in bed reading *Rivers of London*. She looked up at me, mystified. 'Was that you knocking?'

'Why, you expecting room service?'

'No, but it's your room, you muppet.'

'One, I'm your mother, not a muppet—' Daisy snorted and muttered something about looking like Miss Piggy, but I ignored her '—and two, I didn't know if you were still asleep. I didn't want to make you jump by just bursting in.' *And I wanted to give you time to stop whatever you were doing and for your boyfriend to make himself decent or hide in the wardrobe*, I added, but only to myself.

'Oh, right. Fair enough.' She put down her book and sighed. 'You know what? I know it's only been a couple of days but I miss Germaine. She'd normally be asleep on the end of my bed.'

'You're in luck, then,' I said, casually heading over to the wardrobe and opening it. Nothing but clothes... as I'd expected. There was nothing under the bed, either, and no one was hiding in the ensuite. We both showered and dressed, stopping to gaze at the beautiful gown I'd actually be wearing in a few hours (eek!) before heading down to the breakfast room. It was a light, airy room, much more modern in feel than the grand dining room or the Art Deco bar and bistro, but it still gave off an air of understated, sophisticated elegance, with simple white linen tablecloths and clean, minimalist lines.

'It's quiet in here this morning,' I said to the smiling waiter who greeted us at the door.

'Your party are the only guests who have managed to get here in time for breakfast the whole weekend,' she said.

'Don't tell me the rowdy golfers are on the course already?'

She looked around and then laughed, lowering her voice confidentially. 'Doubt it. I suspect they're all too hungover this morning. They were really enjoying themselves at your karaoke session last night.'

'Oh, you've heard about that, have you?'

'Heard about it, seen footage of it online. That elderly lady, Shirley—'

'That's no lady, that's my mum,' I said.

Daisy sniggered. 'I'm telling her you said that...'

'She is an absolute *legend*,' said the waiter. 'I've never heard The Prodigy sung quite like that before.' *That* was an understatement.

'Well, she'll be at the wedding reception later, so stick around, you might get an encore…'

Debbie and Callum were already sitting at a table, tucking into scrambled egg on toast. I sat down next to them and looked at the menu, but my insides were churning slightly at the thought of the ceremony later on.

'You two are up early,' I said. 'I thought you'd be making the most of being childfree and having a lie-in.'

'When you've spent the last twenty-odd years having to get up at the crack of dawn for work, you can't just switch it off, unfortunately,' said Callum. 'It's the curse of the early risers.'

'You certainly rose early this morning,' murmured Debbie, rubbing his arm affectionately. Daisy made gagging noises but Debbie just laughed. 'You wait until you and Joe—'

'Ahem,' I said, coughing and clearing my throat noisily. I did *not* want to talk about that, not until she was a bit older, anyway.

'Here, have some orange juice,' said Callum, peering at me in concern and passing me a glass.

'Thank you.' I sipped at the juice. 'I'm fine. I've just got to come up with a way to persuade the hotel manager to let me have Germaine at the ceremony this afternoon.'

'Germaine's coming?' Debbie's face lit up. 'Aww, how sweet! Oh my God, I know, she could be your ring bearer—'

'And take that job away from Matt? He's already having to deal with Craig muscling in on the best man duties, I can't edge him out even more by giving Germaine that responsibility.' I thought about it. 'I mean, yeah, she would look cute—'

'*SO* cute!'

'—but she'd probably eat the rings. So no.' My phone beeped: another text from Maggie, saying she was outside. 'There she is now.'

Maggie had parked on the hotel drive as close to the front door as possible, and was standing next to her car with Germaine sitting patiently at her feet. Germaine had a long list of random people she loved and several she hated, and one day out of the blue she'd decided Maggie was one of her favourite people, despite the fact she'd only ever met her in passing while we were on walks. Luckily the feeling was mutual. Maggie loved dogs, but running a B&B in town made owning one a bit awkward, as not everyone felt the same way.

'Jodie, I'm so sorry to do this to you,' she said. Germaine leapt to her feet and trotted over to me and Daisy, tail wagging furiously. 'Will she be alright here? I know they're not as dog friendly as some places—'

'It's only for the day,' I reassured her. 'We're paying them enough, they can put up with her until after the reception, when Mum and Daisy can take her home with them.' Nathan and I were spending our honeymoon night at the hotel, along with most of our other guests. We'd planned for Mum and Daisy to stay too, but Mum had already been dropping heavy hints about missing her own bed, so we'd agreed to get her a taxi home with Daisy to accompany her. 'Is Sam okay? And what's happening with the B&B while you're away?'

'He's not too bad, thank you. Truth be told, I'm probably making a fuss, but I always tell him, I'm his mum and that's my job.'

'Hear hear,' I said.

'And I've got Laurel coming in to keep an eye on our guests today and tomorrow, and then Brian's back for a bit anyway.' She hunkered down to give Germaine a kiss on the furry snout. 'Bye bye sweetie, you'll have to come for a sleepover another time.' She straightened up. 'I'd better get off,' she said, and turned away before whirling around again with a look of embarrassment on her face. 'Oh, and good luck with the wedding! I almost forgot!'

'Other stuff on your mind,' I said, waving her away. 'Go on, off you go. Give Sam our best.'

We watched her drive off. I looked at Germaine, then at Daisy.

'Okay, how do we hide a dog for twelve hours?'

Daisy had nothing to do until Joe came back for the ceremony later – other than get into her bridesmaid outfit, get her hair, make-up and nails done, and stop me and Nathan eloping to get married somewhere smaller and quieter (which was becoming more appealing the closer we got to the Big Moment) – so she agreed to take Germaine for a walk around the grounds, trying to keep out of sight of the hotel staff. I gave both of my babies a kiss – one of whom had better-smelling breath than the other – and then went back into the hotel, but I'd barely set foot back in the foyer when I had another text message.

'Oh Maggie, what have you forgotten?' I murmured to myself. But it wasn't Maggie; it was Sunil.

Are you free to talk? I need to ask you something.

I frowned – he must've texted me by mistake. ***Did you text me by mistake? Did you mean to text Nathan?***

Almost immediately my phone rang. Sunil, video-calling me.

'Hi Sunil,' I said. 'Have you rung me by mistake? Did you mean to ring Nathan?'

'No,' he said, looking awkward. 'I just wanted to run something past you before I talk to him.'

'Okay... Well, he's not here, so go for it.'

Even on the small screen of my phone, I could see that Sunil was steeling himself to speak. He took a deep breath. 'How well do you know Craig Carter?'

'Craig?' I asked, surprised. 'Not that well, but well enough... What's going on?'

'I went back to the station last night and gave Mackintosh Kelly's mobile phone. I think she's annoyed that I looked at it.'

'Ignore her. What's that got to do with Craig?'

'Since then she's got me doing all the donkey work. This morning I've been watching the footage from the hotel's CCTV cameras to double check Frankie Lewis's movements.' He hesitated. 'And Craig's on there.'

'What?' I was shocked. Craig had supposedly been

blackout drunk and fast asleep at that time of night, although to be fair neither Nathan nor I had asked him where he was at the actual time of the murder. Sunil, or one of the other members of the investigating team, would've done, though. 'I'm assuming he didn't mention this when you lot took his statement.'

'No, he didn't. Where are you? In Reception? Can Nathan hear you?'

'No, but I'm heading outside now just in case...' I wandered back outside and plopped down onto a stone bench that was to one side of the door. I held out my phone so Sunil could see where I was. 'Right, no one else about. Go for it.'

'Okay. The footage shows all three girls, and your mate Tony, leaving the hotel at sixteen minutes past one, Saturday morning. Tony waves them off from the door and then goes back in – he didn't look too steady on his feet, so he didn't hang around. The victim re-enters the hotel two minutes later—'

'She'd forgotten part of her costume,' I said. 'A pinny or something.'

'Yes. Nathan's friend Ben says she went back to his room, but he had a look and couldn't find the apron,' explained Sunil. 'She didn't go in. So she left the hotel again at one twenty-nine.'

'Making Mackintosh's time of death even tighter,' I said. 'But what about Craig...?'

'The DI has only seen the footage from the front-door camera. As soon as she saw Frankie Lewis leave the hotel she checked the camera on the driveway – the golf course's greenskeeper lives in the gatehouse, and he's got his own security camera up, to stop people sneaking onto the course without paying – and when it was obvious that Lewis hadn't left straight away but had hung around to wait for Kelly, she decided that was enough to charge him. She didn't even ask about any other cameras.'

'There are others? Inside?' I thought back to what the hotel manager, Mr Robbins, had said: enough to make guests feel safe, but not so many that they felt like they were being spied on.

'There's one in the lift, but that's it. And the lift footage matches up with the front-door camera, with Lewis leaving, and then the girls and Tony, and so on. No one else. But there are two other cameras outside, one above the rear entrance, leading onto the terrace, and one covering the side of the hotel and part of the car park.' Sunil smiled ruefully. 'Not the staff part where our victim was parked, unfortunately, just the guest car park.'

'That would be too helpful, wouldn't it?'

'Yes. The footage has Craig leaving via the rear entrance just after midnight. He sits on one of the chairs on the terrace for about an hour – in fact it looks like he fell asleep there. Then he wakes up and walks out of shot, round the side of the hotel towards the staff car park.'

'Where did he go then?'

'I don't know. He doesn't show up on any more footage.'

'What? How did he get back into the hotel, if both entrances were covered by CCTV?'

'I don't know how he got back in, if indeed he did—'

'He did. Ben knocked on his door this morning to wake him up for the axe throwing, and Craig told him in no uncertain terms where he could stick his axe.' I thought for a moment. 'What about the night concierge? Melissa? Maybe she saw him come back in. Or one of the other staff members?'

'She didn't see anyone leave or enter the hotel after the victim left. And there weren't any other members of staff on duty at that point.'

'She was on her own?'

'For the part of the night we're interested in, yes.' I saw Sunil pick up his notebook and refer to it. 'Marissa, not Melissa. The receptionists' shifts are staggered, so there's always at least two people on, except for the period between midnight and six a.m., when there's just one. Marissa came on at ten p.m., and the other receptionist left at midnight. The bar shut at midnight, but the staff have to clear up so it was more like one o'clock by the time they left. They would've locked the door onto the terrace as part of the clean-up, by the way, which explains why Craig couldn't go back inside the same way. The manager, Mr Robbins, lives on site, so even though he's usually in bed by then he's on call if she needs help, but she says she's only ever had to wake him up once. The day shift comes in to relieve her at six.'

'So she's on her own for about five hours? That must be lonely,' I said. 'I don't think I'd be able to stay awake. I'd have a bed set up in the office so I could go and have a kip.'

'Me too,' said Sunil, although I couldn't imagine him doing anything so rebellious as abandoning his post for forty winks, even when everyone else was fast asleep. 'But she told me she's doing a degree in hotel management, so she uses the quiet time to study. It's perfect – no distractions.'

'And she didn't see anyone? She didn't see Craig come back in? Was she definitely at the desk all night?'

'She didn't see Craig, or anyone else – she didn't even see Frankie Lewis come in, because she was upstairs telling the stags to keep the noise down,' said Sunil, with a small grin. 'She admitted she does do a sweep of the ground floor now and then to keep herself awake, and check that the bar staff have cleared up properly, that kind of thing. She couldn't say exactly what time she did her sweep that night, but she thought it was probably about two o'clock, after the victim had left.'

'What does DI Mackintosh say about the CCTV footage?'

'I haven't told her yet. She's convinced Frankie Lewis is our man, so she's happy with the footage from the front-door camera and the one at the end of the driveway, which puts him outside at roughly the right time. But of course the footage I just found from the other camera puts Craig on the spot at the right time, too.'

'Okay…'

'No one else was picked up on any of the cameras. So if it isn't Frankie Lewis…' Sunil left the rest unsaid. 'That's why I wanted to ask you about him before I talk to Nathan. I know they're friends.'

'Yes, they are,' I said, 'but if Craig was there, at that time of night, he might've seen something.' A horrible thought occurred to me, and I realised then exactly why Sunil was dreading telling Nathan about it. 'Or…' Sunil smiled thinly at me, as the penny dropped.

'Or he did it,' said Sunil.

Chapter Nine

Sunil agreed to keep what he'd found to himself for the moment, with the proviso that if Mackintosh asked him outright if he'd seen anyone else on the CCTV footage he couldn't lie, particularly as she was already a bit miffed with him for looking at Kelly's phone. He told me that, as the footage was recorded and uploaded to a cloud storage system, the hotel manager still had access to it if Nathan wanted to watch it himself. Because telling Nathan was obviously my next step.

Or was it? I didn't want to upset him by accusing his best friend of murder, not unless I really had to. And for the life of me I couldn't think what possible motive Craig would have to kill anyone, let alone Kelly. How could a police officer originally from Liverpool but now from New York City, be connected to a topless waitress from Cornwall? Although there was obviously more to Kelly than that; she was more than just her job. Of course, Craig *had* crudely propositioned her the previous night. That in itself seemed out of character for him, but maybe in light of what he'd told me – about his doubts over his relationship with Nicky, or more accurately how other people would feel about his relationship with her – maybe it was a little more understandable. If he'd been feeling shame or anxiety at the thought of being outed as bisexual (although, I supposed, pansexual was probably closer to the truth), particularly in front of Danny, then maybe propositioning her had been an attempt to look more like a 'proper man' (whatever *that* was). At this point Daisy would no doubt have said something about toxic masculinity and the patriarchy being as bad for blokes as it was for women, which was probably true but not that helpful, so I was glad she was off walking the dog.

    I sighed. I didn't know Craig that well, but he didn't strike me as being that kind of bloke, and I couldn't imagine Nathan being close friends with someone like that. Then again, there were plenty of men out there who didn't seem to be 'that kind of bloke', but were *exactly* that kind, especially after a few drinks. Had he been outside, maybe getting some fresh air and trying to sober up, and had seen her heading for her car? Maybe he'd tried to proposition her again, she'd refused, and then… I kicked myself for not asking Sunil if there'd been any signs of sexual assault, which would at least have given someone other than Frankie Lewis a motive, but I thought he probably would have mentioned it if there were. The body – Kelly – hadn't looked like anything of that kind had taken place, but having been in the water for a few hours, it was difficult to tell just by sight. She had at least been left fully dressed, although that didn't necessarily mean anything.

I needed to get a handle on this investigation. Okay, I didn't *need* to – I was supposed to be getting married, not poking my nose into a case that Di Mackintosh probably already had sewn up – but I wasn't going to let a little thing like that stop me. I had *hours* before the ceremony, loads of time to get my hair done and all that malarkey, and I was supposed to be avoiding my husband-to-be, wasn't I? Never mind that I'd already said I wasn't going to be bound by that particular tradition. Plus I should probably go and find Daisy and Germaine, and if that happened to take me anywhere near the crime scene, then so be it…

I stood up and headed towards the guest car park, as if I was just going to get something from my own car, although it wasn't really necessary; the police circus had pretty much gone, apart from the Forensic team's van, although there was no sign of the team themselves. I made my way round the side of the building where Sunil had said the staff car park was. It was full of vehicles (unsurprisingly; the hotel was in the middle of the countryside, and I couldn't see the local bus service being much help to anyone who worked there), but all bar one of them were crammed together at one side of the car park; the police must've stopped them parking near Kelly's car when they arrived for work that morning. An old silver Nissan sat almost in the centre of the gravel, cordoned off with police tape; that must be hers. There were no officers nearby though, Forensic or otherwise, so it obviously wasn't high priority. I ducked under the tape and sauntered across to the car, because the main thing I've learnt since becoming an unofficial investigator is that if you confidently infiltrate a crime scene, people will assume you're allowed to be there. Although admittedly that hadn't always worked.

I had a nose around the car, but there wasn't much to see. I peered in through the passenger window. There was a bag on the rear seat, which had a small white apron sticking out of it; Kelly had obviously found her pinny, after all. In the centre console there was a reusable water bottle and a crumpled-up tissue. I walked round to the driver's side. The car keys were still in the ignition; Kelly must've been about to get in and drive home, when Frankie Lewis (*or Craig*, a treacherous voice in my head whispered) had approached and – and what? Attacked her? Had there been a physical altercation here, in the car park? Or had it happened by the pond?

I shook my head. It was quite possible we would never know exactly what had happened. I wrapped my T-shirt round my hand to avoid touching the handle (which looked like it had already been dusted for prints, going by the black powdery residue on the chrome) and carefully opened the car door. The *bing bing bing* of the alarm made me jump. I pushed the door shut again and it stopped. I looked around, but nobody had come running over to tell me off. Still, I probably didn't need to open it again. I peered through the window. A pair of flat shoes, probably for driving, waited in the footwell of the driver's seat for their owner to return, which for some reason struck me as incredibly sad. Kelly would never wear them again. I couldn't remember – I'd only met her briefly and could barely picture her now – but thinking about the costume, she must've been wearing heels. Had she had them on when we found her body? I hadn't even looked. I was losing my touch. But then it had been the last place I'd expected to find a corpse, even with Debbie on the loose with the bow and arrow.

'Oh my god, don't tell me…' I whirled around to find Debbie (talk of the devil!) standing behind me with a knowing grin on her face. 'Don't tell me, you don't trust the police to get it right and you're investigating?'

'Of course I'm not investigating, this is my wedding party,' I said, but she looked unconvinced and with my record, I could hardly blame her. 'I'm just checking something out…'

'But they've caught the murdering bugger, haven't they?' said Debbie. 'Her boyfriend.'

'Yeah…'

She rolled her eyes. 'Don't you "yeah" me like that, if you know something I want in.'

'What's the matter, are you bored already?' I laughed.

'There's only so many times you can get intimate in the hot tub before the hotel staff throw you out,' she said.

'Ugh no, you didn't? Not in the hot tub? Daisy and Joe were in there yesterday, they better not have been swimming about in your sex lurgies.' I groaned as I thought of something else. 'Oh no, you don't think *they*—'

'I'm kidding! The spa and the pool are fully staffed, you

can't get away with anything like that,' she said reassuringly, although I was less reassured when she muttered under her breath, 'not unless you wait for them to go on a break.'

'Okay, I really don't want to know. I'm just having a look round, that's all.' She raised an eyebrow. 'I can look round, can't I? Sunil's not convinced that it was Frankie Lewis, so I want to make sure it was, just to put his mind to rest.'

'That's good of you,' she said. 'To do that for Sunil.'

'Yep.'

'Not because you're nosey or owt.'

'I'm completely selfless,' I said. 'By the way, can you remember if Kelly was wearing heels last night?'

'Yeah, she was wearing these massive spiky BDSM things. Shiny black, with studs on the bit that went over her toes. Like court shoes, but the heels must've been at least five inches.'

'How do you remember all that? All I can remember is that she wasn't wearing a lot.'

'Callum has a thing about feet.'

'Oh my god, I *really* don't want to know about that.'

'He asked where I could buy a pair of shoes like that, and I said, "They're on special offer in yer dreams, love."' She grimaced. 'I had a pair like that once, nearly broke me ankle trying to dance in them.'

'Bit hard to run away in, then?'

'Impossible.' She sighed. 'Poor girl.' She looked around. 'This place is well posh, innit? How did you and Nath swing it?'

'His parents gave us some money towards it,' I said. 'They were the ones who wanted the big wedding, not us. It was this or Truro Cathedral.'

'This is posher than the cathedral.'

'Yeah, and of course the monks who built the cathedral didn't think to include a golf course, which is what really swung it,' I said, nodding towards the well-kept greens next to the car park. In the distance, a couple of golfers pulled trollies full of clubs behind them, chatting as they made their way towards the next hole.

'That were terribly remiss of the monks,' said Debbie. 'His parents seem nice enough. You get on alright with them?'

'Yeah,' I said, but I was watching the golfers. One of them had stopped to tread down a disturbed tuft of grass. 'Divots,' I said.

'What?'

'Sometimes, when golfers hit the ball really hard, they also chop out a small piece of turf in the process.'

'Oh, yeah. Divots.'

'If a golf club could do that, imagine the damage a pair of five-inch spiky heels could do…' I looked across the course towards the stretch of grass where the archery targets had been set up – they were still there – and the pond beyond them. 'Come on,' I said, heading onto the grass.

'What are we doing?'

'If anyone asks, we're going to find Daisy and the dog.'

'Okay. But what are we *actually* doing?'

'Looking for traces of anything out of the ordinary.'

'Divots?'

'Divots where there shouldn't be any.' I stopped and looked at her. 'When a golfer creates a divot, they're supposed to tread it back into the ground. I can't say they all do that, but I think most of them probably do because they want to keep the course nice. So anything that's not been trod back down—'

'Wasn't caused by a golfer?'

'Possibly. But the main giveaway will be the location of the divots, if we find any.'

She looked puzzled. 'How d'you work that out?'

'Because they should only be on an actual tee, shouldn't they?' I squatted down on my haunches. 'They shouldn't be here.' But there *were* divots, right there in front of me. Two deep grooves puncturing the smooth turf.

'Blimey, exciting, innit?' said Debbie. 'Although I don't have a Scooby Doo what it means.'

'Excuse me!' I called, standing up and waving to the greenskeeper who was walking past, carrying some tools, a few metres away. He looked surprised, but came over. I pointed down at the ground by my feet. 'Do you know what caused those? Could it be a golf club?'

He looked for a moment, then shook his head. 'Nah, that don't look like anything a club would do,' he said. He put down the tools and the heavy-looking bucket he was carrying, reached down and went to tamp the soil back into place, but I put my arm out to stop him.

'What about someone pulling one of them trolley things, with their golf bag on it? Or a buggy?'

'No, they're designed for golf courses, they wouldn't do any damage, let alone deep holes like this.'

'What about high heels?' asked Debbie. 'Really high heels, spiky ones?'

The greenskeeper nodded thoughtfully. 'Yeah, could be... I reckon that'd do it.'

'Kelly could've run onto the course in her high heels, maybe skidded a bit if she was going fast, and that caused these grooves in the ground,' I said. Both Debbie and the greenskeeper nodded in agreement. 'I know you probably want to repair these, but can you leave them until the police have had a look?'

'This is about that young lass, isn't it?' said greenskeeper. 'Terrible business. Sure, I can leave them. If it helps catch the evil sod who did it...'

'I don't suppose you were out here last night?' I asked. 'I don't suppose you saw or heard anything?'

'Nah, 'fraid not. I live way over there...' He waved his hand over towards the other side of the course, where the end of the hotel driveway was hidden by trees. 'I can't see this part of the course from my house.' He picked up the bucket he was carrying. 'Anyway, I'd best be getting on.'

'The guests here keep you busy, do they?'

He laughed. 'The *grass* keeps me busy. Constantly cutting and watering it at this time of year.' He hefted the bucket. 'That and picking up stray golf balls. The amount they leave behind! I give them to my son at the end of the summer season and he sells them online.' He nodded to us and then went back to work.

'Well, what do you think of that, then?' I asked Debbie.

'What am I supposed to think of that? It still doesn't tell us what happened, does it?'

'No, but we're building a picture of the murder, and the fact there's no police tape or evidence markers round this bit tells me this is a bit of the picture the police haven't found yet.' I smiled at her slightly bewildered face. 'Come on, we need to tell Nathan about this.'

Nathan looked at me in exasperation as he poured himself a cup of tea. We were in the lounge, where Nathan was hiding from his mum, who had apparently gone into Mother-of-the-Groom-Zilla overdrive this morning. 'I thought you were out there keeping Germaine out of sight,' he said. 'Not poking your nose in.' He stopped and grinned. 'I should've known really, shouldn't I?'

'Daisy's looking after the dog,' I said, feeling slightly guilty, as I'd got carried away following clues and had forgotten all about my daughter. 'It's not my fault that I stumbled across some evidence.'

'Yeah, you "accidentally" went and looked in the victim's car,' said Nathan, amused. 'It's terrible how easily these things can just sneak up on you.'

'Exactly,' I said. 'Not my fault at all. Debbie can vouch for me.'

'I can?'

'Yes. So anyway, you see what this means?'

'Nope,' said Nathan and Debbie together.

'It means that someone approached her at her car as she was getting ready to leave – that's why the keys are still in the ignition. There was an argument or an altercation of some sort, and she ran off onto the golf course – not the actual golf course, but the bit that leads down to it, and to the bit where the archery targets were set up. She runs onto the course, skids on the grass in her high heels, but the person she's running from is chasing her now, so she carries on – there were two more sets of divots a bit further on – and then she stops, either because he's stopped chasing her, or more likely, because he's caught her.' I could see it all clearly in my head. 'He hits her, knocking her out and causing the bump on her head, then carries her down to the pond and throws her in, where she drowns.'

'What makes you so sure it happened there?' asked Debbie.

'Because that's where the divots stop,' I said. 'If you're being chased you don't stop to take your shoes off, do you?'

'No…' said Nathan, slowly, and I could see that he was replaying the scene in his head too. Our minds really did work the same way when it came to murder. 'Kelly was small and slim, and although Frankie Lewis isn't very big himself, he's quite stocky and I reckon he could easily have picked her up and thrown her over his shoulder.'

'Exactly.'

'So, call me stupid…' started Debbie, and then held her

hand up as she saw me and Nathan open our mouths. 'Don't *actually* call me stupid, you two are so predictable... What exactly is the relevance of any of this? It still doesn't tell us for certain that Frankie Lewis did it, does it?'

'No,' I admitted, 'but there could be evidence that the police haven't found yet, because they've concentrated their search around the pond. They've looked at her car as well, I think, but there's not really anything there.'

'If she was initially attacked on the course, rather than by the pond, then there could be DNA evidence there,' said Nathan. 'It helps to have as full a picture of events as possible, not just the actual scene where the body was found.'

'You'd better ring Sunil, then, and see if this puts his mind at rest,' said Debbie, because of course she didn't know the reason why Sunil was feeling less than sure about Lewis being the killer. Nathan looked at me, eyebrows raised.

'Sunil called me earlier,' I said, trying to downplay it, because I still wasn't sure I wanted to bring up Craig until I knew what he'd been doing outside. But it looked like I was going to have to.

'Why did he call you instead of me?' Nathan looked genuinely mystified, and a bit peeved too. Debbie saw his expression.

'And now I'm going to go and cause trouble somewhere else,' she said. 'Don't forget, wedding in T minus five hours...'

We waited for her to leave the room. I reached down and

picked up the plate of biscuits that had come with Nathan's pot of tea.

'Suggestive biscuit?' I asked him, with a come-hither smile.

'Don't try to distract me with a digestive and a cheeky look in your eye,' he said. 'Although I will take you up on both later. Not necessarily together. What's this about Sunil?'

'Okay, well…' I told Nathan what Sunil had found on the CCTV footage. 'He wanted to ask me what I thought first, as he knows you're close friends. And he didn't want to ask Matt because even in the short time he was here interviewing people, he got the impression Matt wasn't a fan of Craig. He thought I'd be more objective.'

'And he hasn't told Mackintosh yet?'

'He hadn't when I spoke to him, although he did say that if she asks him about anyone else appearing on the footage he can't lie.'

'No, of course not. He should tell her now, without being asked.'

I looked at him in surprise. 'But the footage puts Craig outside at the time of the murder. If anything, he had more time to do it than Lewis did. Going by the footage of Lewis's car leaving, he'd have had to get a right wriggle on to approach Kelly at her car, argue with her, chase her onto the grass, bang her on the head and then carry her down to the pond. But we have no idea what time Craig came back inside. He could've been out there for hours, giving him plenty of time to—'

'To what? Murder someone he doesn't even know?' Nathan shook his head. 'No.'

'You can't say that for certain—'

'Yes I can. I know him, and I know he wouldn't hurt anyone.' I went to speak but he interrupted me. 'This is exactly what happened when we first met, and everything pointed to Tony being behind Mel's death. You knew he couldn't have done it, regardless of having opportunity. It's the same for Craig.'

'Okay,' I said, placating him. 'But we should still talk to him and find out why he was outside. If Di Mackintosh can't pin it on Lewis, then she'll turn her sights on Craig.'

'I thought she was set on Lewis?'

'I think she is. But she's like you – she's a good cop. She'll need as much evidence as she can get before she charges anyone, and if she can't prove that Lewis did it, she'll be looking at other suspects.'

Nathan sighed. 'Yeah, I know. You're right.'

'Always am.'

'I wouldn't go *that* far...' He sipped his tea. 'I don't suppose I can have that suggestive biscuit first?'

Chapter Ten

But the biscuits – suggestive or otherwise – would have to wait, as Nathan's mum popped her head into the lounge and gave a weird victorious shriek when she saw us.

'There you are!' she said. 'What are you doing, sitting here? And together? That's bad luck!'

'I'm hoping we've already had all the bad luck we're due to get this weekend,' said Nathan. Liz looked puzzled.

'Why, what's happened?'

'The poor girl who died, Mum,' said Nathan patiently. 'I don't think us sitting here drinking tea is going to do anything worse than that.'

'No, well… I am sorry for her, and her family – her poor mum must be heartbroken – but you've got a wedding to prepare for.' Liz shook her head. 'Jodie, I can't believe you're sitting here so calmly, when you've got your hair and make-up to do, and your nails, and last-minute adjustments to your dress—'

'The dress is fine,' I said, but she'd put a little bit of doubt in my mind. The dress was gorgeous, but it was so different to anything I'd ever worn before. I'm not a dress person, and this wasn't just a dress, it was a DRESS. It shouted, *Look at me!* in a way that my jeans and trainers never had. I'd be the centre of attention.

'Umm… maybe I should go up and just try it on again,' I said. Nathan reached out and grabbed my hand.

'You're going to look beautiful,' he said, and I melted a little bit. 'You could wear a bin bag and I'd still fancy you.'

'Nathan!' scoffed Liz. 'As if your bride's going to wear a bin bag!'

'There you are!' There was another shriek as Arabella, our wedding planner, descended upon us. She hadn't been involved in any of the previous day's activities and I'd almost forgotten about her, but she was back with a vengeance. She wore a very smart but very lilac suit, with her blonde hair done up in a French plait and her make-up perfect. She also held a clipboard. My heart sank. Well-dressed women holding clipboards terrify me.

She consulted it now. 'Jodie, darling, what are you doing down here? The schedule has you upstairs with your bridesmaids, getting your hair done, time for a few casual behind-the-scenes photos, nails, that kind of thing. Maybe a few glasses of champagne to settle those last-minute nerves!'

'Yes, I was just going,' I said. 'I need to find Daisy, though—'

'That's okay, I found her on my way in.' Arabella

lowered her voice. 'I almost ran over your dog. I wasn't aware your pet would be here.' She sounded slightly disapproving, although I thought it was less about Germaine and more about us springing something unexpected on her and potentially messing up her tight schedule.

'Our dog-sitter had to go away,' said Nathan. 'But don't worry, she's very well trained.'

'The dog-sitter?'

'The dog.'

'Oh yes, of course! Maybe we could involve her in the ceremony? I'm sure I can find some ribbon to tie round her collar or something...' Arabella looked thoughtful.

'That would be lovely,' I said, taking advantage of her pause. 'Think of how cute she'd look in the photos! But,' I said, putting on a disappointed voice, 'I don't think the hotel allows dogs.'

'You leave it to me,' she said firmly. 'You head upstairs and I'll fix it with the manager.'

'You will? Oh, thank you Arabella, you're the best wedding planner I've ever had.'

Arabella smiled and strode purposefully out of the room. Nathan turned to me with a grin.

'She does know she's the *only* wedding planner you've ever had...?'

So instead of questioning Craig, I found myself sitting in my room with Mum, Daisy and Debbie all fussing around me. Carmen arrived, clutching a bottle of bubbly, and with the make-up lady, Natasha, following in her wake. I sat sipping champagne through a straw so as not to smudge my wet nails and watched the four most important women in my life (sorry, Natasha) as they got ready. Actually, more like the *five* most important in my life, if you counted the dog (sorry again, Natasha) who was curled up snoring on Daisy's pillow, worn out after her run around the hotel grounds and hiding from the hotel staff.

As Mum and Debbie tried to persuade Daisy to have her hair in an up-do, Carmen sensibly left them to it and approached me with the champagne. She held it aloft.

'Top up?'

'I don't know… I don't think I should. I'm going to be tottering down the aisle as it is, in me high heels.'

Carmen grinned and turned the bottle towards me so I could read the label. 'It's non-alcoholic,' she said. Across the room, Debbie and Mum exclaimed loudly.

'What? That's not a *proper* drink!' 'And you a woman of the church, too!' I wasn't sure what that had to do with anything. Carmen held up her other hand to quiet their complaints.

'In my defence, I've had a few bridesmaids – and brides, for that matter – too inebriated to make it down the aisle without serious mishap,' she said. 'One maid of honour was so hammered she nearly married the bride's dad. And this way, Daisy can have some too.'

'Aww, that's really thoughtful of you,' I said, ignoring Daisy's scowl at being tricked out of having alcohol. 'And admit it, ladies, you'd never have known if Carmen hadn't told you.'

'I don't drink enough of the fancy stuff to know the difference,' admitted Mum. 'I had some of that expensive stuff at Tony's wedding – the last one, that is, not his first one—' I glared at her and gave a tiny nod towards Carmen, who maybe didn't want to hear about her boyfriend's failed marriages, but Mum didn't notice. 'It was that Mow-It and Chow-Down. Tasted exactly the same as the bubbly Wonky Alice got from Lidl's for her birthday last month.'

Daisy choked. 'Wonky Alice?'

'Yeah. Poor love. A bird flew into her eye when she was at primary school and she's been able to look left and right both at the same time ever since.' Mum shrugged. 'Deirdre Hurley and I were in the same class as her. When she got out of the hospital after months of operations and came back to school, Deirdre said her eyes looked wonky, and that was it. The name just stuck.'

'Thank goodness she had the support of her friends to help her through it,' said Daisy, with a completely straight face. Debbie, Carmen and I – and Natasha – all snorted with suppressed laughter. Mum assumed a pious expression.

'We did an' all. We never called her Wonky Alice to her face.'

'You wouldn't have known which eye to look her in, for starters,' said Debbie, and we all burst out laughing.

Germaine looked up blearily from her pillow, gave a little growl of complaint and then went back to sleep.

'We finish your hair now, yes?' said Natasha, who despite the fact we were drinking non-alcoholic champagne was still the most sober and sensible one in the room. Daisy sighed and resigned herself to an up-do. Carmen plonked herself down on the bed next to me.

'How are you feeling?' she asked. 'Last-minute nerves?'

'A little bit.' I gazed across to the wardrobe, where my beautiful dress hung on the door. 'I'm going to be the centre of attention in that, aren't I?'

Carmen's gaze followed mine. She smiled. 'That dress is amazing. It's very you.'

'Do you think so?' I was surprised. I didn't think *any* dress was me. 'Daisy helped me choose it.'

'Ah, that makes sense. It's *very* Daisy, so it's very you by extension. She's a chip off the old block, from what I've seen.'

'I think that's more flattering to me than it is to her,' I said, laughing. 'She was the one who suggested the colour.'

'Yes, I can imagine that.' Carmen nodded. 'Everyone thinks white is the traditional colour for a wedding dress, but that only started with Queen Victoria.'

'Really?'

'Yes. She wore a white lace dress at her wedding, and everyone wanted to copy her.'

'She was the Kim Kardashian of her day,' I said, and Carmen shuddered.

'Don't. You should see some of the dresses brides wear

these days! Celebrity fashion has a lot to answer for. If I wasn't a vicar and trained to be discreet I'd tell you all about them.'

'Nathan and I have been winding up his mum about the dress,' I said. 'She was the one who insisted we have a big traditional wedding, so I told her I'd gone somewhere between *My Big Fat Gypsy Wedding* and Alice Tinker's Teletubby dress in *The Vicar of Dibley*. A big flouncy shiny satin dress, with animatronic butterflies on it that are programmed to flap their wings when we say "I do."'

Carmen laughed. 'I would pay good money to see you in that,' she said.

'There's not enough money in the world.'

'Anyway, lots of cultures get married in that colour, don't they?' said Carmen. 'It's meant to be auspicious.'

'Yes,' I said, and in spite of myself I sighed. Carmen raised her eyebrows.

'Oh dear, that doesn't sound like a good sigh…'

'No, everything's fine, it's just…' I pulled myself together. 'Can I ask you a question?'

'Of course.'

I lowered my voice. 'Do you think we're right to go ahead with the wedding?'

She looked surprised, but not *that* surprised. 'You mean because of that poor girl?'

'Yes. I know she wasn't part of the wedding party and we didn't know her, but…' I waved a hand towards the window. 'She died, just out there. And she didn't just *die*, it wasn't an accident. Someone killed her. The Forensics team are still out there. There's still police officers on site, although not many, because DI Mackintosh is convinced she's got her man. No one's said anything, and it would be really awkward to cancel it because we've got the cake, and the catering's all sorted, and of course Nathan's mum and dad and his friends have come all the way down from Liverpool – and from New York, in Craig's case…' I still felt uneasy about Craig being outside at the time of the murder, although I couldn't really see him killing anyone. 'But it feels at best inappropriate and at worst, completely heartless to go ahead.'

'I see what you mean,' said Carmen thoughtfully.

'The colour of the dress is meant to be auspicious,' I said. 'But getting married after someone was murdered here – that can only be *in*auspicious, can't it?'

'That's just superstition, though,' said Carmen. 'I would think the real question is, do you want the memories of your wedding day to include a murder investigation?'

'You think we should cancel, then?'

'I'm not saying that. That has to be down to you and Nathan. I don't think anyone would blame you for going ahead, or for postponing it.' She smiled ruefully. 'Sorry, I don't know that that's particularly helpful.'

'No, thank you, it has been helpful to talk about it,' I said. But I still didn't know how comfortable I was with continuing. I looked at my dress again and *ached* to put it on.

I was saved from having to make a decision by a hurried

knock on the bedroom door. We all looked at each other in surprise.

'Who is it?' I called.

'It's Matt. Nathan sent me along in case you were already in your dress.'

I jumped off the bed, pulled my dressing gown tighter around me and opened the door, to see Matt standing there in his best man's suit.

'Nope, as you can see I'm still getting my hair and that done,' I said. 'You scrubbed up well. Is everything alright with Nathan?'

'Yes,' said Matt. 'Well, no, not really. He's fine, but it's Craig. Sunil's here, he said DI Mackintosh wants to bring him in for questioning but no one knows where he is.'

'Oh bloody hell,' I said. 'Where's Nath? And Sunil?'

'Both looking for him,' said Matt. 'I don't get it. I thought Mackintosh was set on Frankie Lewis? Why's she after Craig? I know I wasn't too sure about him at first, but now I've got to know him a bit better he seems like a good bloke.'

'Because the evidence against Frankie is looking weaker and weaker.' Nathan had appeared behind his best man, his eyes averted. I sighed.

'You can look, I'm not dressed yet,' I said. Nathan looked at me and smiled, but he looked troubled. 'Mackintosh jumped the gun, didn't she? Everything she had was circumstantial.'

'And like you said, she's a good copper,' said Nathan. 'She's never going to charge someone based on flimsy stuff like the CCTV footage of the car. Sounds like she's been trying to back it up with hard evidence, but there's none to be found.'

'Which means he's innocent,' said Debbie, because of course my nosey friends had all come over to eavesdrop. Nathan shook his head.

'Not necessarily. He might just be lucky. Finding DNA evidence at a scene like that – outside overnight, with the body left in water – is like finding a needle in a haystack.'

'That's true,' I admitted. 'But Craig... We need to find him and ask him what he was doing outside last night.' Everyone gasped.

'Craig was outside during the time of the murder?' asked Mum. 'Such a nice young man, too.'

'Now don't go assuming that means he did it,' said Matt. 'There could be a perfectly reasonable explanation. Although,' he added, faltering slightly, 'he obviously didn't mention it when he gave his statement.'

'We need to find Craig, and now,' I said, ripping off my dressing gown like Clark Kent discarding his glasses and turning into Superman. And then I realised I was standing there in just my undies, so I put it back on again. 'Um, Matt, can you wait out there until I get dressed?'

Chapter Eleven

'Still no answer?' I asked Nathan. He shook his head and disconnected the call. He'd tried ringing Craig's phone several times, but it was just going through to voicemail. He'd left a message and texted, but no reply. Matt had left us to join Sunil searching for him.

'Where is he?' groaned Nathan in frustration. He looked at his watch. 'The wedding's in less than four hours. I know I've got two best men, but I'd rather not have to go and bail one of them out during the reception.'

'I dunno, you might want to pop out during my mum's speech…'

'Shirley's doing a speech?' Nathan groaned again, and then pulled me in for a hug. 'If we leave now we could be in Gretna Green tomorrow morning, just as the registry office opens.'

'Tempting, but no. And that wouldn't help Craig, would it?'

'No, I suppose not...'

Ben and Danny trotted around the corner of the corridor where we were standing, talking urgently. They stopped in surprise when they saw us.

'Alright? Thought youse two would be getting ready for the wedding,' said Ben, a little awkwardly.

'Have you seen Craig?' asked Nathan. Ben immediately looked guilty.

'No, mate, not seen 'im since breakfast...'

Danny shook his head and looked at Ben, his expression more serious than I'd thought he was capable of. 'Come on, you gotta tell them what you told me.' Ben hesitated. 'I know you don't want to dob him in, but he could be in trouble.'

Ben looked for a moment like he was going to refuse, but then his shoulders sagged and he gave a heavy sigh. 'Alright, yeah. But it don't necessarily mean nothing, does it?'

If it don't mean nothing, then it must mean SOMETHING, I thought, remembering how Davey Trelawney had bamboozled Frankie Lewis, but I said nothing. I wasn't even the Grammar Police these days.

'Spill,' said Nathan.

'I found Craig outside last night, during the time the murder was probably committed,' said Ben.

'We know,' I said. 'Not that you found him, but that he was outside.'

'You do?' Ben looked at me and then Nathan, as if the answer would be there somewhere. 'How?'

'He's on CCTV, going out the back door from the bar,' said Nathan. 'That's why Mackintosh wants him in for questioning. Because he told her he was passed out in bed all night.'

'Mackintosh is looking for him? Shit…' Ben and Danny exchanged glances.

'Yeah, but he didn't do it, did he?' said Danny stubbornly.

'Of course he didn't,' said Nathan. 'But Mackintosh doesn't know him like we do, so we need to find out what happened. Maybe he saw something?'

Ben definitely looked guilty again at that. I reached out to touch his arm gently.

'If you know something, tell us,' I said. 'It's the only way we'll be able to help him.'

'Okay.' Ben took a deep breath. 'I went down to Reception to see if they had any painkillers, because my head was already starting to hurt and I knew if I didn't get a jump on it, I'd be paying for it later.'

'What time was this?' asked Nathan, making a note on his phone.

'About two o'clock, I think? Maybe a bit later. I don't really know, I didn't look.'

'We can always check with the concierge,' I said, but Ben shook his head.

'No you can't, because she wasn't there. There's a staff-only corridor next to the reception desk, so I wandered down there to see if anybody else was about, but then I came across the fire exit. It was propped open.'

'Really?' Nathan raised an eyebrow and looked at me.

'Health and Safety nightmare,' I said. 'Can you show us?'

We headed down to Reception and made our way to the staff corridor, avoiding eye contact with the day-shift receptionist who, luckily, was busy on the phone and didn't realise what we were doing.

'Here.' Ben stopped in front of the fire door and pushed it open, looking round for something to prop it open with, but there was nothing there. 'There was a chair here last night, one of the heavy ones from the bar. It was propped open.' Danny held the door while we stepped through and out into the staff car park. 'I thought it was a bit suss, like, being propped open in the middle of the night, and I remembered what you told me about the manager, Nate – when he asked you what he should do about the staff having it away with stuff. I thought maybe someone was having it on their toes with some hotel bog roll or something.' He gave a hollow laugh. 'If only.'

'If only,' agreed Nathan. 'Then what happened?'

'I stuck me head out but I couldn't see nothing. I was about to head back inside when I heard Craig, making this weird crying noise.' He shook his head. 'No, not crying, sort of keening, you know what I mean? I don't know how to describe it really. But it was obvious he was really distressed.'

'He was out here?'

'Not in the car park, no. It was dead quiet, so I could hear him even though he was a little bit away from me. I followed the sound and I found him over here...' He headed across the car park and stopped near the grass, where I'd found the divots made by Kelly's high heels. Mackintosh had got someone to put evidence markers near them, and a couple of Forensics officers were taking photos. One of them nodded to me and spoke.

'Alright, Jodie?'

'Yeah, good thanks, Robbo. Found anything useful?'

'Some faint shoe-prints, which might be something, but probably aren't. Not down to me to decide that, though. But it's all building a picture, isn't it?' He stopped and looked at me again more closely. 'Aren't you supposed to be getting married today?'

'Oh yeah, we've got hours yet,' I said breezily.

'We're just having a look round,' said Nathan, and I thought he was a bit miffed that the CSI hadn't acknowledged him. 'Don't mind us.'

'Oh, yes, DCI Withers, you help yourself,' said Robbo, getting back on with his job. Nathan looked at me and rolled his eyes.

'You're not even in the force anymore and you *still* know everyone,' he said.

'Penstowan mafia, innit?'

'Okay,' said Nathan to Ben. 'You've found Craig out here, middle of the night, visibly distressed about something. What then?'

'I told him to come inside and go back to bed,' said Ben. 'I'd had a lot to drink and I was starting to feel a bit shady, and I didn't want to start talking about our feelings or any of that touchy-feely stuff, not at two o'clock in the morning.'

'Tell them what he said,' said Danny.

'What did he say?'

'I didn't think anything of it at the time,' said Ben. 'Like I said, after a night on the bevvies I just wanted to go to bed. But he said something about his girl, how he'd been an idiot and he'd hurt her.'

'Him and his girlfriend are having problems?' asked Nathan, although he knew they were – I'd told him that much from my conversation with Craig the day before.

'She ain't here, is she?' said Danny. 'And he's not said two words about her, that's after the way he was going on about how brilliant she was last time I heard from him.'

'And he was definitely talking about her, was he?' I asked. Ben was quiet for a moment. 'Did he actually specifically say his girlfriend?'

'That's just it,' said Ben. 'I don't think he did. He wasn't making a lot of sense. He was talking about a big argument, about her shouting, and then he said he didn't mean to hurt her. I just said something vague like "I'm sure you'll make it right again" but he said it was too late.' Ben looked anxiously at Nathan. 'Of course, at the time I thought he meant his girlfriend, but when you found the body – and it was her, from the stag do…'

'You were worried he was talking about hurting Kelly,' said Nathan. Ben nodded.

'Yeah,' he said quietly.

'But he wouldn't though, would he?' said Danny. 'Not

Craig. He gives it all that, but he's soft as shite when it comes down to women. Always has been.'

'He wasn't soft when he propositioned her at my party,' said Nathan. I fidgeted, needing to tell him about Nicky; the situation with her would explain why Craig had been acting out of character, full of self-loathing for the way he'd treated her, and for his need to prove to the others that he was a 'real' man. God, Daisy was right; the patriarchy had a lot to answer for, not least of all the macho BS some men believed. It wasn't my place to say anything, of course, but I vowed that if it came to it, I would have to tell Nathan. The question was, would it also give him a motive to kill Kelly?

'How did you get back into the hotel?' I asked. 'You're not on any of the CCTV cameras, not even the one in the lift.'

'I hate lifts,' said Ben, looking a bit sheepish. 'I never go in them if I can avoid it, and the one here's ancient, isn't it? It must be a hundred years old. We came back in through the fire exit and I dragged him back up the stairs.'

'Avoiding the night concierge again,' said Nathan.

'I don't know, I wasn't looking out for her,' said Ben. 'I was concentrating on getting both of us back to our rooms before he started being weird again and we had to talk about our feelings or something.' He shuddered. 'I can just about manage that sober if I have to, but not off me head.'

Nathan looked serious. 'Why didn't you tell us any of this earlier? We could've cleared all this up with Craig before Mackintosh even thought about him as a suspect.'

'I was going to,' said Ben. 'I started telling you when we

were helping the archery instructor collect up the arrows. But then of course we found the body, and it went out of my head. And then when I thought of it again, I was worried and I didn't know what to do.'

'So you kept it to yourself,' I said. 'What if he *was* involved, and you covered it up? You're a police officer. It's not a good look.'

Nathan put his hand on my arm and gave me a *You're not helping* look, which was probably true, but it didn't diminish the fact that as a police officer Ben should immediately have come forward. Because how can the public trust the police if they don't follow the same rules everyone else has to? I'd seen a fair bit of that in my time in uniform – covering up for your mates' mistakes, as I had for DI Mackintosh when she was a newbie at Stockwell – but covering up a potential crime, a potential *murder*? Nope. To his credit, Ben looked remorseful.

'He's told us now,' said Nathan. 'Now we have to find Craig, and get him to tell us what happened last night. Any idea where he'd be?'

'No,' said Danny. 'Soft lad 'ere only just told me all this, and we thought the same as you. We tried his room, of course, but he's not there, and no one's seen him. You don't think he's done a runner, do you?'

'He's got a hire car, hasn't he?' I said. 'If you know what car he rented we might as well walk round to the car park and have a look, because the fire exit shut behind us and we can't get back in that way…'

The four of us headed round to the guest car park near

the front of the hotel. Sunil was already there, his search having led him to the same conclusion as ours: we needed to know if Craig was even still on the premises.

'If you're looking for his car, it's gone,' he said. My heart sank; if he'd done a runner, was that a sign of guilt? 'He had a black Toyota with a "Gatwick Car Rentals" sticker on it—'

'Like this one, you mean?' said Nathan, because as Sunil spoke a car exactly like that drove into the car park. It stopped and a cheerful-looking Craig stepped out. He looked over at us waiting for him with an expression of bemusement.

'Alright, lads? Jodie?' he said, reaching back into the car to take out a shopping bag. 'You waiting for me?'

'Where the hell have you been?' asked Danny.

'Truro.' Craig turned to me. 'That shirt I ordered from Next was too small. I've put a bit of weight on round my tummy since I've been in New York. Too many Reubens for lunch.' He patted his stomach. 'I thought I should probably just drive there and try some on. I managed to get one...' His voice trailed off as he noticed that we were all still staring at him. He laughed nervously. 'What is it? Have I got something stuck in me teeth?' He looked horrified. 'I haven't missed the wedding, have I? I thought it was this afternoon?'

'No, you haven't missed it – it's at three o'clock,' I said. 'But Nathan's been ringing you.'

'So have I,' said Sunil. 'And so has my boss.' He looked at Nathan. 'My *other* boss, that is.'

'I left you several voicemail messages,' said Nathan. Craig pulled his phone out of his pocket.

'Yeah, sorry about that… Nicky called and we were talking for ages. I saw you call me, but my phone died before I could call you back.'

'Nicky called you?' I asked, catching his eye.

'Yeah. I left her a message last night, explaining that, er, stuff we were talking about,' he said to me, vaguely so the others wouldn't know what he meant. I nodded. 'She just woke up and saw it, and rang me straight away.' He gave me a broad, relieved smile. 'I think it's all going to be alright. I was sat in the car park FaceTiming her for about an hour. But why were you trying to get hold of me? Have I missed some best man duty or something?'

'What were you doing outside the hotel on Friday night?' asked Nathan. I was a bit surprised that he was just going to go straight into it without explaining; he was treating Craig like an ordinary suspect, not his best mate.

Craig was surprised, too. 'What you talking about, Nath? You saw me on Friday night, I was bladdered. After I left the stag do I passed out on me bed and didn't leave it again until Saturday lunchtime.' But his voice faltered slightly.

'Are you sure about that?' asked Ben.

'What? Yeah, of course I'm sure…' Although he really didn't sound sure now. 'Look, to be honest, I can't remember much at all about that night. I don't remember making a pass at that poor girl, I remember them turning up and getting their kit off, but it's a blur after that.' He shook his head. 'I think I'd remember going outside, though. Wouldn't I?'

'Would you? Even though you don't remember the rest of it?'

Craig groaned and clutched at his head. 'Oh God, what did I do? Why are you asking me this? I honestly can't remember.'

'Have you had blackouts before?' I asked him.

'I... I used to drink a lot, and yeah, I did have a few nights where everything after a certain point was a blank. That's why I cut down. I've not drunk as much as I did the other night for ages. You know why.'

'You and Nicky had argued,' said Nathan. He nodded.

'Not just argued, I thought we'd split up and I was devastated, specially as it was my fault. But when I had blackouts, I don't think I ever really did anything during those periods. I think if I was too drunk to remember, I was probably too drunk to get up to any mischief.' He thought for a moment. 'Other than that time when I was staying at this girl's flat and I got up in the night for a pee, only it turned out to be her airing cupboard and not her toilet.'

'Eww,' I said. But he had a point. If you'd physically hurt – even murdered – someone, surely you'd remember? But then maybe he *did* remember. Amnesia could be a convenient excuse sometimes.

'Why are you saying I was outside, anyway? Did someone see me?'

'I did,' said Ben. 'You were crying on the golf course. I brought you inside.'

'Really?' Craig looked at him, incredulously. 'Nah, you're winding me up...'

'You're on CCTV, going out onto the terrace and falling asleep in a chair for about an hour,' I said. 'And then you woke up and wandered off, and we don't know where you went or what you did until Ben came out and found you.' I glanced at Sunil. 'We need to catch you up on a few things...'

'Jesus Christ, I don't remember any of that,' said Craig. 'Is that it, though? Or is there something else?' His eyes widened. 'Don't tell me. This all occurred during the murder window, didn't it? I was outside while that poor girl was getting killed.'

'Yep.'

'And you think I might have seen something?' He shook his head. 'Mate, I wish I had. But I thought they'd caught the bloke?'

'It now looks like it wasn't necessarily him,' said Sunil carefully. No one spoke. Finally—

'Oh shit, you think *I* did it?' Craig gasped.

'No we don't,' said Danny stubbornly. 'But that Mackintosh bird wants you taken in for questioning.' Sunil drew in a shocked breath.

'That's *Detective Inspector* Mackintosh,' Nathan said pointedly, 'not "that Mackintosh bird".'

'But I can't remember anything!' Craig wailed. 'I was off me tits!'

'It's a good job I'm here, then,' said a female voice behind us. We turned round to see Mum and her friend

Jocasta, who was attending as Mum's plus one. Jocasta had been a high-powered lawyer once upon a time, but she'd moved to Cornwall to 'find herself'. Beneath the New Age nonsense and all the tie-dyed scarves lay a brain that was as sharp as it had been when she'd successfully sued a massive City institution for being a bit dodgy with their staff pension fund twenty years ago.

'Who's this?' asked Danny, warily eyeing Jocasta's armful of silver bangles and her wild, untamed mane of grey hair (which looked awesome – after my own initial doubts about her, and her influence on Mum, I was a big fan of this incredible woman who was determined to grow old disgracefully). 'Nice of you to offer to help, love, but I'm not sure we need anything knitted at this point.' *Rude*, I thought.

'The only thing I do with knitting needles is stab insolent young men,' said Jocasta, and Mum high-fived her. 'But I am skilled in past-life regression therapy.' And BOOM! Just like that I was back to being embarrassed by all the New Age stuff again.

Jocasta looked around at everyone and laughed. 'Well, that went down well,' she said. 'I know what you're all thinking, that I'm some bonkers old loony who discovered Eastern philosophy and mysticism during menopause, and now I'm convinced that wafting burning sage around and drinking soy milk will cure everything.'

'No, no—' 'Course not—' we all protested, though not that strenuously in some cases, and she laughed again.

'Sage is for stuffing chickens with, not smoking out

demons,' she said. 'But I *am* a trained hypnotherapist. When I say "regression therapy" I'm not talking about discovering you were Napoleon in a past life, I'm talking about the recent past. Buried trauma, or,' she looked frankly at Craig, 'alcohol-induced memory loss.'

'She's really good at it, an' all,' said Mum enthusiastically. Jocasta waved a modest hand. 'When I drank too much Baileys and couldn't remember where I'd left my phone, she helped me find it.'

'I rang it and you followed the ring tone, Shirl,' said Jocasta.

'Yeah, but it's the end result that counts, innit.'

In the absence of any better ideas – and aware that we would eventually have to let Sunil take Craig in to face Di Mackintosh's questions – we went inside and prepared for Jocasta to weave her hypnotic magic…

Chapter Twelve

'I got hypnotised once,' said Tony, settling back in a garden chair. We were on the terrace, waiting while Jocasta set up in a quiet corner of the adjoining bar. 'Stage hypnotist. We were on that lads-only holiday to Benidorm, do you remember, Callum?'

'I'm not likely to forget it. That was the one who made you cluck like a chicken, every time someone said "beer",' said Callum, sipping (aptly) at a beer.

'That wasn't me,' said Tony quickly, although from the expression on his face I could tell he was lying, and regretted mentioning the hypnotist.

'Are you sure?' I asked, leaning forward. 'There's nothing be ashamed of if— BEER!' I watched him closely, but he didn't turn into a chicken. Carmen, who was sitting next to him, laughed.

'Maybe it needs to be a specific brand of— STELLA ARTOIS!' She shook her head. 'Nope. Nothing.'

'Oh cluck off.'

Daisy and Joe joined us at the table. Daisy's hair and make-up had been done and she looked beautiful, in a very unnatural-for-her kind of way, and Joe kept stealing little glances at her, his eyes drinking her in. Bless him.

'Scrubs up well, don't she?' I said. Daisy groaned.

'I swear you sound more like Nana every day,' she said.

'Okay, I take it back. Joe, doesn't Daisy look like a complete dog's breakfast?'

Joe laughed. 'Sorry, Daze, you asked for that. And you do scrub up well. You look beautiful.'

Daisy blushed, which was very unlike her. Tony noticed and winked at me.

'If you'd left it a bit longer I reckon you could've made it a double wedding,' he said, winding her up.

'Yes! Mother and daughter walking down the aisle together,' said Carmen. I laughed and clutched my heart dramatically.

'Oh! We could've had matching dresses!'

'Oh shut up, you're not funny,' she said. Joe laughed and took her hand.

'Sounds alright to me,' he said, grinning.

'OH MY GOD, stop encouraging them!' cried Daisy. She stood up. 'I'm going to get a drink.'

'Come on!' said Mum, appearing in the French doors that opened out from the bar onto the terrace. 'Jocasta's all ready to go!'

We followed her in. Jocasta had taken over a dark corner of the bar, closing the heavy velvet drapes to block out the sunlight and muffle any noise from outside. At this time of the day the bar itself was pretty empty – the other, non-wedding guests were either out exploring the local scenery, or on the golf course – and the barman, who didn't have much to do, stood behind the counter polishing glasses and watching us with an expression of bemusement.

Craig sat in a padded armchair. The tables and chairs nearby had been pushed out to the side of the room and he looked a bit lost on his own. Jocasta pulled another chair up towards him and took a deep breath, as if she was about to start. Then she looked around and saw all of us crowded around her.

'We'll need a bit of air if this is going to work,' she said. 'Craig needs to feel relaxed, and I don't know if he'll be able to with you lot all gawking at us.'

'It's fine,' said Craig. 'I've got nothing to hide.'

'Nothing?' I asked, trying to give him a meaningful look without the others noticing. Nathan did notice, I was sure of it, but he didn't say anything.

'Yeah...' said Craig. As the others fussed about around him, I bent down and spoke quietly into Jocasta's ear.

'No questions about the cause of his argument with his girlfriend,' I said. Jocasta looked at me, surprised, then nodded.

'Doesn't sound like that would be relevant anyway,' she said.

'No, exactly.'

'You can all watch if you have to,' said Jocasta, to the

assembled crowd, 'but you do need to give us some room so I can create the right mood.'

'You need some whale music, love?' said Danny, obviously thinking himself a great wit.

'Whale music? Pah!' Jocasta dismissed him with a look. 'Pan pipes are better. But just a bit of hush will do.'

'Can you please hurry up?' asked Sunil, anxiously. 'Mackintosh will be on the warpath if I don't get him back to the station soon.'

'Too bloody right she will be.' Sunil went pale and we all turned to see DI Mackintosh and another officer standing in the door of the bar. 'What the bloody hell's going on here? DC Bakshi, why isn't Mr Carter on his way to see me already?'

'Um, we only just found him, Guv – Ma'am – and he says he can't remember anything that happened, so Mrs—'

'Ms,' Jocasta corrected him.

'Ms, er, Jocasta, is helping him remember.' Sunil looked terrified of Mackintosh, who was eyeing him the way an orca eyes a baby seal in a wildlife documentary.

Mackintosh gave a snort of derision and opened her mouth to speak, but Jocasta, who had dealt with her fair share of stroppy police officers during her legal career, spoke over her.

'Yes, and I've just put Mr Carter into a suggestive state – a kind of pre-hypnotic mode – and it would be very dangerous to leave him like that.' She was polite but firm, despite the fact that she was completely bullshitting the DI, and I could see Mackintosh weighing up if it was worth forcing the issue; but she just smiled back, a thin smile that didn't quite reach her eyes.

'Go ahead. I've got all the time in the world.' She nodded to Sunil. 'DC Bakshi, if you wouldn't mind filming this.'

'Yes, Gu— er.' Sunil took out his phone.

Jocasta took a deep breath, then unexpectedly stretched out her arms and cracked her knuckles. 'Okay. Craig, are you comfortable?'

'Yes,' said Craig, somewhat uncomfortably.

'I want you to close your eyes and take some nice, deep breaths. In through the nose for the count of five...' She counted to five. 'Hold it for the count of five... and out through the mouth for the count of five. Be aware of the soft cushions of the chair around your body, and the carpet under your feet. Feel your fingers become heavy and let them relax. Let that heavy feeling travel up your arms and into your body, let yourself sink into the chair, all the time breathing in through your nose and out through your mouth.' Jocasta breathed deeply herself, Craig following her rhythm. In spite of myself I felt my eyelids start to droop. I gave myself a shake.

'I want you to go back to the events of Friday night,' said Jocasta.

'The stag party,' said Craig, thickly. Jocasta looked up at me, although the investigation had nothing to do with me. I glanced over at Mackintosh.

'We know what happened at the party,' I said. 'If you're

keen to get to the juicy part, we should skip on to Craig being in bed and deciding to get up.'

'You've left the party,' said Jocasta soothingly, not waiting for a response from Mackintosh. 'You're in your hotel room. What's happening?'

'Spinning,' said Craig. 'I've drunk too much. I had a little sleep, but I've woken up again and I feel terrible.' He frowned. 'Someone's shouting.'

'Where? In your room?'

'No, somewhere else.'

'That could be when Frankie Lewis confronted Kelly at the party,' Matt murmured, and Nathan nodded.

'What are you going to do now?' asked Jocasta.

'I need some fresh air. Or some more alcohol...' Craig gave a small laugh, eyes still shut. 'Nah, that's not a good idea. I'm going downstairs.' He frowned again. 'I can't find the lift but the stairs are right there...'

'You're at the bottom of the stairs,' said Jocasta. 'Where to now?'

'I'm in the bar.'

'Anyone else there?'

'No... Wait, yeah, the barman's still here, but he hasn't seen me because he's behind the bar, clearing up. I think he'll throw me out if he sees me.'

'What are you going to do?'

'The door out onto the terrace is unlocked. I'm going out there.' He gave a big sigh. 'It's nice. I'm going to sit out here for a bit and get some air.'

'This all ties in so far,' said Nathan.

'What a surprise,' said Mackintosh. We all ignored her.

'Time's passing,' said Jocasta. 'What's happening?'

'It's a bit cold out here,' said Craig. 'I must've fallen asleep. I'm trying to go back inside, but the door's locked. All the lights are off. The barman's gone. Maybe I should walk round to the front of the hotel? Not sure which way that is, though.'

'Is there anybody else out there?'

'No... Although I can hear voices.'

'How many? Do you know who they are?'

'No... I can hear lots of voices, laughing, in the distance.'

Nathan and I exchanged glances. We hadn't been expecting that. Who did all these voices belong to?

'Are they male or female?' asked Nathan.

'I don't know... male, I think. They're too far away to hear properly, but they're low-pitched.' He assumed a look of intense concentration, like he was listening. 'No, I can't really make them out. But there's other voices.'

'Closer?'

'Yes. A woman.'

'Is she alone?'

He paused for a moment, again, as if he were listening to their conversation in real time. 'I don't think so – it sounds like she's pausing to let someone else speak – but I can only hear her.' His fingers clenched and he began to look distressed.

'Craig, this is just a memory, okay? It can't hurt you, or anyone else,' said Jocasta, soothingly. Carmen came over and crouched next to him, and took his hand, looking askance at Jocasta, who nodded and whispered, 'Yes, that's fine.'

'She sounds really angry,' said Craig.

'Angry? Or scared?'

'No, angry. Definitely. She's furious, she's shrieking at the other person—'

'Can you hear what she's saying?'

'No... I'm going to get closer.' Craig was silent for a while, then: 'I can't hear them. They must've moved on.' He looked upset. 'I hope they're okay.'

'Why are you getting upset, Craig? Can you tell me?'

'Because all that shouting is making me think about the argument I had with Nicky before I came here. I'm such an idiot. I really hurt her. I don't know if she'll ever forgive me. *I'd* never forgive me.' He swiped at his eyes, where tears were forming. 'I'm all on my own again...'

'That's enough,' said Nathan.

'Is it?' Mackintosh was standing with her arms folded, watching. 'I was just starting to enjoy myself.'

'Di!' I said, shaking my head. 'There's no need for that.'

'Ask him if he killed her,' said Mackintosh, ignoring me.

'It doesn't really work like that,' said Jocasta.

'Did you kill Kelly?' Mackintosh spoke directly to Craig.

'What? Who?'

'Kelly. The young woman who you made a pass at earlier in the evening, and who rebuffed you forcefully in front of your friends.' Mackintosh watched Craig closely. 'Did she make you feel stupid? Did you see her outside and decide to teach her a lesson?'

'Di, for God's sake—' I said.

'Did her body end up in the pond because she hurt your male pride?'

Nathan grabbed her arm and pulled her away. 'That's enough, DI Mackintosh. I might not be leading this investigation but I'm still your superior officer and I will not have you questioning a witness—'

'Suspect.'

'—*or* a suspect while they're in a vulnerable state, and without a lawyer present. I'll remind you that this is being recorded, at your own request. Do you want the Chief Super at Exeter to see this?'

She finally turned away from Craig and looked at Nathan. 'You wouldn't. Craig Carter is your best man, you're hardly in a position to dictate how he's treated. You're not exactly an impartial bystander.'

'Impartial or not, there are rules when it comes to interviewing a suspect,' said Nathan. Craig, who had woken up or come out of his trance – whatever the technical term was – and who was being fussed over by Jocasta and Mum, looked up sharply.

'Suspect? I really am a suspect? Even though I told you what happened?'

'You remember it now?' I asked, and he nodded. Mackintosh scoffed.

'I'm sorry, but this little parlour trick might impress some people, but do you think it'll stand up in court?' she said. 'DC Bakshi. Please escort Mr Carter to the car and tell DC Walters to take him to the station, where I'll interview him *properly*.' She turned back to the rest of us. 'Amnesia is a handy excuse if you need more time to come up with an alibi or a convincing story,' she said. 'Just because he *said* he didn't remember, it doesn't mean that he didn't know all along what went on that night. And just because he's now come up with some story about hearing voices – even though we've interviewed everyone who was on the premises at the time and no one else has reported hearing them – that doesn't mean he's telling the truth, does it?' She looked at me and shook her head. 'I thought you were a better cop than that, Jodie. I can see now why you quit.' And with that she swept out of the room, leaving me uncharacteristically speechless.

Chapter Thirteen

'Well, that one's a right cow,' said Danny. 'She were well out of order.'

We were sitting in the bar, completely shellshocked after Mackintosh's exit. I was shellshocked and embarrassed too, by her last remark; after everything I'd done for her when we'd been at the same nick! We hadn't exactly been friends, but I'd stood up for her when male colleagues had made comments like, well, like the one Danny had just made. But this time I didn't feel like defending her.

'Unfortunately, she isn't wrong,' said Jocasta, and we all stared at her, horrified. She put up her hands in defence. 'Not about Jodie, of course, and she wasn't exactly professional towards the end. But she's not wrong about suspects who claim amnesia.'

'You can't seriously believe Craig was putting that on?' asked Ben, and Jocasta shook her head; but I could see some of us were thinking, *Could he have been?* Because at the end of the day, Nathan, Danny and Ben knew him, but we didn't.

'That's not what Jocasta's saying,' said Nathan. 'But you have to admit, if you had someone in the frame and they'd left something that important out of their statement, and then when you pulled them up on it, with proof, they just said they couldn't remember... would you take their word for it?'

'But we just stood there and watched him going over the events of that night,' said Ben. 'Did it look like he was making all that up on the spot to you?'

'No, of course not,' said Nathan. 'But that's because I know him, and quick as he is, I don't think he'd be capable of doing that off the top of his head. Put yourself in her shoes. What would you think?'

'I'd still be thinking the no-mark boyfriend would be a more likely suspect,' said Danny, and the rest of us nodded in agreement. Frankie Lewis was a much more palatable suspect. 'I don't get why she's turned the heat off him.'

Sunil joined us. 'Lewis is out of the picture,' he said. 'The time of death meant his window of opportunity was always very narrow, and we just got a look at his phone calls on the night of the murder.' He reached out and picked up a glass of whisky that was on the table. 'Whose is this? Can I?'

Tony nodded. 'Be my guest.'

Sunil knocked back the whisky in one and gasped.

'Woah, Sunil!' said Nathan. 'You don't drink!'

'I know, Guv,' he croaked. 'But it's through choice, not religion. Just thought it might help...'

'Did it?'

'Only to remind me why I don't drink.' He coughed. 'I shouldn't be telling you any of this, but DI Mackintosh and that Exeter lot can get stuffed.' He slapped a hand over his mouth. 'Sorry.'

'Sunil, after her attitude just now, I think we all agree with you.' Nathan waved at the barman, who brought a glass of water over and placed it in front of Sunil. Nathan waited until he'd gone, and then said, 'So what about these phone records?'

'Lewis had a phone call at one forty,' said Sunil. 'He didn't answer it, which is probably why he forgot about it and didn't mention it to us. But he did see it, and declined it.'

'At one forty?' I asked. 'Right in the middle of the time he was supposedly murdering his girlfriend?'

'Dunno about you, but I think I'd let it go to voicemail in a situation like that,' said Danny.

Sunil nodded. 'It *did* go to voicemail. And then at one forty-six, Lewis listened to it.'

We all stared at him, incredulous. Sunil sat back, enjoying his moment in the spotlight, I thought, but also looking slightly green around the gills after knocking back that whisky.

'Right,' said Nathan, 'so that's why he didn't pass the camera at the gatehouse until one fifty – because he was listening to a message, rather than dumping the body in a pond?'

'Yup.'

'Who called him?'

'His brother, Ian. Frankie had spoken to him earlier that night, and Ian could tell he was winding himself up about Kelly doing the waitressing job. He'd tried to call him about midnight to make sure he wasn't going to do anything stupid, but there was no answer. He knew Frankie hadn't just gone to bed, because he could see he was online on Facebook, right up until around the time the girls left the hotel. So he gave him one last call to make sure he wasn't waiting up for Kelly to get home and have an argument with her.'

'That worked well, didn't it?' said Ben.

'We only heard about it when we spoke to Ian Lewis, because Frankie had texted Kelly saying he'd stayed at his brother's overnight. Frankie told us something completely different, of course, so we had to check, and that's when Ian told us he'd tried to call him.'

'So where *did* Frankie spend the night?' I asked.

'It looks like he was telling the truth when he said he'd slept in his car on top of the cliffs,' said Sunil. 'ANPR from a camera at the petrol station on Clifton Park Road puts him there at just after two a.m. And the same camera picked him up going the other way at eight thirty. Ian told me that their parents used to take them up there when they were kids, and Frankie often goes up there now when he needs space to think, or to calm down.'

Nathan handed Sunil the glass of water, then picked up his own glass of cola and raised it in a small toast. 'Well done, Sunil. You had doubts about Frankie Lewis from the start, didn't you? I told you, trust your instincts and you can't go far wrong.'

'Which is all well and good,' said Danny, 'but what does that mean for our lad Craig? Has she got anything on him, other than him being outside at the right time? Or the wrong time.'

'I don't know,' said Sunil. 'And I can't find out, because Mackintosh took me off the case.'

'What?' Nathan looked annoyed.

'I didn't follow her orders, which were to bring Craig in as soon as I found him. I went into the victim's phone instead of passing it on to her and letting her do that. She told me I was insubordinate and incompetent.' Sunil looked glum.

'No, I'm not having that,' said Nathan. 'You're a good copper, Sunil. I'm lucky to have you on my team.'

'Thanks, Guv,' said Sunil, brightening up a bit. 'I really appreciate that, coming from you.'

'So what happens now?' Matt, who had been standing outside talking on the phone, came back into the bar. 'I just spoke to one of the lads from Exeter, Martin – I went to school with his brother, so he didn't mind filling me in, although I think Mackintosh has got them all on a tight leash. He doesn't think there's enough to charge Craig, not yet anyway, but he reckons she'll keep him there for as long as she's allowed to.'

'He's not making it back for the wedding, then,' I said, and Matt shook his head.

'Not a chance.' He looked awkward. 'I was a bit put out when I realised you were going to have two best men, not gonna lie, but it feels wrong to be doing it on me own now.'

'Yeah…' said Nathan, glancing at me. I sighed.

'I think you and me need to have a chat, don't we?'

Nathan and I went for a walk in the grounds, to get away from everyone else. It was a beautiful day; the sun was out and it would've been quite hot, but for the gentle breeze that rustled the trees and shrubs planted around the formal garden we found ourselves in.

'Perfect day and perfect place for wedding photos,' I said, and Nathan nodded. He took me by the hand and led me over to a stone bench that overlooked another – thankfully corpse-free – ornamental pond. We sat and looked at the water for a moment without speaking.

'I think we need to—' 'I think we should—'

Nathan stopped and looked at me. 'You first.'

'Do I have to?' He nodded. 'I think we should postpone the wedding.'

'Oh thank God for that,' he said. 'That's what I was thinking, but I didn't want to upset you, if that wasn't what you thought.'

'No, and to be honest it's not just this thing with Craig,' I said. 'I was talking to Carmen about it earlier. It feels really wrong to get married after someone was murdered here. I know she wasn't really part of our group, but we're the reason she was here. And it just feels heartless to carry on, regardless of how many best men you've got.'

Nathan heaved a big sigh of relief. 'Yes, that's exactly how I've been feeling. I know we said life goes on and everything, but… My mum's going to go spare.'

'I know.'

'What do we do?'

'We can't send everyone home, can we? We talked about that before. Your lot have all come from miles away, which makes it awkward. And of course we've paid for everything already – the reception, the cake, all the food…'

Nathan took my hands. 'I was looking forward to seeing you in your dress.'

'You'll still get to see that. We'll still get married, just not today. And not here. We're not forking out all that money again.'

Nathan laughed and put his arm around me. 'Always the romantic.'

'You said it yourself, we could've bought a new car with the money.' I reached up to kiss him. 'Not that we need a new car. And we have had some fun in that big posh four-poster bed…'

'That's true… Expensive fun, though.'

I laughed. 'I'm worth it.'

We sat in silence for a while, watching the insects buzzing around the pond.

'I think we should still have the reception,' I said. 'We've paid for everyone to stay another night, and for the dinner. I think rather than a wedding, we should celebrate having all our family and friends around us, because the events of this weekend have proved you never know how long you've got with them.'

'That's a cheery thought,' said Nathan. 'I do like that idea, though. It feels a bit more respectful of Kelly than a big knees-up.' He laughed. 'Although with Danny and Ben around, it will probably still turn into a big knees-up.'

'That's okay. We will get married, and soon, and this way the only members of the Devon and Cornwall Constabulary in the photos will be off duty.'

'That's agreed, then. Now what can we do to get Craig out of there?'

What could we do? That was the question. With the weight of the wedding gone from our shoulders – and I realised with a start that that's exactly what it had become, a burden, which absolutely confirmed that we were making the right decision – it meant we could concentrate on proving Craig's innocence. But how would we do that?

We told the rest of our party that the wedding was off. Liz looked like she was going to faint, and I could tell that Mum was disappointed, but everyone accepted it and understood why we were postponing. And of course they all cheered right up when we told them the party was still on. Carmen took me to one side after we'd announced it and told me that we'd made the right decision.

'Why didn't you say that before?' I asked.

'Because it wouldn't be the right decision for everyone,' she said. 'You and Nathan had to work it out for yourselves. But I could see it was really troubling you.'

'Yeah, it was. All we have to do now is find another venue where we can get married as soon as possible, although,' I said, as a thought struck me, 'we'll have to work it around when Liz and Roger, and maybe Nathan's mates too can get back down here.' I groaned. 'It's going to be a pain in the backside. Maybe we should just elope.'

'Don't do that,' said Carmen, with a grin, 'because I may be able to help you out there…' She wouldn't say any more.

'So, what's the game plan? How are we getting our lad outta the nick and back here where he belongs?' asked Danny.

'The best way to prove someone's innocence is to find out who's actually guilty,' I said, and Nathan nodded.

'Yep. We do what DI Mackintosh should be doing. We start at the beginning and find out who the killer is.'

Debbie and Arabella appeared, wheeling a big whiteboard between them. They stopped in front of us, heralded by a bark from Germaine, who clearly no longer had to hide upstairs with Natasha the make-up lady.

'Ta da!' said Debbie.

'You had your hair done?' I asked.

'Well I was stuck in *your* room, looking after *your* dog while all the excitement was going on down here, with only an experienced hair and make-up artist for company, so *duh. Of course* I've had my hair done.' She patted a curl. 'Like it?'

'It's very glamorous,' I said. 'But the whiteboard...?'

'That was my idea,' said Arabella. 'When I heard what was going on, and that you'd postponed the wedding ceremony, there wasn't much for me to do, so I thought I'd come and join your gang of detectives...'

'Gang of detectives?'

Debbie had the decency to look a little bit embarrassed. 'I may or may not have told Natasha and Arabella all about our previous exploits. Like the murder at Kingseat Abbey, when we were catering that Christmas party and got snowed in. And then last year, when Lee Roskill got bumped off...'

'It all sounded very exciting,' gushed Arabella. 'So I thought, how can I help? What do they normally do on the television?' She indicated the whiteboard. 'Murder board. And I have marker pens.' She proudly held up a blue marker.

'That's great, thanks Arabella,' I said, because she was so enthusiastic I could hardly tell her to go away. And she *had* worked her magic with Mr Robbins and convinced him to let Germaine stay at the hotel.

'If I may?' said Nathan, politely taking the pen from the excited (but now unneeded) wedding planner. He turned to face our motley crew of investigators. 'We have several lines of enquiry.' He wrote on the board. 'Number one. Our victim. We need to dig into her background, find out if she had any enemies, anyone likely to want to do her harm. They may not have set out to kill her, but they definitely had mischief in mind.' He turned to Daisy and Joe, who had been lurking at the edge of the crowd. 'Are you two on social media?'

Daisy rolled her eyes. 'Yes, grandad.'

'See what you can find out on her social media accounts. Facebook, Instagram, Twitter…'

'Facebook is for old people,' said Daisy.

'Oi! I've got a Facebook account!' I said.

Mum nodded. 'So have I. We just proved her point.'

'Just have a look and see what you can find. Who her friends are. Particularly if there are any who are friends with Frankie Lewis, as well.' Nathan ignored my grumbles about not being old.

'Why him?' asked Joe.

'He might not have killed Kelly, but he's not exactly pure as the driven snow,' said Matt. 'Someone might've got at her, to get at him.'

'Exactly. It's a long shot, but it's worth looking at,' said Nathan. 'Shirley and Tony. You know where to get all the good gossip—'

'They spread most of it,' muttered Debbie.

'Get on the phones and ask around. Basically do the same thing as Daisy and Joe, only with real-life people.'

'Sir yes sir!' said Tony, snapping off a salute. 'I think me and Shirl can manage that, don't you?'

'You want us to dig the dirt and spill the tea on Kelly,' said Mum. 'Gotcha.'

'Number two. We need to look at the crime scene again – that's not just the pond, but those grooves in the grass. Jodie, you'll have to do that, as you seem to know the entire Forensics team.'

'Only Robbo,' I protested. 'Unless Gary's working. In which case Lisa could be on as well.'

Nathan grinned at me. 'Like I said, you know the entire Forensics team…'

'Okay. What am I looking for?'

'The usual – anything weird or out of place. And although the cause of death was drowning – is that official, Sunil?' We all looked over at Sunil, who nodded. 'Although she died from drowning, there was a big lump on her head, wasn't there? We need to know what caused that. If that's been found it could have DNA or some kind of evidence on it.'

'Righto,' I said.

'Three. We need to look into Craig's evidence. He reckons he heard lots of voices in the distance. Did he really? If so, who are they and why haven't they come forward?'

'Thieving staff members,' said Ben. 'That's what I thought, when I came across the fire exit propped open. Could be them.'

'It could be, although Robbins did say they were only nicking toilet rolls and bleach…' said Nathan.

'Yeah, but look at Robbins. He's—' I started.

'He's my father,' said Arabella. So that was how she'd persuaded him to let Germaine stay.

'—a very good manager, but does come across as very principled and maybe a little strict.' I was quite proud of how quickly and smoothly I changed what I was about to say. 'If there were any staff members outside engaged in nefarious deeds,' *Nicking loo paper,* I thought, 'then they might be worried about losing their jobs if they came forward, even though I'm sure, in such circumstances as these, a manager as skilled as Mr Robbins would be sure to overlook their indiscretions.' I smiled at Arabella, all the time thinking, *Oh my God, I should've gone into politics or the diplomatic service.* I risked a glance at Nathan, who was grinning broadly and who had obviously spotted my linguistic gymnastics.

'Anyway, Ben, you should go to the station and amend your statement, tell them what you told us about finding Craig, while Danny, you could ask around the staff members, see what you can dig up,' said Nathan.

'The kitchen staff are all here,' said Arabella. 'And the wait staff are setting up in the dining room, for the reception. I need to talk to them about the change in plans anyway, so I'll come with you.'

'Good idea. What about the receptionist? The one who was here on the night of the murder?'

'She's doing night shifts, obviously,' I said. 'I don't know what time she'll be in. Might be worth finding out who else was on duty, see if they could be the mysterious bog-roll burglars.'

'What about me?' asked Debbie. 'What can I do?'

'Oh, you're with me,' I said. 'You can flirt with Robbo

and get him to talk.' Callum, who had been sitting nearby with a pint and quietly taking everything in, as was his way, raised an eyebrow. '*Mild* flirting, of course. Just a bit of giggling and flicking her fancy new hairstyle and going, "Ooh you must be *so* clever!" occasionally. She's good at that.'

'Hmm,' said Callum mildly, which meant he wasn't best pleased but was resigned to it. Debbie giggled, flicked her hair and leant down to kiss him.

'Ooh, you're *so* handsome when you're moody,' she said, because Callum was so lovely and easygoing, that *was* his version of being moody, 'there's no way I could *ever* love any other man!'

'Hmmph,' said Callum, which was his version of, *Yeah, alright, I know you're taking the mickey out of me but I love you anyway.*

'She'll make it up to you in the hot tub later,' I said, and Callum laughed.

'Not the hot tub, there are bits of me that are all wrinkly that shouldn't be, and bits that are wrinkly anyway that are now even more wrinkly.'

'Okay,' said Nathan, cutting off that area of discourse before anyone could start imagining which bits he was talking about. 'You lot know your jobs. The rest of you, just relax, get ready for the meal and the party afterwards, which starts in—' he checked his watch, '—two hours. And keep your eyes peeled for anything odd.'

Chapter Fourteen

'Anything odd.' Easy to say, not always so easy to spot. But we had to try.

Debbie and I set off for the golf course, heading first to the spot where I'd earlier seen Robbo photographing divots. The area was still taped off, but the Forensics officer was gone; to be fair, there wasn't a lot to see there, and there was no undergrowth for any hitherto undiscovered clues to be lurking in. We didn't loiter there, but followed the vague path the divots in the grass had marked out and made our way to the pond.

The scene was a hive of activity. Robbo had moved on there, helped by Gary (who was married to an old school friend of mine) and Lisa (her mum worked at the local hairdressers and had styled all three generations of the Parker women at some point). A place like Penstowan, where everyone knew who you were, could be your worst nightmare sometimes, but at other times – like when you were an unofficial busybody trying to find out information you had absolutely no entitlement to – it was a dream.

They weren't the only ones there, though. A diver in a wetsuit sat on the stone bench at the side of the pond, peeling off his rubber gloves and drying his face on a towel.

'You been searching the pond?' I asked, surprised. He nodded. Robbo saw me and came over, leaving the others to take photographs and catalogue their findings.

'Mackintosh has pulled out all the stops this time,' he said, gesturing towards the diver. He looked around and lowered his voice. 'I think she got caught out earlier, with that Frankie Lewis. It doesn't do to put all your investigative eggs in one basket.'

'No,' I said. 'So what are you looking for? Did he find anything?'

'And I should tell you why?' He smiled at me and Debbie.

'Because I'm a caterer, and I hear you just got engaged,' I said. Debbie nodded.

'Expensive things, weddings,' she said sagely. 'Be handy to have a caterer who gives you mates' rates…'

'Exactly,' I said, although I hoped he wouldn't expect too much of a discount if he hired me, because a woman's got to make a living, and with the number of favours I owed friends, most of them incurred during murder investigations, I'd be filing for bankruptcy if I wasn't careful.

He laughed. 'I've heard what happens when you're involved in wedding parties,' he said. 'No offence, but I don't think we'll be hiring you. But you can still come and have a look at what we found.' He shrugged. 'There isn't much...'

He wasn't kidding. A tarpaulin had been spread out on the grass, and the fruits of the diver's search were laid out on it. It was a sparse offering.

'Four empty beer bottles and a load of golf balls,' I said.

'Yep. Not a lot to go on,' said Robbo. He squatted down and poked the bottles with a pencil. 'These look like they've been in here a long time,' he said. 'The labels have soaked off in the water, and they're full of silt.' He moved on to the golf balls. 'Hard to say how long they've been in the water. Some of them are dirtier than the others – you can see how the mud has collected in the dimples on the surface – so they'll probably have been in the water longer, but other than that they haven't deteriorated.'

'They could've been in there days, or weeks, or months,' I said. 'Golf balls are pretty tough, aren't they?'

'Yes.' Robbo looked across the grass towards the golf course proper. 'There must be some terrible golfers out there if their balls have ended up here. I know a lot of golf courses drain any water traps and ponds once a year, clean off the golf balls and sell them.'

'What about around the edge of the pond?' asked Debbie, getting into her role as investigative sidekick.

'Lots of shoe-prints in the mud,' said Robbo. 'A couple of actual footprints as well, but I think that might be from when DCI Withers and Matt Turner went in to get her.'

'Yeah, they both took their shoes off,' I said.

'Talking of shoes, did you find the victim's?' asked Debbie.

'Now's not the time to be thinking about Callum's foot fetish,' I said. Robbo's eyes widened, but Debbie shook her head, exasperated.

'I'm not. But you asked me before about her shoes, so I'm assuming she wasn't wearing them when Nathan and Matt pulled her out of the water,' said Debbie. I wrinkled my nose, thinking hard.

'No… I don't think she was. I can't really remember.'

'Believe me, if she'd been wearing them you'd have noticed,' said Debbie, and from her earlier description of them I thought she was probably right.

'We've not found any shoes,' said Robbo. 'They might be caught up in the reeds or something.'

I stepped forward and looked at the muddy patch where numerous shoeprints (and two sets of footprints) had congregated. 'There's no puncture marks in the grass,' I said to Debbie. Robbo looked at me quizzically. 'She was wearing spiky high heels,' I explained.

'Oh yes – hence the divots in the grass back there,' he said. 'We've not found anything like that near here.'

'We thought before that the murderer must've picked her up and carried her over here, then chucked her into the pond,' I said, 'and that still seems the most likely explanation because of the lack of heel marks, but if that's the case I would've expected her to still be wearing her shoes when we found her, or for them to have fallen off and be in the water. Would the murderer really have stopped and taken them off her before they threw her in, and then what – kept them?'

'Maybe he had a foot fetish like your husband,' said Robbo, grinning at Debbie. 'Do you know where he was at the time?'

'I have intimate knowledge of his whereabouts at the time of the murder,' said Debbie, 'and I can tell you that he were well occupied for at least an hour either side of it.' She thought for a moment. 'Well, occupied for some of it, asleep for most of it.'

'Sounds more likely,' I said.

'Maybe she lost her shoes while she was running away?' suggested Robbo. 'That would also explain why there are no more divots in the grass.'

'But it still doesn't explain where they are now,' I said. 'You must've searched around that area?'

'Of course. There's not much in the way of undergrowth there, though.' He looked thoughtful. 'These shoes could be important, do you think?'

'No idea,' I said. 'It's just odd that they're not here.'

'Yes, that's true. Okay, leave it with me. I'll get the diver to go back in again and give the reeds one more going over, and see if we can get some more bodies over here and get them searching the rest of the course, see if we can find them. Although,' he warned, 'even if we do, they might not tell us anything.'

'No. But you never know if something's going to be the final piece of the puzzle until you find it, do you?'

'No. It's normally not, though…'

'So what do you think?' asked Debbie excitedly, as we left Robbo and the gang and headed back towards the hotel. 'Do you think it's a serial killer?'

I stopped and looked at her in amazement. 'A serial killer? You do know what the word "serial" means, in this context? More than one murder. Unless you're expecting another body to pop up in a bunker? Or a corpse on the final tee?'

'Well – that might happen…' said Debbie. 'But I was thinking about the shoes. Maybe the killer's kept them as a trophy or something?'

'A trophy?'

'Yeah. You know, like, a finger or the victim's wedding ring or something. Or in this case, shoes.' Debbie's eyes gleamed enthusiastically and I thought, *I have created a monster*. 'I were watching that true crime thing on Netflix—'

'Which one? Half of Netflix is true crime documentaries.'

'The one about the postman in Alaska.' She stopped and put on a terrible American accent, several octaves lower than her normal voice. '"They thought he was just an ordinary mail man, but he brought death to the small town along with their post."' She lowered her voice even further until it was almost a growl. '"It was murder – by special delivery."'

'You enjoyed saying that far too much.'

'Missed me vocation, didn't I? Should've been a

voiceover artist. But anyway – the shoes. Could they be a trophy?'

'I suppose they could,' I said. 'But I bloody well hope not. One dead body's put enough of a dampener on the weekend as it is.'

'True, that.'

'What have you learnt?' asked Nathan, as we walked into the bar to find him staring at the murder board.

'One, that Debbie's watched too many true crime documentaries, and two, there are a lot of golfers about with terrible aim.' I sat down on an armchair. 'Honestly babe, I'm not sure we're going to solve this one. There's just no evidence of anything, anywhere.'

'This is not like you,' said Nathan, sitting next to me and putting his hand on my leg. 'Where's the outlandish theories? The wild speculation?'

'I'm not that bad,' I protested, but weakly, because he was kind of right. 'I suppose I just didn't expect to be playing Sherlock Holmes this weekend.'

'No, me neither,' he said. 'But I don't see that we've got much choice. We're here, we're not getting married today now—' I knew we were only postponing it, and it was my choice as well as Nathan's, but it still caused a pang when he said that. 'And Craig's still at the station.'

'She can't seriously charge him,' I said. Nathan shrugged.

'No, I hope not. But as much as we can't find anything to prove who did it, we've also not found anything to prove he didn't.' I looked at him, shocked. He shook his head. 'I'm not saying I think he's guilty – I still can't imagine him killing anyone – but then he was acting out of character when he first got here, and the whole of that night.'

'Yeah…' I said, because of course I knew why. And I knew that I had to tell Nathan what Craig had told me. So, after looking around and making sure no one would overhear us – Debbie had wandered off to find Callum, and everyone else was either preparing for our no-wedding reception or still following up on the investigating task Nathan had given them – I did.

Nathan's jaw dropped.

'So you see,' I finished up, '*that's* why he's been behaving so odd. He's not some sexual predator, he was just very confused about who he is and how he felt, and *that's* why he propositioned Kelly the way he did. It's like he was trying to prove something to the others, and maybe to himself as well.'

'That he's a "real man", whatever that is,' said Nathan, rolling his eyes, and I smiled, because that was just one of the reasons I was marrying him. At some point. He was comfortable enough with himself that he never had to try and prove his masculinity. He could be tough at work when the situation called for it, but equally I'd seen him cry at a film (to be fair, it was *The Book Thief*, and if you don't cry at *that*, you are basically made of stone). 'To my mind, real men love who they want to love and don't care what other people think. I mean, look at me, marrying you…' He grinned at my outraged face. 'But seriously, why on earth didn't he tell me about Nicky? Surely he didn't think I'd have a problem with her?'

'No, he did say he wasn't worried about you, but the others... They do take the piss, don't they? I can imagine them saying something, even if they didn't actually mean it in a nasty way. They might think they were being funny.'

'Yeah, that's true. But he seems to think he's made it up with her, so hopefully the engagement is still on.'

'If he's ever allowed back on the plane and isn't kept here to face a murder charge,' I said, and we both sat for a moment in grim silence.

'Hopefully one of the others will have come up with something,' said Nathan. 'I think they're all getting ready for the party now.'

'Maybe we should too, then,' I said, standing up and pulling him to his feet. I put my arms around him and gazed up into his eyes. 'Will you not marry me, Nathan Withers?'

'It would be my absolute pleasure not to,' he said, and then his grin disappeared. 'I mean, to not marry you *today*. I'm desperate to actually marry you, anywhere there's no dead bodies.'

'That rules out the church, then,' I said. 'It's surrounded. The graveyard's full of 'em.'

'Are you still going to wear this amazing dress I've been hearing about?' he asked.

'I don't know. It *is* a wedding dress, and as we just agreed, it's not a wedding.'

'But...?'

'But if I save it for when we do get married, no one will see it, will they? Because we probably won't have this many people at the next one. We've got half of Penstowan coming along just for the reception.' A thought occurred to me. 'Oh God, do they all know the wedding's off? I know Mum and Tony spread the word, but are people going to turn up with wedding presents?'

'They shouldn't,' said Nathan. 'We told people not to buy anything.'

'Yeah, but you know some of them still will,' I said. 'Oh God, we're gonna have to stand up in front of everyone and tell them—'

'Don't panic,' said Nathan, brushing hair off my face and cupping my cheek in his hand. 'They're all coming because they love you—'

'Us.'

'Well, most of them don't really know me, but they grew up with you, so yeah, I reckon they're coming because they love *you*,' he said, smiling. 'You are quite lovable, so I get it. They'll understand why we've cancelled, and they'll have a good time anyway, because have you seen the amount of food and booze the hotel have laid on for this?'

'No.'

Nathan laughed. 'Nor have I, but we gave them a lot of money so they'd better have.' He bent down and kissed me on the lips. 'Why don't we go upstairs now and help each other get dressed?' He gave me a seductive smile. 'Which of course involves getting undressed first.'

'Ooh, DCI Withers, and us not even married yet!'
We took the stairs up to the honeymoon suite at a run.

Chapter Fifteen

So that was how I found myself in my wedding dress, even though there was no wedding. After Nathan and I had, er, consoled ourselves about the postponement of the ceremony, I made my way back to my own room, having first sent out the Bat signal (or a group WhatsApp message saying **Bridal Party Assemble!**) to my girls. Daisy, Mum, Debbie and Carmen (and Germaine) were back on the (non-alcoholic) champagne when I got there, along with Natasha the make-up lady, who'd been more than happy to hang around because I was paying her by the hour *and* we'd agreed to pay for her to have lunch at the hotel. And, she said, she had nothing better to do and it was almost as exciting as one of those true crime documentaries, wasn't it? Debbie's eyes had lit up and they were soon discussing (cue ridiculously deep and gravelly American voice) *Murder by Special Delivery*.

'Okay, Debbie's happy,' I said. 'Everyone else okay?'

'Oh yes,' said Carmen. 'I've been watching a masterclass in rumour gathering.'

'My mother is a world-class gossip,' I said, and she laughed.

'I'm not talking about Shirley, I meant Tony,' she said. 'He's worryingly good at charming information out of little old ladies.'

'I taught him everything he knows,' sniffed Mum. 'I would've taught him everything *I* know, but it would've taken too long.'

'Did any of you find anything out?' I asked. Daisy, who had been feeding Germaine sausage rolls pinched from the buffet, which they'd just started to lay out on the tables in the dining room, nodded.

'We did. We found her Facebook page—'

'Hang on,' I said. 'How come she had a Facebook account? She wasn't old.'

'Oh, ha ha. The waitressing was just a side hustle, to earn money while she went to college.'

'What was she studying?' I asked.

'She was training to become a veterinary nurse,' said Daisy, making a fuss of Germaine, who was nosing around hopefully for more sausage rolls. 'She used to volunteer at the RSPCA.'

'Oh,' I said, feeling even sadder at the thought of her young life being snuffed out, because in my book anyone who wants to devote their lives to looking after animals is bound to be a nice person. 'What about friends?'

'Loads of them,' said Daisy, a little unhelpfully. 'Everyone loved her.'

'Not everyone, obviously,' said Natasha, and we all looked at her in surprise. She grinned. 'I'm part of your gang now, yes?'

I spread my arms out wide. 'Of course. Everybody's welcome, as long as they can help us prove Craig didn't do it.'

'Hmm,' said Natasha. 'I finish your face now.' So she obviously didn't have any theories.

'What about you and Tony?' I asked Mum, as I sat myself in the make-up chair. 'Anything to add? Or did you find anything out about Frankie?'

'Only what we already knew,' said Mum. 'That he's a right little wotsit. Gave Gavin Matthews a black eye a couple of years ago.'

'Yeah, but Gavin Matthews is a little sod himself,' said Debbie. 'His gran's on my round. I go round there to keep an eye on that nasty leg ulcer—' Daisy and I looked at each other and grimaced.

'Oh yeah, poor old Bonny,' said Mum. 'She came on that trip to Tavistock the community centre organised back in April. It were too much for her leg, walking from the bus stop to the café. By the time we sat down to eat, oozing, it was. *Oozing.*'

'Yikes,' said Daisy.

'Bright yellow, it was. And me about to eat a custard tart. It put me off for a moment, I can tell you.'

'Okay, let's skip to the part about Gavin...' I said. Debbie nodded.

'Oh yeah. He's been round there a few times when I've gone to change the dressing, supposedly to do some shopping for her. But when he does it the supermarket always seems to only have half the stuff she wants, and they charge twice as much for everything they *have* got.' She sighed. 'Bonny knows he's stealing from her, but he's her grandson.'

'Sounds like he deserved that black eye,' said Natasha, and I couldn't disagree with her, primarily because she was waving a mascara wand around near my eye.

'Gavin Matthews is a git,' I agreed, 'but I hardly think he's going to knock off Kelly to get back at Frankie for a black eye from two years ago.'

'I dunno, you know what they say,' said Mum, and we all waited for her to tell us what they apparently say, but she didn't. After a quiet pause, Natasha stood back and admired her handiwork critically.

'Yes, I think you do very nice,' she said, nodding and stepping out of the way so I could see myself in the mirror.

'Oh my – is that me?' I asked, turning my head this way and that to get a proper look at what she'd done. Because she'd managed to tame my unruly hair, as well as hide the bags under my eyes, and the reflection of this glamorous and, yes, I'm going to say it, beautiful woman stared back at me.

'Oh, Jodie, love,' said Mum, and I could hear in her voice that she was trying not to get too emotional. We

Parker women are brilliant at holding it all together, until we're not, and then the floodgates open and suddenly we're knee-deep in Kleenex. When I had Daisy, my mum and dad had come to visit us in hospital, driving all the way up to London at the crack of dawn just to be our first visitors (my ex-in-laws lived about three miles away from the hospital, but they still didn't make it until the next day). My Mum had taken one look at Daisy, then one look at me, and then we had both immediately fallen apart. Mum had grabbed me for a cuddle and we'd had a good sob (happy tears, obviously), while my dad and Richard, my useless cheating ex, had looked at each other, completely bemused – Richard no doubt wondering what on earth he'd married into. At the thought of my dad my own eyes started to water, but I sniffed furiously, not wanting to ruin my make-up.

'Is waterproof mascara,' said Natasha, smiling.

'Just as well,' muttered Daisy. 'What are these two like?' She turned to Debbie, but she was gurning and making weird faces, and I realised she was struggling not to cry as well. Daisy rolled her eyes. 'Oh my God, the menopause has got a lot to answer for.'

'Cheeky mare! I'm not menopausal just yet,' said Debbie.

'That's worse, then. You can't even blame your hormones.'

Carmen laughed. 'There's something about weddings that sets everyone off,' she said. 'But you look so different. You look beautiful.'

'What do I normally look like, the back end of a bus?' I

said, but I was laughing because I knew that wasn't what she meant.

Daisy stood up decisively, making the dog bark, and clapped her hands together. 'Come on, it's dress time!'

She'd thrown on a pair of shorts and a T-shirt when our preparations had been interrupted earlier, but now she threw them back off again.

'You *are* wearing your dress, aren't you?' she said, hesitating as she reached out for the hanger that held her own beautiful outfit.

'I haven't decided yet,' I admitted, and everyone groaned.

'You're going to be making an entrance, guest of honour at this party—' started Debbie.

'Guest of honour, not bride,' I pointed out.

'Whatever. You're going to be walking in there with all eyes on you in about twenty minutes, and you still haven't decided?' Debbie's eyes weren't on me, they were rolling.

'What else have you got to wear?' asked Mum, her arms crossed on her chest, which was her *just try me* stance from when I was a teenager. I knew I was in trouble.

'Well – just my ordinary clothes,' I squeaked. 'I've got the sundress I had on last night—'

'Jodie!' 'No. Just no.' 'For heaven's sake, Mother!' They all groaned at me again and I put my hands out in defence, and defeat.

'Okay, okay. Looks like I'm wearing The Dress…'

I'd love to be able to say that my entrance to the party was just like the movies, where the heroine sweeps into the room looking amazing, and everyone gasps at her transformation from mousey, bespectacled librarian-type to glamorous, sophisticated princess slash supermodel. But this was real life, and Cornwall at that, where we don't really go in for supermodels. I staggered into the function room, my feet encased in unaccustomed high heels, and most of the guests didn't even notice me; they were too focused on the buffet table or getting a drink at the bar. Nathan stood talking animatedly to Matt, looking in completely the wrong direction.

'So much for my grand entrance,' I muttered, wishing now I'd worn that sundress. But then Matt spotted me over Nathan's shoulder and his eyes widened, his hand (which was clutching a canapé) stopping halfway to his mouth. He looked at Nathan and said something, nodding towards me, and Nathan turned round.

THIS was the reaction I'd wanted. Nathan gazed at me in absolute astonishment, his eyes roaming over my face and body, and then his own face split into the most enormous grin. He held his hands out as he came over to me. He took my hands and then stood back again to look me up and down.

'Oh my God,' he said, 'you look absolutely amazing.' He pulled me close and whispered in my ear, 'I am the luckiest man alive.'

'I haven't married you yet,' I said lightly, trying not to burst at his look of pride.

'I'll be the even luckier luckiest man alive when you do,' he said, kissing me.

'Wow, Jodie, you look fantastic!' said Matt, coming forward and kissing me on the cheek.

'Thank you.' I could feel myself beaming. Suddenly everyone else was noticing what was going on, and they were coming over to say hello and tell me how good I looked. *I could get used to this*, I thought, but it wasn't long before it started to feel a bit weird and awkward, and it did make me wonder what they thought of me when I was dressed in my usual uniform of jeans and T-shirt.

'You and Daisy chose well,' said Nathan, looking at my dress and then smiling at Daisy. He reached out and put an arm around her shoulder as well, so we were engulfed in a family hug. 'You both look incredible, but I have to say your mum beats everyone.'

'My mum?' I asked, and he laughed.

'I was talking to Daisy,' he said, 'but Shirley's pulled out all the stops as well, hasn't she?'

'All fur coat and no knickers,' said Daisy, and we all giggled.

'I love the red,' said Nathan, running a finger across the bodice of my dress. 'I suspected you wouldn't wear a big flouncy white frock, but this is a surprise.'

'Red is an auspicious colour in a lot of cultures,' said Daisy. 'In Asia, lots of women get married in red. And can you see Mum in frills?'

'No, I can't,' said Nathan. He bent slightly to murmur in my ear. 'I like the way it hugs all your curves…'

'I can hear you, you know,' said Daisy, pulling away. 'I'm off to find Joe.'

'She looks lovely as well,' said Nathan, as we watched her walk away, Germaine (in a little red and gold bow, to match my dress) trotting behind her, nose twitching at all the exciting smells. 'So grown up. Daisy, that is, not the dog. Although…' He put a hand on his heart. 'I feel like a proud dad.'

'Aww, bless you,' I said. We had a little cuddle, but there were guests to be attended to and food to eat.

The function room looked absolutely *magnificent*. Everything had been polished and buffed and primped to within an inch of its life. Although it was still daylight outside, the lights inside were on, and three chandeliers glittered above us, the intricate design of crystal droplets sparkling like frosted spiderwebs catching rays of early morning sun. The walls were hung with a gorgeous chinoiserie paper; golden trees dotted with pink and white blossom grew across a pale-blue background, while brightly coloured birds nestled among the leaves or took flight. A stunning floral display took pride of place on a table at one end of the room, all whites and pale yellows and pinks. Next to it was an empty spot, waiting for the wedding cake. Glasses shone, cutlery gleamed, and the buffet table was covered in so much food that I was a little worried it would buckle under the weight. We'd originally – well, *Liz* had originally – wanted a sit-down meal, but everyone seemed to have different dietary needs. Some of our guests were vegan, some gluten-free and/or dairy free; we had friends who didn't eat pork for religious reasons, others who didn't eat chicken because they just didn't like it, and some who turned their nose up at anything green or remotely healthy. After looking back at the weddings I'd catered for, there were so many where the guests had only picked at the stuff on their plate (and not because of my cooking, before you say it), it did feel like a waste of food and money to do a big meal. A buffet meant we could have such a wide variety of dishes that it would cater for everyone, and people could take as much, or as little, as they wanted. And after the main buffet was finished, we were bringing out the big guns: a dessert buffet, with not just the wedding cake but trifles, muffins, mousses, fruit platters and chocolate.

I stared at the food critically. Obviously I'd chosen the dishes, but I hadn't cooked any of it because it was my wedding. It all looked and smelt really good. I'd catered for another caterer's wedding myself three years ago, and it had been probably the most nerve-wracking gig I'd had. I picked up a canapé – a disc of roasted sweet potato topped with whipped feta cheese and avocado – and studied it.

'You're not on duty now,' said Tony, coming over. 'You're allowed to just eat it.'

I smiled and then popped the whole thing in my mouth. I moaned with pleasure. 'Oh damn, that's good.'

Tony smiled. 'You look beautiful, by the way. Far too good for Nathan.' He laughed at the brief look of alarm that flashed across my face before I could stop it. 'I'm kidding. I'm really happy for both of you – at least, I will be when you actually tie the knot.' He shook his head. 'What do you say to the happy couple when they've decided not to get married but are still having the reception?'

'We decided not to get married *today*,' I said. 'It's not called off, it just didn't feel right here and now. Your girlfriend helped us decide that.'

'I thought she might have.'

'You two next?' I asked cheekily, but to my surprise he didn't immediately laugh it off. Instead he just smiled enigmatically.

'Might be…'

'Ooooh, yes! Third time's the charm, eh? Although maybe get someone else to cater this time.' Tony's ill-fated second wedding had been my first catering gig after I'd moved back to Penstowan, and let's just say it hadn't gone to plan, least of all for Tony's ex-wife. Or for Tony.

The next couple of hours were spent eating, drinking and talking to all the guests. We'd booked a DJ that Matt's girlfriend Chrissie knew from her days back in London, and she was brilliant, managing to avoid too many cheesy wedding classics but still getting everybody on the dance floor.

Danny and Ben had been very complimentary about my dress, and had slapped Nathan heartily on the back, so I got the impression that despite the jokes about 'losing another good man', they actually approved of us getting married. Not that we had yet. They had a few drinks, and they seemed to be enjoying themselves, but after a particularly energetic turn on the dance floor I wandered off and found them sitting in a corner, talking quietly between themselves.

I sat down next to them and slipped my shoes off.

'Alright, lads?' I asked. 'Looking a bit serious there.'

'Yeah, just talking about Craig,' said Ben, and I immediately felt bad because, even though the hours leading up to the party had been spent investigating Kelly's murder, the moment I'd got that dress on I hadn't thought about Craig at all. As if reading my mind, Ben said, 'I know it's your wedding party, and everyone's here, and we shouldn't really be talking about that now, but—'

'No, no, it's fine,' I said. 'You changed your statement, then?'

'Yes,' said Ben. 'For all the good it's done. Mackintosh just said they'd make a note of it, but their enquiries were ongoing.'

'That's as expected,' I said. 'Danny, you and Arabella were talking to the hotel staff, weren't you? Did you find anything?'

'I don't know,' said Danny carefully. 'Most of the ones we spoke to weren't on duty that night, they're the day shift. And those that were had already left by the time the murder happened, so none of them saw anything. One of the bar staff said he *might* have seen Frankie waiting in his car when he left at one o'clock, but we already knew that.'

'But you did say one of the cleaning staff noticed something strange the next morning when they came in,' added Ben, 'but you didn't know if they really did, or if it's relevant.'

'What did they say?'

Danny looked at Ben and shook his head, dismissing it, then turned to me. 'The washing machine was on a setting they never use,' he said.

'What? What does that mean?'

'Absolutely bugger all,' said Danny.

'Says the man who doesn't know how to use a washing machine,' said Ben. 'There's a laundry room, next to the staff room. Most of the time they don't use it, because the hotel uses an industrial laundry service. They drop off clean bedding and towels and that three times a week, and pick up dirty stuff at the same time. The laundry room here is only really for emergencies, like during bad weather if the laundry lorry can't get along the muddy country lanes.' He grinned. 'Or if the bride has too many Bacardi Breezers at the reception and falls headfirst into the cake.'

'I'd like to see someone try to get *this* frock into a washing machine,' I said, belligerently. 'Over my de— Anyway, how do they know the machine was on a different setting?'

'One of the cleaners has been bringing in her own laundry,' said Ben. 'I went and checked her out after soft lad here told me about it. Her washing machine packed up a few weeks ago and she can't afford to buy a new one, so she's been bringing it here and washing and drying it while she's working. She said she went to put some clothes in this morning and the machine was on a quick-rinse, half-load setting, which she never uses.'

Danny shook his head again. 'Which tells us absolutely

nothing. She could've just set it wrong the last time she used it, or one of the other staff members has used it. Or someone's brushed against it as they've walked past and it's moved the dial.'

'If she was washing a full load of clothes, I think she'd have noticed it was the wrong setting when she took them out of the machine,' I said. 'They wouldn't have been washed properly.'

'The machine's tucked away in the corner of a tiny room that no one even goes in,' Ben pointed out. 'No one's walking past it. And the machine is practically brand new, so the dial's too stiff for it to move if someone did knock it.'

'So someone else used it.' Danny shrugged it off. 'But we don't know who, and we don't know when. It ain't necessarily suspicious.'

'No, except she last used it on Friday, so whoever used it on quick rinse did so between four p.m. that day, when she emptied it just before she knocked off, and this morning at eight when she put it on again.'

'Okay...' I said, thinking. 'But all the staff know it's there, yeah? And there's nothing to stop them using it?'

'Yes, and no.'

'Did you manage to talk to everyone who's been on duty since that time on Friday?'

'Nope,' said Ben. 'I spoke to a few after I got back from the station, but there's still several staff members who are on the later shifts who aren't in yet.'

'And this cleaner was one of the last people I spoke to,' said Danny. 'For some reason,' his voice was heavy with sarcasm, 'I didn't think to ask the others about whether they'd used the washing machine or not.'

'Alright, I admit it could be nothing, and I *am* grasping at straws,' said Ben. 'But do you want to risk missing something important and leaving Craig at the mercy of DI Mackintosh?'

Chapter Sixteen

I went back to the party, but I was coming to the conclusion that (un)wedding receptions didn't feel quite as jolly when one of the best men was being held by the police on suspicion of murder.

But everyone else was having a good time. My soon-to-be in-laws Liz and Roger were cutting a rug on the dance floor, watched with varying degrees of embarrassment by Nathan (on a scale of one to ten, he looked like he was averaging around a five, although when his dad picked his mum up and swung her over his head, giving everyone a brief flash of her knickers in the process, it went all the way up to eleven). Matt and Chrissie stood next to him, clapping and whooping and encouraging Roger to swing Liz higher and higher. Not that he needed anyone egging him on. Daisy and Joe were in a corner of the room, laughing and teaching Germaine to stand up on her back legs. She was easily taught, as long as there were some nice titbits of food being offered as rewards. I realised the dog and I had a lot in common.

Tony and Carmen were dancing in a four with Debbie and Callum, both men jigging about to the beat of their own drum (which sadly didn't match the rhythm of the song the DJ was playing). Debbie waved her glass at someone across the room and half of her wine sploshed into Carmen's face, but the off-duty vicar just laughed.

Mum had found Jocasta, who was sitting at a table with my old school friends Nina and Lily, and their respective partners. Jocasta was reading Nina's palm, but I got the impression that none of them – not even Jocasta – were taking it seriously; there was a lot of laughing going on, and as I passed them I heard Jocasta say, '… which could either mean the Liberal Democrats will win the next General Election, or Cornwall will finally join the international space race and launch a pasty into orbit.'

What a waste of a good pasty, I thought. I headed over to Daisy and Joe.

'Nice party,' said Joe, politely. I smiled.

'Thank you,' I said. 'I know my mum was planning on making a speech at some point, although I suppose she might save it now for when we actually get married, but if the two of you want to escape before then I totally understand.'

'Thanks for the heads up,' said Daisy, but Joe laughed.

'Are you kidding? I wouldn't miss that for the world!' He pulled himself together. 'Sorry, no disrespect to Shirley, but—'

'She's bonkers,' I said. 'No, it's fine. She's daft but loveable and occasionally very entertaining. I think she needs a bit of air.' I nodded down towards Germaine, who was panting. 'I meant Germaine, not my mum...'

'We'll take her outside,' said Daisy, but I shook my head.

'No, I'll take her. I could do with some fresh air too. This whole day's been emotional.' Daisy practically threw the dog at me then, no doubt concerned that I was about to start sobbing and getting all clingy with her in front of Joe. Not that I do that sort of thing. Very often.

I gave her a cuddle, picked up the dog and then headed out of the function room, walking through the bar and out of the French doors, onto the terrace. It was early evening now, and the sun was starting to get low, but it was still lovely and warm. I put Germaine down and let her sniffle around the tables for a while. There were a few party stragglers, as well as one or two other hotel guests, sitting outside enjoying the sunshine, and they all cooed over her. A couple of them congratulated me on my wedding day, so I just smiled and thanked them; it was easier than telling them we'd called it off because of a murder. Particularly as the murderer was still on the loose somewhere...

Sunil was sitting on the terrace, nursing a glass of water; that hasty glass of whisky earlier had played havoc with him, and although he was alright now, he was staying clear of alcohol. We'd invited him to the wedding, but hadn't expected him to make it, what with the murder investigation. But now he'd been thrown off the case he was available again. That still annoyed me – and I knew Nathan was furious about it – but I was glad he'd been able to stick around and join in, because I didn't feel like I knew him that well; certainly not as well as I knew Matt. He smiled as he saw me.

'Jodie! I haven't had the chance to tell you yet, but you look great,' he said. 'I love the colour of your dress.'

'Would your *nani* approve?' I asked, giving him a twirl, and he laughed.

'She'd love it. She'd pretend to be shocked at how tight it is, but secretly she'd approve.' He looked around. 'I did ask Eesha if she was coming, but she said she was too tired.' Sunil's wife was eight months pregnant with twins.

'Poor thing, I bet she is,' I said. 'Do give her our love, and remember, if you need any help when the babies are born, Nathan's always available for babysitting…' I sat down at his table and took a deep breath, closing my eyes and enjoying the sun on my face. It had been quite a day, and it hadn't exactly turned out how we'd expected, but it was lovely to be sitting here on this warm evening, surrounded by the scent of rosemary and lavender from the plant pots dotted around the terrace. Germaine gave the sort of heavy sigh that only a pampered dog without a care in the world can give and plopped herself down on the floor, resting her head on my feet.

'Excuse me, Miss?' I opened my eyes and saw the greenskeeper that I'd spoken to before. He looked at my dress. 'Although it's probably Mrs by now, innit?'

'Not yet. Long story,' I said. 'Everything okay?'

'Well, I don't know.' He reached into his pocket and brought out a golf ball. 'You're police, aren't you?'

I opened my mouth to say yes, but Sunil interrupted me. 'I am.'

'I were talking to them CSI lot, round by the pond,' he said. 'Just passing the time of day and that. And I saw they'd got a load of golf balls out of the water.'

'That's right,' I said. 'They couldn't tell how long they'd been in there.'

'No. Well we last cleaned the pond out end of last summer. We do that every year, at the end of our busy holiday period. Clean 'em up and sell 'em on. So some of them could've been in there for months. Maybe even almost a year now.'

'Okay,' said Sunil, eyeing the golf ball in the greenskeeper's hand. 'Is that one of them?'

'No,' he said. 'I found this one, and a couple more just like it, when I were checking the course yesterday morning. I give it a once-over every morning, just to make sure everything's okay, and I always seem to come across a few stray balls.'

'Right...' I said, glancing at Sunil, who, like me, was obviously wondering where this was going.

'I didn't think nothing of it at the time, but see this?' He held the ball up and pointed to a mark on it. 'It's monogrammed. A lot of golfers do that, or mark them in some way, so they don't get mixed up with other people's balls when they're playing in a group.'

'Okay...'

'I always do a quick sweep of the course in the evening, when I know the last lot of players have come in,' he said. 'Course, I might've missed them on Friday evening, but I don't think I did. They were there Saturday morning.'

'Wait – so you think someone was on the course on Friday night?' I said, looking again at Sunil, but this time in excitement. 'You think someone was on there when they shouldn't have been?'

'Like I said, I could've missed them on Friday, but… yeah, I think maybe there were someone on there, after I'd finished for the day.'

'You mean later that night?' asked Sunil.

The greenskeeper shrugged. 'Can't say for certain, like, but if they was on there while it was still light, someone would've seen them, I'd have thought. And they'd have rung me to check they were okay to be on there.'

'Would someone really try to play golf in the dark?' I said.

The greenskeeper laughed. 'I don't think they was properly playing golf,' he said, 'more like larking around. They weren't aiming towards any of the holes – if they were, they were well off target. I found a couple not far from your divots,' he nodded to me, 'and then guess where another one ended up?' Sunil and I both shook our heads. 'One of you lot found one in the pond.'

'In the pond? Definitely from the same group of golfers?'

'Same monogram, see. Looks like initials – "SR"?' He peered at it closely.

'Could we take that?' I asked. Sunil held out his hand

and the greenskeeper dropped the ball into it. 'Thank you, you've been really helpful.'

'You're welcome. And congrats again on your wedding,' he said.

'Thanks,' I smiled as he left us, then turned to Sunil. 'So, who do we think could've been on the course late on Friday night?'

As if on cue, there was a loud burst of laughter from the bar.

'I wonder…'

I went and found Nathan, who'd finally noticed that his almost-bride had disappeared. Sunil and I (with some cute but not very helpful input from Germaine) told him all about the golf balls, and what the greenskeeper had said about somebody having a clandestine round of golf late Friday night or early Saturday morning.

'In the dark?' Nathan was incredulous.

'Yep.'

'But – how would they see where they were aiming?'

'I think that's the whole point,' I said. 'They obviously couldn't.'

'Hence the balls being all over the place, and one in the pond,' said Sunil.

'That's true,' said Nathan. 'But if they couldn't see where they were aiming, they probably also couldn't have seen anything to do with the murder.'

'Which is more than likely why they didn't come forward,' I admitted. 'But you know as well as I do, sometimes people do see or hear something, and they don't mention it because they think it's not important.'

'Hmm…' said Nathan. 'Well, Craig did say under hypnosis that he could hear men's voices, laughing. I think we've got a good idea who that was, haven't we? Let's go and ask them.'

We headed back into the hotel bar, where our hen party and karaoke night friends, the golfers who were there celebrating a friend's birthday with a lads-only golfing trip, were continuing the theme of the weekend and drinking heavily, this time still in their golf clothes.

'Oi oi!' said one of them, lifting up his glass in a toast as he saw us. 'Here's the happy couple!' And at that the whole group cheered and gave us a rousing (but inebriated) chorus of 'I'm Getting Married in the Morning', even though, as far as they were aware, we were already married.

'Congratulations,' said another one of them, who from what I could remember of Friday night was the birthday boy, Stuart. 'Many happy returns.' He frowned. 'Nah, that's birthdays, innit? What do you say when someone gets married?'

'"Here's the number of a good lawyer,"' quipped one of the others, and they all laughed uproariously, as if he'd made some comment worthy of Oscar Wilde. The wit winked at me and gave me a cheeky grin. 'Nah, only joking love, happy wedding day.' He nudged one of his friends. 'And even happier wedding night.' They all cheered and drank a toast to us again.

'Thanks,' said Nathan. He held up the golf ball. 'I think one of you lost something the other night.' He tossed the ball to the closest one, who luckily didn't have a drink in his hand and managed to catch it. He peered at it.

'Stu, one of yours!' He tossed it to Stuart, who fumbled and dropped it. They all laughed again. Honestly, it wasn't that funny, but maybe it was if you'd had that much to drink.

'Cheers, mate,' said Stuart. 'I thought we'd found them all.'

'The greenskeeper found quite a few,' I said. 'And the CSI team found one in the pond, as well.'

At that they all quietened down and looked a bit shifty. Stuart laughed and tried to style it out.

'You know what it's like, trying to play a round when you've had a few drinks,' he said.

'Yes,' said Nathan. 'Although the greenskeeper said they were so far off course that it looked like you'd been playing with your eyes shut.' He paused for effect. 'Or in the dark.'

At that they all looked even more shifty.

'Why didn't you tell us you were on the course late on Friday night, early Saturday morning?' asked Sunil. I nodded to myself approvingly; he hadn't asked, *Were you on the course?*, because they still could've said no. Wording it this way meant it sounded like we'd already confirmed they were there, so there was no point them denying it. 'None of you mentioned it in your statements to me and my colleagues.'

They all looked at each other, probably to get their stories straight, but unfortunately for them they were all a bit too drunk to communicate telepathically.

'We didn't see or hear anything,' said one of them. 'We didn't know anything about that poor girl getting bumped off, so we didn't think it was worth mentioning.'

'But someone heard *you*,' said Nathan, 'which means you might well have heard something and not realised it. You should have told us, and then let us decide whether you knew anything or not. How did it not occur to you that coming forward was the right thing to do?'

'Well, er…' Stuart looked awkward. 'We weren't supposed to be on the course, for starters.'

'I think helping in a murder investigation trumps playing an unauthorised round of golf, don't you?' I said. 'Unless there was more to it than that.'

Stuart sighed. 'Yeah, okay…' The others all looked at him, wide eyed, as if they were desperately trying to get him to shut up. 'We've all known each other since we were teenagers. We used to go to raves and all that, have mad weekends. And then we got married and had kids, and – well, to be honest it didn't all completely stop, but as we got older we all calmed down a bit. Got a bit boring.'

'Speak for yourself,' said one of them.

'Don't get me wrong, we're all quite happy being a bit

boring – well, apart from Ryan—' He nodded at the one who'd just spoken, who grinned. 'But every now and then we like to get together and relive our misspent youths.'

'You mean,' I said, 'that you were off your tits on the golf course.'

They all laughed, and then stopped, looking anxiously at Nathan and Sunil (but not me – to be fair, I didn't look much like law enforcement in that dress). Nathan held up his hands.

'I don't care what you were up to,' he said, 'I'm more interested in finding the killer.'

'Dominic brought a load of pills with him and we'd all taken one,' blurted out Ryan. One of the men – Dominic, I assumed – groaned.

'Thanks, Ry. Ever heard of "intent to supply"?'

'He told us, he don't care,' said Ryan.

'I don't,' said Nathan, although I could see Sunil studying Dominic carefully. Just in case. 'Go on.'

Stuart took over. 'We'd had a bit to drink at the bar – you saw us, love – but of course they chucked us out at midnight, so we went back up to my room and necked some pills. Then the night concierge came up and told us off for making too much noise, but we weren't really in a position to stop partying and go to sleep…'

'So you went out onto the course?'

Dominic nodded. 'Yeah. We'd all had a right mare trying to get over one of the water traps earlier in the day, so we started talking strategy about how to get over it, only then it started to get a bit silly. We decided to go out and have a go at it, but it was so dark and we were so out of it I couldn't tell me arse from me elbow, and nor could the others.'

'So we were just messing around really,' said Stuart. 'Just started hitting balls all over the place.'

'How did you get in and out of the hotel?' asked Sunil. 'You weren't on the CCTV cameras, and no one saw you.'

'We were going to get in the lift, but we knew the scary woman on Reception would see us when we got out of it, so we sneaked down the stairs instead,' said Stuart. 'Comical, it was. But then we still had to get outside without her seeing us. Luckily Ryan spotted the fire exit, so we propped it open and went in and out that way.'

'When you came in, did you shut it behind you?' I asked, and he nodded.

'Any idea what time you came back inside?' asked Nathan. They all looked at each other, then shook their heads.

'Nah, not really. Sorry. It was after two, I think?' said Dominic. 'Must've been. It would've been about half twelve, quarter to one when we went out there.'

'Right.' I looked at Nathan and Sunil. 'So during the murder window, then.' All four golfers went pale.

'Shit, that was when she died, was it?' Stuart looked round at the others. 'We didn't realise it was right then.'

'And you're sure you didn't hear anything?' asked Sunil. They all shook their heads.

'Well, thank you for your help,' said Nathan. 'But next time – if there's a next time – come forward.'

'Will do, officer,' said Ryan smartly. *Yeah, like hell you will,*

I thought. We started to walk away, but then something occurred to me and I turned back.

'What made you decide to come back indoors?' I asked. They looked surprised. 'I mean, if you only took the pills when you got back to your room – around midnight – you'd still be buzzing at two o'clock. I don't suppose you were ready to go to sleep for a good few hours after that.'

'No – no, we weren't.' Stuart thought for a moment, looking puzzled. 'Dom, you were the one that said we should go in, weren't you?'

'Was I?' Dominic now looked puzzled as well. Then his face cleared. 'Oh yeah, I thought we should go in because I thought I heard someone...' His voice trailed off as he realised what he was saying. 'Bloody hell, I'd forgotten all about that.'

'Can you remember who you heard? And what they were saying?' asked Nathan.

'No... Sorry, I couldn't even say if it was a bloke or a woman,' apologised Dominic. 'I don't know if I really heard them, more like I just sort of knew someone was out there. If you get what I mean?'

'The person they heard could've been Craig,' said Nathan, after we left them and headed back out onto the terrace, where it was a little quieter. 'Or Ben, going to get him back inside.'

'Or it could've been Kelly,' I said. 'Or the murderer.'

'None of which really helps, does it?' asked Sunil.

Nathan shrugged. 'Not in isolation, no, it doesn't. But

it's another piece of the puzzle, isn't it? We still don't have the full picture.'

'Who's that, waving at you?' asked Sunil, looking out across the grass. 'Isn't that one of the Forensics team?'

'Robbo,' I said. 'Maybe he's found something else.' I hitched up my skirt and headed down the steps from the terrace, onto the lawn. Nathan and Sunil (and Germaine) followed.

'I thought that was you,' said Robbo, trying not to look at my cleavage. 'You look a bit different in that dress…'

Nathan almost threw himself in front of me in an attempt to preserve my modesty, but the poor CSI man managed to tear his eyes away. I couldn't blame him. That dress had all sorts of nips and tucks and hidden scaffolding, and it had completely changed my shape. I had a mental image of all the different bumps and curves that had been forced into such unnatural, unaccustomed positions holding the shape of the dress for thirty seconds when I took it off, before suddenly cascading back to their normal positions in an avalanche of saggy bits. Sexy…

'Found something?' asked Nathan, in a *let's concentrate on business, shall we?* tone of voice.

'Not found, so much as I've had a thought,' said Robbo. 'I spoke to the greenskeeper earlier, about the golf balls we found in the pond—'

'So did we,' said Nathan. 'Apparently one of them is from a group of golfers who were on the course during the murder window.'

'They were?' Robbo nodded, thoughtfully. 'Then that

backs up what I was thinking. Look.' He took out his mobile phone and pulled up some pictures. 'The victim had a small but quite significant bruise on her head. Here.' He showed us a photograph, which had been sent through by the medical examiner. 'It's almost perfectly round.'

'But this wasn't the cause of death, was it?' asked Sunil. 'That was drowning?'

'Yes, we've heard back that there was water in her lungs,' confirmed Robbo. 'But the ME asked us to have a look to see if we could find what caused the bruising, because it's fresh. And whatever it was would have to have hit her quite hard to cause such a deep bruise.'

'Okay…' I said, but I was starting to get an image of what object it could have been. 'Something hard and round.'

'Something like…' Robbo pulled a golf ball, wrapped in a plastic evidence bag, out of his pocket.

'Bloody hell,' said Nathan. 'You think she got hit by a golf ball?'

'It's not down to me to decide that,' said Robbo, 'so the ME will have to confirm it, but… Unofficially, I reckon she did. The greenskeeper said there were several balls, completely off course. I reckon one of them – probably this one, as it was found near her, in the pond – hit her on the head.'

'People have died after being hit by stray golf balls,' I said. 'It's even happened at golf tournaments, when the crowd have got too close and been hit. But this didn't kill her.'

'Maybe it stunned her, or even knocked her out,' said Nathan.

'So it was an accident, after all?' said Sunil. He sounded almost disappointed. 'She got hit by a ball and fell in the pond?' Nathan and I exchanged thoughtful glances.

'I don't think so, do you?' he asked. I shook my head.

'No. I can't see how she ended up in the water.' We all turned to look in the direction of the pond, although the lie of the land meant we couldn't actually see it. 'The edges of the pond are pretty shallow, and full of reeds. Even if she was standing right next to it and got knocked out, if she'd fallen over she'd have ended up in the reeds, wouldn't she? I know it's possible to drown in just a few inches of water, but we found her in the middle of the pond. How did she get there? The reeds would've held her at the edge.'

'What if someone pushed her, hard?' asked Sunil. 'Would that get her past the reeds?'

Robbo looked doubtful. 'I don't think so. It would have to be a very hard push, and even then...' He shook his head. 'That's the bit we still don't know.'

'Any luck finding her shoes?' I asked, and he shook his head again.

'No. The diver went back in for another look, and we searched the nearest bushes and undergrowth, but nothing. They might've ended up in the bushes further onto the course, but that's a big area and we haven't been able to search it all yet.'

Germaine barked and ran off back towards the terrace,

where Daisy and Joe were standing, looking around. Daisy looked up at the sound of the dog and waved at me.

'Better go,' I said. 'This is supposed to be our un-wedding reception, after all.'

'There you are!' said Daisy, exasperated, as we joined her. 'Nana's getting all twitchy around the wedding cake—'

'*Un*-wedding cake,' I corrected her.

'Are you planning on doing that for the whole day?' She rolled her eyes. 'Whatever, Nana thinks you should cut the cake, and then…'

Joe rubbed his hands together, his eyes gleaming. 'And then the speeches!'

Chapter Seventeen

So we headed back to the function room, where our guests had only started to miss us as they began to want cake. The hotel's catering staff had played a blinder with the buffet, and there was very little of it left by the time they set out the dessert table. The puddings on offer looked incredible. Mini trifles and tiramisus (basically the English and Italian versions of the same dessert); three different types of cheesecake, including my favourite – a vanilla 'New York'-style baked one, served with a selection of juicy berries; and a huge bowl of warm chocolate fondue, with cubes of moist sponge cake, mini chocolate muffins, strawberries and bananas to dip into it.

But the crowning glory went to the wedding cake. I'd originally planned to make it myself, but then we'd originally planned a small wedding with the reception back at ours; things had escalated somewhat, so I'd had to get someone else to do it for me. A couple of years previously

Daisy and Nathan had secretly entered me into one of the most popular cooking contests on TV, *The Best of British Baking Roadshow*. I'd made the final of the local heat, although I hadn't won it, and I'd stayed in touch with my two fellow finalists, Elaine and Martin. Both of them were much better bakers, and certainly much better cake decorators than me, so I'd asked if either one of them would be interested in making my cake. Elaine had immediately leapt at the chance. And here she was now, helping to carry it in and put it into position.

'Jodie!' she cried, coming forward to give me a hug. 'You look fabulous!'

'So do you,' I said, because she did. Since winning the Cornish heats and going on to represent the county in the grand final – where she'd come second – Elaine had had a new lease of life. She'd told us she'd entered because she wanted a chance to be someone other than 'Mum' for a while. She'd certainly managed that. She'd written a successful cookbook, and she was a regular guest cookery presenter on one of the daytime TV shows. She was absolutely glowing.

'I heard about that poor girl they found,' she said, lowering her voice. 'Murder seems to follow you around, doesn't it? Are you and that handsome police officer of yours investigating?'

'Unofficially,' I said. 'Officially, it's time to unveil the cake. And eat it!'

The cake was amazing. I'd asked for a chocolate fudge cake, which was a favourite of the Parker women and, luckily enough, Nathan. It's difficult to make a big gooey chocolate cake look pretty, but my friend had done us proud. Elaine had given us three heart-shaped tiers, covered with intricate swirls of chocolate frosting. A series of piped rosettes covered the top tier, and in the centre of each one was a white-chocolate-dipped strawberry. The bottom tier was ringed with handmade chocolate truffles, rolled in desiccated coconut.

'I hope it's alright,' said Elaine, with characteristic modesty. Behind us, my guests started to gather round to look.

'Oh. My. GOD!' breathed Debbie, gazing at the cake in wonder. I smiled at Elaine.

'Yeah, I think that means we're happy with it.'

Nathan and I cut the cake – which was just as amazing on the inside as the outside – and posed for a few pictures. We'd booked Leo Adams, grandson of ex-Penstowan desk sergeant Harry, who was enjoying retirement and was currently living it up abroad somewhere.

'Grandad sends his love,' said Leo. 'Can you just turn the knife that way, so we lose the reflection?... Great...'

'Where is he now?' I asked.

'Portugal. I get the feeling him and Nana might not come back...'

Brief photoshoot finished, Roger picked up an empty wine glass and tapped it, which is universal sign language for *Everyone shut up because I want to say something.* Nathan groaned and muttered in my ear.

'God help us...'

'Just you wait,' I whispered back. 'There's no way my mum's going to let an opportunity like this slip by.'

'I remember the first time Nathan told us about Jodie,' said Roger, smiling at me and then looking around the room. 'He rang me up and said, "Dad, I've met this woman… and she's driving me mad."' Everyone laughed, and Nathan clapped a hand to his forehead. 'He said, "She won't keep her nose out of this case I'm investigating. Everywhere I turn, she's there, waiting for me. I might have to arrest her."'

'I never said that!' Nathan protested, laughing.

'Yes you did,' I said. 'You threatened to arrest me.' I waited for him to open his mouth to refute it, and then interrupted him. 'Twice.' Our guests laughed again. Roger smiled affectionately at us both.

'And I knew at that moment, that this was the woman for our Nathan,' he said. 'He's a bit of a know-it-all sometimes—'

'Oi, Dad!' said Nathan. 'Remember, I'll be the one choosing your nursing home.'

'—and he needs someone to pull him up now and then. Jodie, thank you for taking him on. I hope you know what you've got yourself into.' Roger raised his glass to me, and Liz came over and hugged me. 'To Nathan and Jodie,' he toasted, and everyone joined in.

'My turn now,' said Mum.

Tony winked at me. 'This should be good,' he said. Mum reached over to clip him round the ear, but he dodged it.

'That's enough of your cheek, Tony Penhaligon,' said

Mum, although she wasn't really angry with him. 'I've known you since you were in short trousers.' She turned to look at me and Nathan. 'Look at the two of you, worrying about what I'm going to say. I can almost see you both thinking, *I hope she keeps it brief.*' Everyone laughed, some – those who knew Mum well enough – maybe a little louder and more emphatically than others.

'As if,' I said.

'Well, I *will* keep it brief. I just wanted to say that on days like this, when all our friends and family are here—'

'Apart from Aunty Wendy,' said Daisy, and I rolled my eyes, but Mum just laughed.

'Apart from Aunty Wendy,' agreed Mum, 'it just brings it home that there's one important person missing. Your dad,' she said, looking at me. *Oh God, don't make me cry*, I thought, but I suspected it was a bit late for that. 'Nathan, I know you've heard a lot about the famous Chief Inspector Eddie Parker, and that you've had big shoes to fill in Penstowan, but fill them you have. You also had a big space in Jodie's heart to fill, and you've done that, too. I wish you could've met him, but I know that Jodie's dad would've loved you, and he would've been happy to trust his daughter's happiness to you. I love you too, darlin', and so does Daisy.' We were all sniffing furiously by now. Actually, that was a bit of a lie, because I was well past sniffing and only one step away from absolutely howling. 'And Jodie. I am so proud of you and the woman, and mum, you've become.' She smiled at me and raised her glass. 'And now I need a drink. To family!'

'To family!' said everyone, relieved that one, Mum hadn't said anything embarrassing or inappropriate (first time for everything), and two, that she'd stopped before we all dissolved into a puddle of sentimental tears.

I took a big swig of my wine, then went over to Mum and pulled her into a hug. 'Thanks, Mum,' I whispered huskily. 'That was perfect.'

'Sorry,' she said, 'I had a load of jokes prepared and everything, and they all went out of me head the minute I started talking.'

'Thank God for that.'

'Although I did remember the one about the nuns and the one-handed lion tamer—'

'Don't spoil it, Mother.' I kissed her on the cheek. 'I'm so glad you approve of Nathan.'

She cackled.

'Like it would've put you off anyway,' she said, but then she softened and added, 'I meant what I said about Dad, though. I can just imagine the two of them gossiping together like a couple of old ladies.'

'Like us, you mean.' I laughed. 'Yeah, I think they'd have got on like a house on fire. And even *Tony* likes him now, which is no mean feat when you consider the first time they met, Nath was trying to arrest him.'

'And that means a lot to you, doesn't it?'

'Of course it does. Tony's my oldest friend. He's like a less-annoying brother. Less annoying because I could always tell him to go home when he started irritating me.' I gazed round the room at all my friends – only now they were all *our* friends, because despite being a bit of an arrogant git when I'd first met him (which was basically a type of armour, designed to show the locals that their new DCI wasn't in over his head or anything…), Nathan was really easy to get on with. Even some of the people he'd nicked had grudgingly admitted to some level of respect for him.

'Yes, it makes life easier when everyone likes your partner,' agreed Mum. 'Poor Kelly never had that.'

'No?'

'No. I never told you the stuff me and Tony found out, did I?' she said, brightening up at the thought of passing on some gossip. Not that she'd looked glum or anything before that, but, you know – *gossip!* 'So I spoke to Margie Glossop – you know, her with the husband with arthritis and the son with a lazy eye, who works in the frozen food department at Morrisons?'

'Who does? Margie, or her husband? Or her son?'

'Her son, of course. Well, he was in the same year at school as Kelly.'

'Did he know her?'

'No.'

'Right…'

'But his girlfriend's *sister* used to have a Saturday job with her at the café at that garden centre just outside Bude—'

'And they kept in touch?'

'No. But his girlfriend's sister's *next door neighbour* used to live next door to Kelly's family, and *she* reckoned they were always arguing.'

'Who, Kelly and Frankie?'

'No, Kelly and her family. This was not long after they first started going out together, apparently, but they ain't changed their opinion of him. Said he was a wrong 'un, which he is, to be fair.'

'Right...' Which was sort of interesting, but not very helpful.

'It wasn't just her family who had an issue with her seeing him,' said Joe, leaning across me to help himself to a tiramisu. Behind him, Daisy sighed.

'Here we go. I swear the urge to gossip just rubs off on other people, the more time they spend with you two.'

'Oi, cheeky!' I said, turning round and giving her a playful poke with my finger. 'There's nothing wrong with taking an interest in the local community. Or gossiping, for that matter. Who else had a problem with her seeing Frankie?'

'Here...' Joe handed Daisy his tiramisu and took out his phone. 'This is her Facebook account...' He pulled up the page and handed me the phone. I scrolled through the posts – the most recent ones now addressed to her expressing shock and sorrow at her death – and what Daisy had said before (somewhat dismissively) looked to be true; she had loads of friends, and they all loved her.

'She was very popular,' I said, not sure what I was looking for.

'Among her Facebook friends, yes,' said Joe, taking the

phone from me and finding what he was after before handing it back. 'But she set her profile to public, so not everyone commenting on here was a friend…'

Kelly had posted a photo of her and Frankie, a selfie of them in each other's arms, laughing. Behind them was a group of presumably real-life friends, male and female, all in their twenties. It looked like they were in a pub garden, enjoying the sunshine.

'That's the Brendon Arms, in Bude,' said Mum, peering over my shoulder. 'They do a cracking scampi and chips in there.'

I read the text that accompanied the photo: *Celebrating our first anniversary!* It was dated three months earlier.

'They'd been together a while, then,' I said. 'Over a year.'

'Yes,' said Mum, nodding. 'That's what Margie said.'

'How does Margie Glossop know so much about Kelly's love life?' asked Daisy. Mum shrugged.

'Her murder's all over the town by now,' she said. 'All the gossips will have been out in force from the moment the news got out.' She managed to sound disapproving, even though the only reason she knew what the gossip was, was through gossiping herself.

'I still don't know what I'm looking for,' I said, scrolling through the comments, and then I saw it. *It won't last, you ugly slut.* 'Woah.'

'You found it?' asked Joe.

'Yeah. This "Medea" really isn't a fan, is she?' I wrinkled my nose, thinking. 'Why do I know that name? Who is she?'

'She's not real,' said Daisy. 'She's the title character from a play by Euripides. Unless she's unlucky enough to actually share her name with an ancient Greek character, I'd say it's an alias.'

'Have you looked at her bio?' I asked, clicking on the name. But the so-called Medea's own Facebook page was bare; no profile photo, no cover photo, no 'About' details, and no posts, apart from a few more similarly unfriendly comments on other posts by Kelly. Nathan came over to see what we were talking about, and I showed him Joe's phone.

'Oh, nice,' he said. 'I think we – or DI Mackintosh – needs to talk to this Medea.'

'Except that's probably not her real name,' I said, musing. '"Medea". Hmm. Bit of a niche source for a poison pen name, isn't it?'

'Not really,' said Daisy. 'We looked at *Medea* in Ancient History.'

'You did?'

'Yeah. Well, some of us in the top stream did.' My daughter, clever lass that she is, was in the top class for most of her subjects. 'Miss Norrie told us you can choose between Greek and Roman theatre or Architecture in the A level, which Lorelei and I want to do, so a few of us thought we'd have a go at reading it. Miss Norrie let us put aside some time for it near the end of the lesson. It was a bit confusing, but it was more fun than learning the difference between Ionic and Doric columns.' She screwed up her face. 'Oh God, I am *such* a geek.'

'So this Medea – she—'

'Or he,' said Joe. 'You never know.'

'True, but there's no suggestion that Frankie Lewis likes men as well as women,' said Nathan, 'so I think we're probably safe to assume Medea is female. Whoever they are, they must be intelligent, or at least think they are. That's a very literary alias.'

'Maybe they were a student at Penstowan Comprehensive, like Daisy,' I said. Nathan nodded.

'Yes, although that's the biggest school in the area, so most of the young people round here probably went there,' he said. 'So it doesn't narrow it down that much.'

I handed Joe his phone back. 'What's *Medea* about?' I asked Daisy.

'Medea is married to Jason – you know, that awful old film you made me watch, *Jason and the Argonauts*?'

Nathan clutched at his heart. 'Terrible? That film is a stone-cold classic.'

'Yeah, maybe if you're watching it in 1978… Anyway, *that* Jason. She helps him steal the Golden Fleece, and they get married and have kids, blah blah blah, only then he dumps her for a younger model. And so she swears revenge and it all goes a bit *Fatal Attraction* after that.' I stared at her, seriously impressed and proud beyond measure that my daughter's breadth of knowledge took in ancient Greek theatre *and* 1980s erotic thrillers.

'So – if the alias is relevant, and not just picked at random – this could be an ex-girlfriend of Frankie's, jealous of Kelly's relationship with him?'

'Or they could've just picked it at random from

somewhere,' said Nathan. 'There's probably a kebab shop or a Greek restaurant somewhere called Medea.'

'Or they were the Greek entry for Eurovision,' said Joe, and we all laughed.

'But would she really be jealous enough to kill Kelly, her rival?' I asked. I shook my head. 'I dunno, I wouldn't have thought he was that much of a catch.'

'The heart wants what the heart wants,' said Mum, sagely.

'I know, but, *Frankie Lewis*?!'

Nathan laughed. 'I know, it seems unlikely. Have you still got that Facebook page open, Joe?' Joe hadn't, but he opened it up again quickly and handed Nathan his phone.

'What're you looking for?' he asked. 'I scoured all Kelly's posts, and there's a few other nasty comments from Medea, but that's the worst one.'

'I was wondering if she could be in any of these pictures,' said Nathan, and we all crowded around him, peering at the tiny screen. He looked up at us. 'I know you're keen, but give us some space…'

We all stepped back about half a centimetre and watched as he scrolled through, zooming in on the pictures that Kelly had posted.

'Too much to hope that in one of them, there'll be a girl with a furious expression and a knife aimed at Kelly's back,' I said.

'Yeah,' said Mum. 'That would be – hold up!' She looked up at Nathan. 'Go back to that last one… There!' She stabbed at the screen. 'Her.'

'Your thumb's in the way, Shirley,' said Nathan. Mum moved her hand away.

'The one with the blonde hair,' she said. 'Although most of them have got blonde hair… That one, in the green top.'

In the picture, a group of young women – most of them with the same long blonde hairstyle – stood on a beach. The sky was a deep blue and there were a few palm trees scattered around the edge of the frame.

'Looks exotic,' said Nathan. Mum cackled.

'Nah, that's St Ives,' she said. I was about to be impressed with her powers of deduction until I read the caption: ***Fantastic weekend in St Ives with these beauts!***

'Very clever,' I said. 'What about her? She looks like she's having a good time, they all do. There's not even a hint of side eye.'

'I recognise her,' said Mum. 'She was on Reception.'

Nathan and I exchanged surprised looks. 'What? When?' I asked, because I was sure I hadn't seen her.

'She was on Reception Friday morning, when we checked in,' said Mum. 'I recognised her because she looks just like Deirdre Hurley did when she was that age, only blonde.' Nathan raised his eyebrows at me, but I shrugged; I'd never even met Deirdre, who'd gone off to London as a teenager in the Sixties to become a successful model, and I had no idea what she looked like as a young woman.

'Are you sure, Mum?' I asked, trying to stop a note of doubt creeping in.

'Yes, I am.' Mum crossed her arms stubbornly. 'I also recognise her because she was wearing that same necklace, and I asked her where she'd got it from.' All of us leaned in even closer to peer at the necklace. It was quite distinctive, a thin gold chain with a red enamelled heart-shaped pendant or locket on it.

'Has she been in since Friday?' asked Nathan.

'If she has, I ain't seen her,' said Mum. 'But that doesn't mean she hasn't been.'

'And it doesn't mean she's done a runner,' I said. 'She might just have had the weekend off.'

'So she works here, and she was a friend of Kelly's,' said Nathan. 'That might not mean anything. And if she was on in the morning when we arrived, she would've gone home long before Kelly and the other waitresses got here. She might not even have known she was working here that night.'

'Although they were obviously close, if this picture's anything to go by,' I said. Joe took back his phone and clicked on the photo. Some of the other women were tagged in it, and he clicked on their names until he was taken to the page belonging to our mystery receptionist.

'Heidi Monroe,' he said. 'Her bio says she works here.' He looked up at Nathan. 'And she went to Penstowan Comp, so that's where she could've heard about *Medea*.'

'I wonder when she's next on duty?' I said, and then Fate gave us the perfect opportunity to ask. Only we didn't get a chance to.

Chapter Eighteen

'Hi, sorry to bother you...' We turned around, Joe hastily shutting down his phone. One of the receptionists I'd spoken to earlier, Chelsea, was hovering behind us. She smiled. 'Sorry, I know it's your wedding reception, or your sort-of wedding reception, anyway...'

'What's the matter, lovey?' asked Mum.

'Some of you are police, aren't you?'

Nathan nodded. 'I am. Has something happened?'

'Not yet, but I think it might be about to...'

Nathan and I hurried after the anxious young woman, collecting Sunil and Matt in our wake; they'd seen us across the room and had immediately decided that whatever was making us rush off warranted them joining us. Honestly,

I'm not the only nosey person in Penstowan, despite what some might have you believe, not by a long shot.

A knot of hotel staff were gathered outside the staff room, muttering angrily. They turned as they saw Nathan.

'He's really overstepped this time,' said one of them, angrily. 'Sending the police in now, is he?'

'I'm just here to keep the peace,' said Nathan, holding up his hands. 'Can someone tell me exactly what is going on?'

Mr Robbins appeared from inside the staff room. He looked a little bit embarrassed when he saw us, but he rallied and pulled himself up to his full height. It wasn't that impressive.

'I am conducting a search of staff lockers,' he announced. There were mutterings from the staff. 'If you look at your contracts, you agreed to random security checks, which includes bag and locker searches.'

'Why are you conducting a search?' I asked, although I could guess why; someone had been nicking the loo paper again. The manager seemed more upset by the petty pilfering than the murder of a young woman in the hotel grounds.

'A large quantity of hotel property has gone missing, sometime between Saturday morning and this afternoon,' he said. *Bingo*, I thought. 'The thief, or thieves, seem to have taken advantage of the sad situation that occurred on Friday night, and have helped themselves while everyone has been distracted. Even the presence of police,' he said, his lip curling slightly as he looked at us, 'has not deterred them. I had been willing to overlook some level of petty theft, especially in the current economic climate, but not this much. I feel like my good nature,' here there were a few hastily muffled sniggers from the staff, 'has been preyed upon. Well, no more.'

'Okay,' said Nathan, in his most placatory tone of voice. 'I understand that tensions are high at the moment. Why don't we all take a deep breath and give everyone some time to calm down. Maybe—'

'I'm perfectly calm!' shrieked Robbins, spittle flying from his lips. He looked a bit shocked at his own outburst, as did everyone else. 'I'm sorry, I just…'

'It's been a difficult time, hasn't it?' I said sympathetically. He nodded, a look of misery crossed with fury on his face. 'No one expects to have a dead body turn up, especially not when you've got a hotel full of guests to reassure.' I realised that, while my lot hadn't really batted an eyelid at the death (I mean, we were upset, but no one had freaked out), others at the hotel had probably been ready to pack up and leave, or cancel before they even got here. My lot were all used to it to some extent, all being either police officers, married or related to police officers, or in some cases part of my unofficial investigating team (in other words, just plain nosey). 'I'm sure the rest of the staff understand.'

'We do,' said Chelsea, putting her hand on his arm.

'At the same time,' said Nathan, 'if someone is stealing stuff, they need to stop.' The rest of the staff looked around at each other, although I noticed in a couple of cases they avoided each other's eyes. Hmm…

'Can I make a suggestion?' asked Sunil. He was so polite, but firm, that no one could refuse. 'It probably is in your contract that you agree to occasional searches,' he said, and everyone groaned. 'I'm sorry, but it's a standard clause in a lot of contracts. However, there are good ways and bad ways of going about it. I suggest Mr Robbins takes you into the staff room one at a time and asks you to open your locker, so you're there to witness it. That should reassure you that it's all above board.' There were a few moans.

'If you haven't done anything wrong, you've got nothing to worry about,' said Matt, a phrase which I've never found particularly helpful in crowd situations, and there were more groans.

'Unless he wants to get rid of you, and he stitches you up,' murmured one of them in a low voice.

'Yeah, like they did with Janette,' muttered another. *Who's Janette?* I wondered. But this probably wasn't the time to ask.

'Would it help if one of us was present when the search took place?' I asked. There were a few hesitant nods, and then the one who'd moaned about being stitched up looked at me and did a double-take, his gaze travelling up and down and apparently only just noticing the red and gold dress I was wearing.

'Hang on, aren't you the bride?' he asked. He looked at Nathan. 'Isn't this your wedding day?'

'Yes,' said Nathan. 'We've taken the time to come and

help you sort this out, when we should be talking to our guests at our reception.'

At that there were a few ashamed faces and murmurs of 'sorry'. It reminded me of the time I'd volunteered on a trip to London Zoo when Daisy was at primary school, and I'd had to tell a couple of the boys off for throwing stuff into one of the animal enclosures (I was furious and they were lucky I didn't throw *them* in). They'd been shamefaced for the rest of the trip and on the coach back to school had shuffled over and apologised.

'I'm happy to stay and help,' said Sunil.

'Me too,' said Matt. 'If you all form an orderly queue, the happy couple can get back to their party. We'll get this over and done with in no time, and you can all get back to work as normal.'

Everyone seemed, not exactly happy at that suggestion, but a lot less likely to go into full-blown revolt, so we left Matt and Sunil to it and went back to eat cake. I was a bit miffed because I realised I'd missed the perfect chance to ask Chelsea about her colleague, the mysterious Heidi (possibly Medea), but a few mouthfuls of the delicious, rich chocolate cake – and a chocolate-dipped strawberry – made me feel much better.

'You want me to take a photo of you feeding each other cake?' asked Leo, appearing at my side. He'd been going around the room taking photos of our guests, because Nathan and I had both agreed that other than a few photos of the special moments (us saying 'I do', for example, which hadn't happened, and us cutting the cake, which had), what we really wanted in our wedding photos was a record of our friends and family having a lovely time.

'Humph umm umm,' I said, because my mouth was already full of cake.

'It's alright, I speak fluent Jodie,' said Nathan with a grin. 'I think that was, "Just let me finish this mouthful."'

'You've got to admit, it's bloody good cake,' I said, swallowing. I was about to answer Leo when my eyes found Matt, standing in the doorway of the function room. He saw me and waved. 'Uh, maybe later? I think we need to be somewhere else…'

'What's going on?' asked Nathan, as we joined Matt.

'You are not going to believe this…'

We stood in the staff room, in front of the open locker, with our jaws almost on the floor.

'Whose locker is this?' asked Nathan.

'Heidi Monroe's,' said Sunil. We all looked at each other, thinking, *Holy crap! We've only gone and solved the murder!* At least that's what I was thinking; the others were probably far too professional for that.

'Is she here?' I asked, looking round. Matt shook his head.

'No. Robbins was only supposed to be opening the ones with staff present, but he got a bit carried away and opened this while I was escorting the next staff member in.'

'That's them, isn't it?' said Sunil. 'They're Kelly's shoes.'

'I reckon so, from the way Debbie described them,' I said. 'Although Callum might be a better person to ask...' Sunil and Matt looked at me. 'Don't ask. How did Robbins get into it, if Heidi's not here? Wouldn't she have the key?'

'There's a master key,' said Sunil.

Nathan stepped forward and reached in his pocket for some gloves, but he was in his wedding suit and obviously didn't have any. Instead he leaned in as close as he dared and studied them. 'Dirt on the heels,' he said, turning to me. 'From your divots, I expect.'

'So how did they end up in here?' I asked. 'What are we thinking? Other than, "Oh bugger, we have to ring Di Mackintosh now and admit that we've been doing a bit of unofficial investigating."'

'Yeah, we'll let you do that,' Matt told Nathan, grinning.

'I thought you would.' Nathan stepped back, thinking. 'Craig heard a woman arguing with someone. So maybe that was Kelly and Heidi arguing? Maybe Kelly had run onto the golf course to get away from Frankie, causing the damage to the turf with her heels. When she realised he wasn't chasing her, but had gone back to his car to listen to the voicemail from his brother, she relaxed, took her shoes off – which is why there are no more divots in the grass – and then... what?'

'She's joined by Heidi? But she's not worried, because she's her friend?' I suggested. 'They walk down to the pond together. Maybe Heidi's persuaded her to stay out there a bit longer, to make sure Frankie's gone before she heads back to her car.'

'Okay... And then?'

'And then they start arguing. Maybe Heidi – or Medea – tells her that she doesn't deserve Frankie. Maybe,' I said, 'rather than her being one of Frankie's ex-girlfriends, maybe he's cheating on Kelly with her? Maybe she tells her that and they argue? That could be what Craig heard.'

'He did say she sounded furious, rather than scared,' said Matt.

'And then as they're standing there, the golfers, who are further down the course but high as kites, hit a golf ball back towards the pond and hit Kelly on the head, knocking her out?' said Sunil.

'Or stunning her,' I said. 'Because next, Heidi has to get her in the pond, and if she's unconscious on the ground, I think she'd struggle. Going by that picture on Facebook, Heidi isn't any bigger or stronger than Kelly was, and I don't think she'd be able to pick her up.'

'She could've dragged her into the pond,' said Matt.

Nathan shook his head. 'The ground round there is soft,' he said. 'There were too many shoe-prints to find anything distinctive enough to identify anyone, but there would've been a trail if a body had been dragged along there.'

'Okay, Kelly is stunned, staggering around a bit, unsteady on her feet,' I said. 'So Heidi doesn't have to drag her, she can kind of propel her into the water, pushing her in front of her.' I clicked my fingers. 'Heidi had to go into the water herself a little way, getting her clothes wet and muddy, so when she's finished drowning Kelly she goes into the hotel and sticks them in the washing machine on a quick programme to clean off any evidence.'

'Except there's no footage of anyone going back into the hotel,' groaned Sunil. 'I should know, I watched it enough times.'

'What time did you watch up to?' asked Nathan.

'Four a.m.' Sunil looked resigned. 'You're going to tell me to watch it again, aren't you?'

But it wasn't down to Nathan to tell Sunil anything, as neither of them were officially on the case. Nathan rang DI Mackintosh who, as predicted, was furious with him for sticking his nose into the investigation, but she couldn't say a lot as he was her senior in rank. Sunil was ordered to stay at the hotel and guard the shoes until someone came to collect them, but whether he was reinstated or not was anybody's guess.

'She's not happy,' said Nathan.

'That's a shame,' said Matt, unconvincingly. I shook my head.

'She's not done herself any favours with this investigation,' I said. 'I'd normally be telling you off for not supporting a fellow officer, but…'

'She *is* following the process,' said Sunil, carefully. 'She's not done anything wrong, as such. But unlike you, Guv – er, Nathan – she doesn't encourage her officers to think outside the box or question her, so if she's following the wrong line of enquiry she has to follow it all the way to the end before anyone can say anything.'

'Her way or the highway,' I said. 'Yeah, I think she was a bit like that at Stockwell, only she wasn't high enough rank for it to have much of an effect.'

'Excuse me...' Chelsea, the receptionist, was back. 'Did you find something? Only Mr Robbins has shut himself back in his office, and all he'll tell us is that there won't be any more searches today. Which is good, but he only searched half the lockers, so everyone's wondering if he found the thief?'

'No,' said Nathan. 'Not exactly.'

'Oh.' Chelsea looked mystified. 'Alright, it's just I sent a message to the staff WhatsApp group, telling everyone to come in if they were worried about him searching their locker without them being here – I know you told him not to, but I wouldn't put it past him to search them anyway when you've left.' On cue, her phone pinged. She took it from her jacket pocket and glanced at the screen. 'One of the other receptionists has just come in, she's wondering whether to get him to search it now she's here.'

'No,' said Nathan. 'The staff room is out of bounds at the moment, so please tell her, sorry, but she's had a wasted trip.'

'Okay, I'll tell her to go home, then. Poor Heidi, she's been really upset this weekend, what with the murder, and now I've dragged her in here for nothing—'

'Heidi?' I said, glancing at Nathan. 'Heidi Monroe?'

'Yes.' Chelsea looked surprised. 'Do you know her? Poor

thing, she was friends with the girl who was murdered. It can't have been easy for her, coming back here, knowing that her friend's body was found in the grounds. I wouldn't be surprised if she quits after this.'

'Where is she?' asked Nathan, carefully, not wanting to alert Chelsea to the fact that we suspected Heidi – or Medea – had had a hand in her friend's death. 'I'd like to have a word with her about Kelly.'

'She's out by Reception,' said Chelsea, tapping on her phone. 'Do you want me to tell her you're coming?'

'No, that's fine,' said Nathan, quickly. We didn't want Heidi doing a runner at the sight of the police, and luckily we didn't look much like police officers in our wedding outfits. 'We'll just head out there now…'

Chapter Nineteen

'It's just so horrible.' Heidi Monroe dabbed at her eyes with a crumpled tissue. They were red-rimmed, and it looked like she'd been crying a lot over the last couple of days.

'You were close friends?' I asked, sympathetically, although of course if Heidi really *was* Medea, and really *had* bumped Kelly off, they were crocodile tears. Or maybe they were tears of guilt and remorse.

'We were like sisters,' she sniffed. 'We've known each other since primary school. She was always there for me, through the bad times and the good, and I was for her.'

'Bad times? Like splitting up with boyfriends, that kind of thing?'

'Yes, stuff like that, but also other, more important things.' Heidi blew her nose and made a visible attempt to pull herself together. 'When my mum was diagnosed with cancer, it was awful. I tried so hard to be strong for her, but inside I was, like, falling apart. Kelly was my rock. And now she's gone. Someone took her away from us.' She burst into tears again. Nathan and I exchanged glances. This did not sound like someone who would get into a murderous rage over her friend's relationship with Frankie Lewis. But then some murderers were very good actors.

'How is your mum?' I asked, softly.

'She's fine now, but for a long time I thought I was going to lose her,' said Heidi. 'I don't know what I would've done without Kelly...' She dissolved into more tears, and I felt terrible. If Heidi *was* acting, she deserved a BAFTA, an Oscar, a Golden Globe and an Emmy. And she'd have been a shoo-in for a *TV Times* Readers' Choice award.

'I'm sorry to question you about it, Miss Monroe,' said Nathan. 'Only I don't think DI Mackintosh has sent anyone to talk to you about Kelly's death, has she?'

'No, she hasn't.' Heidi mopped herself up. 'But then I finished my last shift Friday lunchtime, and I'm not due back in until tomorrow, so I wasn't here when it happened.'

'No,' said Nathan, noncommittally. 'What time did you finish?'

'I was on the early shift, six in the morning until two in the afternoon,' she said.

'Okay. Did you return to the hotel at any time after that?' he asked.

'No. Why would I?' She gave a small smile. 'I don't get paid enough to come in when I don't have to.'

'Although you have come in today.'

'Yeah, Chelsea said Robbins was on the rampage, so I

thought maybe I should be here. What is going on with that? I thought he was searching all the lockers, but now he's just stopped?' She shook her head, angrily. 'As if any of that matters now. He's more bothered about someone stealing toilet rolls than about Kelly getting murdered outside his precious hotel.'

'Was there anything in your locker that you didn't want Mr Robbins to see?' asked Nathan.

'In my locker? No, of course not. There's nothing in there at all.' Nathan and I looked at each other again, and she noticed this time. 'What? I don't even use my locker when I'm here most of the time, I leave everything locked in my car. What's going on?'

'Can you tell me how Kelly's shoes ended up in your locker?' asked Nathan. Heidi looked at him in complete amazement. *And the Oscar for most convincing disbelief goes to...*, I thought, but really it looked genuine. Which meant we were barking up the wrong tree. Again.

'Her shoes? Her *shoes*? What the – what are you talking about?' Heidi looked confused, and she was starting to get angry. 'Why the hell would her shoes be in my locker? Who cares about her shoes, anyway? Why aren't you trying to find the person who did this?'

'We are,' said Nathan calmly. Heidi looked at him for a moment, then me, and then her mouth dropped open as the penny dropped.

'Wait – you're not saying that I did it?' she scoffed, but I could tell she didn't think it was funny. She was horrified, horrified and furious. 'I don't believe this. Why would I kill

Kelly? I loved her. She wasn't just a friend, she was like a sister to me.'

'Can you just answer the question, please, Miss Monroe,' said Nathan. She gave a big dramatic shrug of her shoulders, exasperated with him.

'What the bloody hell do you want me to say? I didn't put them in there. Are you sure it's my locker? And that they're Kelly's shoes? For God's sake…'

'Heidi,' I said softly, 'I know you're grieving, and I know none of this makes sense to you. But when Kelly was found her feet were bare, and despite a search of the grounds and the pond, her shoes were never recovered. We do have a description of them, and a pair of shoes matching that description has just been found in your locker. We have reason to believe that whoever killed Kelly took her shoes – we don't know why. We think Kelly may have taken them off shortly before she was killed. Maybe the murderer found them afterwards and panicked, not knowing what to do with them, so they picked them up and hid them somewhere until they could get rid of them properly. And the hiding place they chose was your locker.'

Heidi was speechless with shock for a moment. 'No… no, that's ridiculous…'

'How could someone else get into your locker, Heidi?' asked Nathan. 'Think about it. Do you take the key home with you?'

Heidi shook her head. 'No, I leave it in the desk at Reception.'

'Who knows about that?' I asked.

'Everyone, I'd have thought,' she said. 'Everyone knows I don't normally use it, so it's kind of like a spare locker if anyone needs it. They can just get the key from the desk drawer. And a couple of months ago I organised a card and a whip-round for the assistant manager, who was leaving to have a baby, and I left it in my locker so people could go and write in the card and pop some money into the kitty when they got a moment. It made it easier, with people being on different shifts and everything. It meant I didn't have to, like, try and catch people before they clocked off or whatever.'

'So anyone on the staff could've had access to your locker?' asked Nathan.

'Yes. And of course there's the master key. Robbins keeps that in his office, but it's easy enough to get to.'

'Okay...' Nathan looked thoughtful. 'Did you know Kelly was working here as a waitress on Friday night?'

'Oh, yes. When I saw I was on the rota for Friday we actually joked about me joining her when I finished my shift, but of course I'd finished well before she got here.'

'What did you think of Kelly's job?'

Heidi crossed her arms over her chest. 'Judging her, are you?'

'Not in the slightest. It was my stag do,' said Nathan. Heidi set her lips in a thin line.

'Well, I admit I didn't like her doing it. I thought she was worth more than that. But it didn't make her a slut. It's the blokes paying for that sort of thing who are the real saddoes.'

'I totally agree,' said Nathan. 'Frankie Lewis didn't like it, did he?'

'Frankie?' She rolled her eyes. 'That's something else she was worth more than.'

'Not a fan?'

'You could say that.' She sighed. 'You met him?' We both nodded. 'Then you know what I mean. Oh, he could be like, really sweet with her – I think he thought he was in love with her – but he could be so possessive, so jealous.'

'Enough to punish her for coming to work that night?' I asked.

'No.' She answered quickly – too quickly, maybe? Or was I reading something into nothing?

'No?'

'Not punish as in *murder*. I wouldn't have been surprised if he'd screamed in her face or something, but I don't think he ever physically hurt her.' She turned to me. 'Stuff like that escalates, doesn't it? It starts off with a push, then a punch, then a beating… and then maybe a fit of, like, murderous rage.'

'What makes you say that?' I asked.

'Kelly and I used to watch those true crime programmes—'

'Netflix?' I asked. Netflix had a lot to answer for, turning ordinary people into amateur criminologists and detectives…

'Yeah. And I said to Kelly, half joking but not really, you know, I said, "You know what to look out for, then," and she told me that he had a mean temper but the first time he hit her would also be the last.' She stopped and looked absolutely devastated again. 'Maybe it was. The first *and* the last.'

'I'm sorry,' I said, putting my hand on her arm. 'We'll let you head home in a minute, we just have a couple more questions for you. We saw on Kelly's Facebook posts, there were a couple of nasty comments from a user calling themselves "Medea".'

'Oh, *that* bitch. Yeah, we saw them.'

'Did you or Kelly have any idea who was behind those comments?'

'No. We did try to work it out, but did you look at their profile? There's nothing on it.'

'Was Kelly upset by them?' asked Nathan.

'Of course she was. Every time she posted a picture, that cow would pop up with a nasty remark. I told her to ignore it and block them, but she didn't.'

'Why didn't she block them?' I asked. 'If someone was making nasty comments on my posts, I wouldn't want to see them.'

'No, that's what I thought at first – but she said she wanted to know if they were still out there, or if they'd given up. She said she needed to, like, keep her friends close and her enemies closer.'

'Yeah, I kind of get that,' said Nathan. 'But you had no idea who it was? Did you manage to discount anyone, or was there anyone you thought it *could* be?'

'Like who?'

'I don't know. Maybe an ex-girlfriend of Frankie's?'

'Nah. I know two of Frankie's exes, and both of them were glad to get shot of him.'

'Really?'

'Yeah. Although…'

'Although what?' I asked. We needed a breakthrough of some kind. Could this be it?

'One of them did say that Frankie was a changed man now he was with Kelly.' She snorted. 'If that was him as a changed man, he must've been a right idiot when he was with her.'

'Did she seem envious about that? Like she wished Frankie had been like that with her?' asked Nathan.

'Nah. She's engaged to someone else now. She was happy for him.'

'What about the name itself? "Medea". We think it's probably an alias. Do you know anyone it would be significant to? Someone who would be likely to use it?'

'No. She's like that monster with the snakes in her hair, yeah? I know a few people it would suit, but none of them would choose it…'

'That's Medusa,' I said. 'Medea was actually married to Jason, who stole the golden fleece. Until he dumped her for someone else.'

Heidi chuckled softly. 'Really? And there we were, looking for someone with snakes in their hair,' she said. 'No wonder we couldn't work it out. If Kelly was still here she'd have a right laugh at that…'

'Thoughts?' asked Nathan, as we walked out to the car park with Heidi and watched her drive away. We'd warned her that DI Mackintosh would want her to make an official statement and tell her what she'd told us, but as far as I could see, that was another suspect ruled out.

'Not guilty, m'lord,' I said. 'You saw her, she's devastated. And she's given us a very checkable alibi for Friday night.' Heidi had been at a nightclub in Exeter with her boyfriend until three o'clock Saturday morning, and it had been closer to four a.m. by the time she'd got back to the house that she still shared with her mum. There were plenty of potential witnesses to corroborate her story, along with traffic cameras that would have picked up her car as they drove home – she'd been designated driver for the night, a necessity when you live somewhere like Penstowan, as God knows you can't get a bus home at that time of the morning, and as for a train – what's a train? Nothing like that round here… Mackintosh would be the one to check those cameras, of course, or more likely one of her team, but the chances of her lying about it felt slim to me.

'Yes,' said Nathan. 'And as far as we can tell, she's not one of Frankie Lewis's ex-girlfriends.'

'You definitely think that's what we're looking at? A jilted ex?'

'It seems the most likely motive, after a jealous boyfriend, and we've ruled him out.' Nathan sighed. 'Thank God I'm not dating anymore, it's a minefield.'

I laughed. 'You got a lot of exes, have you? Did you

leave a string of broken hearts behind you in Liverpool? Do I need to watch my back?'

'With *this* face? What do you think?' Nathan grinned and attempted to give me a smouldering look. He went a bit cross-eyed, but to be fair it still did it for me. 'The streets of Merseyside are full of ladies wishing they were in your shoes.'

'They can have them,' I said, slipping off my heels. 'They're starting to hurt my feet. But talking of shoes, if it wasn't Heidi, who put them in her locker?'

'It's got to be someone else on the staff, hasn't it?' said Nathan. 'What do we know about the receptionist who was on duty that night?'

'Marissa?' I said. 'Not a lot. One of the other receptionists made a snooty comment about her being very career-orientated and focused, and Sunil said she was studying for some hotel management qualification – she uses the quiet time when everyone's asleep to study. She was the only member of staff on duty during the murder window.'

'Was she, now?'

'Yep. The bar staff had all left by one, and Robbins was asleep, although he was on call if she needed him.'

'And she was on the Reception desk all night?'

'More or less…' I tried to remember what Sunil had told me. 'She said she did go and do a bit of a sweep of the ground floor at some point, although she couldn't remember when exactly, to check everything was cleared up and all the doors were locked, that sort of thing.'

'Why did she do that? Did she have reason to suspect that anything was wrong?'

I shook my head. 'No, it sounds like she does it every night, to keep herself awake as much as anything.'

Nathan thought hard. 'Okay... Ben said when he came downstairs about two o'clock, he was going to ask if she had any aspirin but she wasn't there. So she must've done her sweep about then.'

'But if she *had* done it then, surely she'd have spotted that the fire exit was propped open and shut it? But it was still open when Ben brought Craig back inside, and it stayed open until the golfers came back in and shut it behind them.'

'Yes... I don't think you'd be able to see that fire exit from Reception, but the minute you started walking around you'd spot it.'

Daisy and Joe appeared with the dog. 'Go on, Germaine, get on with it,' said Daisy.

'Hello, you two,' I said. 'Everything okay?'

'Germaine needed to do her business,' said Daisy. 'Why are you lurking out here in the car park?'

'Just getting some air,' I said. 'We'll come back to the party in a minute. I'll keep an eye on the dog if you want?'

'Be my guest,' said Daisy. 'She takes so long to have a wee, honestly, it's embarrassing.' She turned away, and then turned back to us with a grin. 'This is just the sort of wedding reception you two *would* have, isn't it? One where you can cut the cake and then nip out to do a spot of investigating.'

'It's more fun than watching Nana do the Macarena, like she did at your Uncle Kevin's wedding,' I said. 'It's definitely less embarrassing…'

Nathan and I led Germaine across the car park, heading, without meaning to, towards the spot where Kelly's heels had caused so much damage to the turf. We turned right, away from the markers CSI had left behind to mark the spot, and walked in the opposite direction from the pond, which we'd seen more than enough of that weekend. Germaine's ears pricked up and she gave a little bark of pleasure as she spotted some likely-looking bushes to wee on (honestly, my dog is so fussy). As usual, she took ages to actually get on with the job in hand, Nathan and I looking away and giving her some privacy (plus who wants to watch a dog have a wee? Weirdos). My eyes followed the line of the river that cut across the golf course and led back towards the hotel, which was now lit up as dusk was falling. As I watched, a member of staff came out and stashed a box behind some wheelie bins. Maybe the random security search today hadn't put the thief off…

'What if Kelly's death had nothing to do with her love life?' I said suddenly.

'What?' Nathan looked surprised.

'Well, we've assumed from the beginning that it was something to do with her relationship with Frankie – which is understandable, seeing as we all thought it was him.'

'Apart from Sunil. But yes, once we discounted him and started looking into Kelly's background, that was the only real motive we could come up with,' said Nathan. 'Apart from Craig suddenly turning into a sexual predator, which I don't believe for a moment.'

'No, although unfortunately Di Mackintosh seems to think it's a possibility,' I said. 'But what if it's got nothing to do with that? Or even with Kelly herself? What if she was in the wrong place at the wrong time?'

'What, like she saw something she shouldn't have done?' Nathan mused for a moment. 'Yeah, it's possible, but what? Don't tell me – she spotted the phantom loo-roll nicker and he bumped her off?'

'Oh my God, you sounded like Mum then,' I said, shuddering. 'But yes. Not the loo-roll nicker, I mean – but maybe there's more to these thefts than Robbins is letting on?'

'Maybe, although if there was you'd expect him to either go to the police – the *actual* police, not an off-duty officer staying here for his wedding – or, if he's involved, keep quiet about it.'

'Maybe it's something that he doesn't know about,' I said. 'Maybe Kelly saw someone stealing something valuable from a guest, and the thief saw her and had to stop her reporting it?'

'But as far as we know, no one's reported anything missing,' said Nathan. 'If Robbins bothered us about toilet paper, he'd definitely have mentioned something big being stolen, particularly just now when he was searching the lockers. Although that might explain *why* he suddenly decided to search them.'

'Yes, it might,' I said. 'Although I have to admit, I put

that down to the stress of the murder investigation getting to him. He was already pretty tightly wound when we got here, wasn't he?'

'True.' We turned to look at the dog, who was sitting there watching us with an expression on her face that said, *What are you two waiting for?*

'Okay Germaine, let's go and see if there's any sausage rolls left for you…'

We entered the hotel through the front entrance into Reception, where Chelsea looked up from her computer behind the desk and smiled at us.

'Heidi okay, was she?' she asked.

'Yes, poor thing,' I said. 'She was obviously very close to Kelly.'

'Like sisters, from what Heidi used to say about her. Her real sister was a waste of space. They didn't get on, Heidi reckons.'

We were about to head back into the function room, but Nathan stopped. 'Your colleague who was on duty on Friday night—'

'Marissa,' I added.

'Obviously we haven't had a chance to talk to her yet—' Nathan started. Chelsea looked confused.

'Oh no, I'm sure she's given the police a statement,' she said.

'Yes, yes she has,' said Nathan quickly. 'But we're

conducting a parallel investigation – following up a few different leads to the official one.'

'After all, we're here, on the spot,' I said.

'Oh right, yes. Go on.'

'I just wondered if you could tell us anything about her? Did she know Kelly?' asked Nathan.

'I wouldn't have thought so,' said Chelsea. 'She's not from round here.'

'Not from Penstowan?'

'Not from Cornwall. She's from somewhere upcountry – Birmingham, I think. She puts on this posh accent, but every now and then it slips and you can hear her real voice.'

'Really?' I lowered my voice, as if inviting a bit of gossip from her, in confidence. 'I thought when she came up to tell Nathan and his stags off for being noisy, she was a bit hoity toity…' I silently begged Marissa's pardon, because I'd thought nothing of the sort, although I definitely hadn't heard any Brummie in her voice.

Chelsea sniggered, then put her hand to her mouth and looked around to make sure no one had seen her. 'Yeah, she is a bit. I felt sorry for her when she first started here, because she didn't know anyone, but she wasn't interested in making friends.'

'No?'

Chelsea shook her head. 'Not amongst us lot, anyway. Happy to be friends with the boss…'

'Really? Are they friends or are they *friends*?' I asked.

'Some of the others think more than friends, but I don't think she'd go *that* far.'

'You said earlier that she was very career orientated,' I said. 'But not career orientated enough to…'

'No. Ew.' Chelsea looked faintly disgusted, but also thrilled to be getting this off her chest. 'No. She's Robbins's favourite, though, that's for sure.'

'Yeah?'

'Yeah. You know I sent out that WhatsApp message, about the searches? She's the only one who didn't bother to reply, although I can see that she read it.' She folded her arms, like *that* said it all.

'She wasn't worried about him searching her locker?' asked Nathan.

'No. Because she knew that he wouldn't try and stitch her up by putting something in there. Some of the others, they've had a few run-ins with him, that's why they wanted to be there when he opened their lockers, just in case he was using it as an excuse to get rid of people.'

'Do you really think he'd do that?' I asked.

'Well – no, probably not. But…'

'But it happened before, with Janette?' I said, and both she and Nathan looked at me in surprise.

'How do you know about Janette?' asked Chelsea.

'I heard one of the other staff members mention her name,' I said. 'Who is she? What happened?'

'She was a housekeeper. It was about nine, ten months ago. One of the guest rooms was burgled and an expensive watch was taken,' she said.

'And Mr Robbins accused Janette?' asked Nathan.

'No, Marissa did. She said she saw her put the watch in

her locker.' Chelsea looked disapproving. 'I told you Marissa wasn't out to make friends.'

'Did Robbins call the police?' I asked.

'No, he confronted her about it and she admitted she did it.'

Nathan and I exchanged bemused looks. 'So she *did* do it?' asked Nathan.

'Well, yeah. But it wasn't very nice of Marissa to grass her up, was it?'

'I don't know about that,' I said. 'If it meant the hotel could just clear it up without calling the police, it means Janette got away without getting a criminal record.'

'Still got sacked though,' said Chelsea, although what else she thought Robbins could've done in the circumstances I didn't know. 'And he wasn't thinking about her, he was more worried about the hotel's reputation.'

The phone rang then, so we left her to answer it and headed back to the party, where the DJ was still playing but a lot of our guests were starting to look worn out. That's what happens when most of your friends and family are over forty. We're happy to party all day – as long as we don't have to start until after lunch – but we do need to be in our jammies by nine.

'Robbins trusts Marissa,' said Nathan, handing me a glass of wine. 'He trusts her, and she knows it and takes advantage.'

'How'd you work that out?'

'She wasn't worried about her locker being searched. Admittedly, anyone who hadn't stolen anything should be okay with being searched, even if they don't particularly like it. But she knew she was okay because he trusts her.'

'And presumably because she knew she didn't have anything in there,' I said. 'We can't start making something out of nothing. And she'd already proved to him that she was trustworthy when she told him about Janette.'

'True, but she *does* take advantage, because it sounds like she's not the most conscientious employee. She studies during her night shift, which he might be okay about because it's to do with hotel management—'

'He might be grooming her for a managerial position,' I said. 'Heidi said the assistant manager had left to have a baby. There doesn't seem to be anyone else filling that position at the moment, so maybe he's thinking of replacing her with Marissa, if she doesn't come back from maternity leave?'

'Yes, okay, that's true. But also, she wasn't at her desk all the time she was supposed to be. Not when Ben went to see her. The golfers *and* Craig all managed to avoid her – they said it was because they were actively trying not to be seen, but what if she didn't see them because she'd wandered off? Or more likely, gone for a kip in the office?'

'That's *exactly* what I said I'd do, if I was on my own overnight,' I said.

'She was supposed to keep an eye on things, but she didn't see the fire exit was propped open,' added Nathan. 'I know you can't see that from the reception desk, but she was apparently wandering around checking everything, and she missed it.'

'So, what? What are you saying? That she killed Kelly? Why?'

'I don't know. What does she look like? I know I spoke to her, but I was a bit drunk…'

'A bit?' I rolled my eyes. 'She's like the rest of them – young and blonde.'

'Blonde? And pretty?'

'Well, not my type, you know… I don't know, attractive enough, I suppose?'

'Blonde and attractive enough, whatever that is. And well educated.'

'How do you know that?'

'She's studying. No one else has mentioned doing that.' Nathan looked at me as if he'd just said something of great significance, but I was still in the dark.

'Sorry babe, you're going to have to give me more than that,' I said.

'Davey Trelawney said he saw Frankie Lewis having a set-to with a blonde girl outside the pub a few months ago, yes?' I nodded. 'And Frankie told him that she wouldn't leave him alone, like she was obsessed with him.'

'Yes…'

'Marissa is blonde and, possibly, well-educated enough to have at least heard of the classics…'

'Marissa is Medea?' I asked, surprised, although it actually kind of made sense. At least, no less sense than anyone else being her.

'Why not? Chelsea said she didn't really know anyone round here, but maybe that would explain why she found it hard to accept it was over when Frankie dumped her – because there was no one else out there to replace him.'

'Hmm, that's a stretch,' I said, but was it? People did get obsessed over the most unlikely objects of affection.

'There's a picture behind the reception desk,' said Nathan. 'I think it's a photo of the staff. Let's go and have a look…' He bent down to pick up my shoes, handing them to me with a grin. I sighed.

'My poor feet have been in and out of these instruments of torture all evening,' I said, bracing myself as I slipped the high heels on. 'Next time we get married I'm wearing my trainers.'

We left the party again, although it took a while because there were a few guests we'd hardly spoken to, and when they accosted us on the way out we could hardly ignore them. But finally we stood at the desk, looking up at the picture. It was a photograph of everyone smiling, smart in their uniforms, with the caption 'Meet the Team' underneath. Chelsea looked at us quizzically.

'Everything alright?'

'Is Marissa in that photo?' asked Nathan. 'Could we have a look?'

'Sure…' Chelsea looked mystified but lifted the picture off the wall and placed it in front of us. 'That's her.'

I recognised Marissa from the brief interaction we'd had on the Friday night, but only just. She looked older than I'd remembered her – I think all of the receptionists had kind of merged in my mind into one generic staff member, which I felt bad about, but then I'd not really spoken much to any of them except Chelsea.

'She's older than Kelly,' I said quietly to Nathan. 'And Frankie, for that matter. Getting dumped is bad enough, but dumped for someone younger…' I didn't have to imagine how that felt, as my useless ex had been having an affair with someone younger than me. It wasn't the main reason it had hurt, but it hadn't helped. 'That could tie in with choosing "Medea" as an alias.'

'Yeah… I wonder if it really *was* her that Davey saw?'

'If who was what now?' And as if by magic Davey himself stood there, like a genie freshly escaped from a bottle.

'How did you get here?' I asked in surprise.

'Usual way. In a car.' He grinned at me. 'DI Mackintosh sent me to collect some evidence from Sunil. The Forensics lot have all gone home and no one wants to pay them overtime. Apparently I'm also meant to tell you two off for encroaching on her investigation, but I might skip that bit.'

'Yeah, I would if I were you,' said Nathan. 'You remember you told us about Frankie Lewis arguing with a blonde girl outside the pub, a few months back? Could you have a look at this photo, and tell us if she's in it?'

'I'll have a go, but like I said, they all look the same to me these days…' Davey took the photo and peered closely at it, studying it carefully.

'Any luck?' I asked. Davey put the photo down and smiled.

'Oh yes, she's in it alright.'

Chapter Twenty

'But that *can't* be her,' I said. 'She's got an alibi.'

'For Friday night, yes,' said Nathan. 'She didn't kill her friend, but she was definitely arguing with her boyfriend…'

Davey had been absolutely adamant, and to be fair when you saw the young women next to each other they didn't look anything like each other, except of course for the hair.

'Marissa wasn't obsessed with Frankie,' I said, 'but does that mean Heidi was?'

'Frankie said that she wouldn't leave him alone,' said Davey. 'I didn't believe him for one minute. She were furious with him, proper angry. I got the impression she were telling him off for something he'd done.'

'Cheating on Kelly?' I said. Davey shrugged.

'Maybe. Wouldn't put it past him.'

'Then who's Medea?'

Davey looked bewildered. 'Buggered if I know, but there's a lot of people down here who do give their kids some weird names. I know someone who called their daughter Moonpie. Sweet enough when she were five, not so good now she's a bank manager in Barnstaple.'

'True... I still think it's a false name, though,' I said. 'Heidi said she and Kelly tried to find out who it was and they couldn't. There can't be many Medeas in the whole of the UK, let alone Cornwall. So if it was a real name they wouldn't be that hard to track down.'

'We need to ask Heidi about this,' said Nathan.

'Yeah, but we can't exactly go round her house at the moment, can we?' I said.

'You want her phone number?' It hadn't looked like Chelsea had been loitering, but she obviously had. I admired her ability to eavesdrop so discreetly that we hadn't noticed, although I also hoped she hadn't heard too much.

Nathan took the phone number and wandered away to a quiet corner, where Chelsea wouldn't be able to hear. I hoped she couldn't lipread.

The conversation didn't take long. Nathan came back to where Davey and I were standing, which was now out of earshot of a certain receptionist. 'Yes, she confirms it was her arguing with Frankie. She remembers that "lovely copper" who came to her rescue when Frankie started to get out of hand.' He nodded at Davey, who gave a little bow. He was as big and strong as an ox, but Davey Trelawney could be as gentle as a lamb when the situation called for it.

'What were they arguing about?' I asked.

'She says someone had told her they'd seen Frankie getting off with another girl, a brunette this time, not another blonde… She didn't know whether to tell Kelly about it or not, so she decided to ask Frankie about it first. He denied it and things got nasty, but she still wasn't sure if she believed it. She reckons Frankie went round to hers the next day and admitted that he had kissed another girl when he was very drunk, and that he regretted it and he wouldn't do it again. She said he seemed sincere, so she decided not to tell Kelly. But she warned him if he did it again she'd grass him up. And after that, they actually got on better than they had done before.'

'So this other girl, the mysterious brunette – maybe *she* could be Medea? She could be the one who left nasty comments on Kelly's posts?'

'She could. But that doesn't mean she killed her, does it? And we don't know who she is. Heidi said the person who'd told her hadn't been able to make out who the girl was, because Frankie had been all over her. When they tried to find out who Medea was, Heidi thought it could be the same girl, but it didn't help her find her.' Nathan gave a rueful smile. 'Of course, if we were *officially* on the case and not in the middle of our sort-of wedding reception, we could go and ask Frankie. But…'

'So we're back to – unknown jilted woman kills her rival, or unknown person kills her for an unknown reason.' I groaned. 'Aargh! This case.'

Davey patted me on the arm in a way I hated intensely

from anyone else, but actually didn't mind from him, as he'd known me since I was young. 'Maybe you both need to step away from this one, and concentrate on your party,' he said.

'Yeah, you're probably right...' I shook my head. 'Come on, we'll take you to the staff room. Sunil's waiting for you.'

We walked through Reception and down the corridor to the staff room, the entrance to which had been blocked by a chair. Sunil sat on it, watching something on his phone. Nathan assumed a stern expression and cleared his throat, making him jump.

'DC Sunil, I hope you're not watching TikTok videos when you're supposed to be on duty...'

Sunil leapt to his feet. 'No, Guv—'

'It's alright, Sunil, I was just messing with you. You're not strictly on duty, are you?'

'No. But I was watching something that I think you'll want to see.'

'Is it three kittens and a gerbil dancing to Michael Jackson?' I said. 'We've already seen that one, it's awesome.'

'No... I downloaded the link to the security footage of the front entrance from Friday night so I could watch it on my phone,' said Sunil.

'Seriously, the kitten video is much more entertaining.'

'I think I've found something.' Sunil pulled up the camera recording and we all stood round him, peering at the little screen over his shoulder. 'When I originally looked at the footage, it was on a bigger screen. I fast-forwarded through it until I saw someone appear and then I slowed it down so I could identify them. Otherwise it would've taken me hours to watch it.'

'Fair enough,' said Nathan.

'But being on a small screen, I thought it would be easier to miss something, so I've been watching it at normal speed. I've been concentrating on the period after the time when we think the golfers shut the fire exit. Because at that point, the murderer would only be able to re-enter the hotel through the front door.'

'Okay.'

'And I think the murderer was probably still outside when the golfers shut the fire exit, because they reckoned they heard voices and that's what made them come in.'

'Yes, that's right,' said Nathan. 'So what have you found? Did someone run in so fast they were a blur or something?' He was joking, of course, but Sunil nodded.

'Yes. Not about them running in, but about the blur. Look.' He played the footage slowly and, sure enough, at one point the picture blurred. It was only a little bit, and just for a split second, but it was there.

'Play that again,' said Nathan, leaning forward even more. Sunil rewound and then hit play again. 'There. It's barely noticeable, but it's like the footage jumps or something?'

'There's a shadow,' said Davey, and I jumped then because I'd almost forgotten he was with us. 'Just on the edge of the frame.'

We watched it again, and Davey was right. There was no one there – and then suddenly right at the edge, there was a shadow. It disappeared again as quickly as it had appeared.

'Wow,' I said. 'You know what that means?'

'Someone's tampered with the footage,' said Sunil.

'Someone was caught coming in through the front entrance, and the footage was edited to take them out,' agreed Nathan. 'They didn't have to cut out much – just a few seconds – but they missed the very last couple of frames that show the light changing as someone moved out of it.'

'Who has access to the footage?' I asked Sunil.

'Robbins. We asked the receptionist who was on duty on Saturday to give us the link to it, but she said he was the only one who had access to it, so we had to find him first.'

'But why would he tamper with it?' I asked. 'Is there any connection between him and Kelly?'

'None that we could find,' said Sunil. 'But then we weren't looking at him as a suspect.'

'What about between her and Marissa, the receptionist?' asked Nathan. 'We can't overlook the fact that she was the only staff member on duty that night.'

'No connection,' said Sunil. 'DI Mackintosh did briefly look into her as a suspect, of course, but she only moved here a year ago and she doesn't seem to have any friends.'

'Apart from the manager,' I said, looking at Nathan. 'That's what Chelsea said. And there's another thing she said that's been bugging me. She said that Kelly and her sister didn't get on, that her sister was a waste of space. And yet on Friday night, when we suggested Kelly stay somewhere else to give Frankie a chance to calm down, she texted her sister and asked if she could stay with her. Why? One of the other girls was really keen for her to go back and stay at hers, which would've been the easiest option, but instead Kelly woke up a sister she didn't even like very much and arranged to stay there.'

'They might have reconciled,' said Nathan. 'But you're right, it would've been easier to go with the other girl.' He thought for a moment. 'Okay, I think we need to talk to Robbins first about this footage.'

'And then?' I asked.

'And then we probably need to bring Mackintosh in.' Nathan smiled at our glum faces. 'I know, but like you said – she's a good copper, she's just following each lead until it ends before she starts on the next one. We're only ahead of her because we know Craig, and we know he didn't do it. But obviously that's not enough to satisfy her, nor should it be.'

'Oh God, you're so sensible,' I grumbled, but he was right.

Davey headed back to the station, clutching an evidence bag containing Kelly's high heels and instructions to discreetly look into Kelly's family background – particularly her sister. There could be a myriad of reasons why Kelly had chosen to stay at her sibling's that night – although of course she hadn't made it – but it still niggled me.

There was another receptionist on duty now, and I realised that the shift must've changed. She was chatting to Arabella who, wedding planner duties duly executed, seemed a lot more relaxed. When we asked to see her father she raised her eyebrows.

'Guest complaint or unofficial investigation?' she asked.

'Unofficial investigation,' I said.

'In that case, I'm coming in with you…' She knocked on the office door.

Mr Robbins ushered us into his office, anxiety radiating off him as he fussed around trying to get us all chairs, even though we'd already said we were happy to stand.

'How can I help you?' he asked, in the voice of a man who was already having the worst weekend of his life and just did not want to know how much worse it was likely to get.

'Who has access to the security camera footage?' asked Nathan, although of course we already knew that.

'Anyone with the link can watch it,' said Robbins, nodding to Sunil, 'as I explained to you before, officer.'

'Not just to watch it, but to delete it, or edit it,' Nathan clarified. Robbins frowned.

'Edit it? No one.'

Arabella cleared her throat. 'That's not strictly true, Daddy…'

Robbins was unabashed. 'Yes, *technically* I can, of course, but I've never needed to and I wouldn't know how.'

'No? Then can you explain to me why the footage from the time of the murder has been tampered with?'

Robbins went pale. 'Tampered with? How?'

'And when?' asked Arabella. 'My father was in bed at

the time of the murder. He always goes up about ten thirty, don't you?' Robbins nodded.

'And no one else could get into the system?' asked Nathan.

'Not as far as I know. But if what you're saying is true, they must have, because I didn't do it…' Robbins frowned again, then looked up at us, his face clearing slightly. 'The log.'

'Log?'

'There's a security system activity log,' said Arabella. 'It records things like system outages, times when the cameras might be offline, that kind of thing. I think it shows when people have logged in, too. Let me see if I can find it…' Arabella gently moved her unresisting father out of the way, reached over to his computer keyboard and hurriedly typed in some commands. The activity log came up on screen and she scrolled down to Friday night. 'Here we go… nothing there… Oh…' She looked at Robbins. 'Here.'

'That's my login,' said the manager. 'Someone accessed the system using my login details at just before four a.m. Saturday morning.'

'Can you restore the footage that was tampered with?' I asked. 'We think this person deleted a few seconds of footage from the front-door camera taken at some point between two a.m. and two thirty.'

'I don't know,' said Arabella. 'We've never had this happen before.'

'There is a help desk, but they won't be there at this time

on a Sunday night.' Mr Robbins looked worried. 'They used my login details, but it wasn't me. I was asleep.'

'Who else knows your login?' asked Nathan.

'No one.' But Robbins seemed hesitant.

'You're sure about that?' Arabella looked at him, seriously; she obviously had someone in mind.

'Well – there *is* one person who might know it, but I'm sure she wouldn't…'

'Oh *Daddy!*'

'Marissa?' I asked. Robbins looked surprised. 'Lucky guess. Not that lucky, admittedly – she *was* the only member of staff on duty at the time.'

'She's worked here for just over a year, she's one of my best staff members.' Robbins was practically wailing. 'She's got a real passion for the hotel business. I've been grooming her to take my place.'

'*Your* place?'

'Yes. I want to retire soon, but I've worked so hard building this business up, I couldn't bear to see it passed on to someone who didn't appreciate what we have here and didn't keep it going to the same high standards as me.' He looked a little embarrassed. 'I know it's not down to me to choose my successor, it's down to the owners, but I know that they would take my recommendation when it came to it.'

'Wouldn't the assistant manager be a more obvious choice?' I asked, but he scoffed.

'Her? No. She's gone off to have a family. They'll always come before the hotel, won't they?'

'Well, yeah,' I said, because as much as I'd loved my job in the Met, when I had to put Daisy first I'd quit. 'How well do you know Marissa?'

'As I said, she's been here just over a year. She came with glowing references from the previous hotels she'd worked at. I trust her implicitly.'

'Did she tell you why she'd moved down here?' I asked. 'One of the other girls said she came from upcountry somewhere.'

'Yes. Certainly the hotels she worked at were up North somewhere.'

'Birmingham?'

Robbins thought for a moment. 'No... not Birmingham. Manchester, I think. It's all in her HR file.'

'Could we have a look at that?' asked Nathan.

'Of course. But I still can't believe she would do anything wrong...' Robbins got up and opened a filing cabinet, searching through until he found a file. He handed it to Nathan, who passed it to Sunil. 'I'm a bit old school, I'm afraid – everything on paper.'

'So how would she know your login?' I asked.

'A couple of months ago I had to have an operation. A slightly embarrassing one. I didn't tell the staff about it,' he said. Arabella took his hand.

'He didn't even tell me about it,' she said.

'You'd already booked your trip to America,' he said. 'I didn't want you cancelling it for me. I soldiered on, but Marissa spotted my discomfort and offered to take on some of my workload. She was so helpful. She took on some of my administration work, which she would've done in here, and my passwords…' He glanced down at the top drawer of his desk.

'Let me guess: they're all written down on a piece of paper in that drawer?' said Nathan, and Robbins nodded. 'So Marissa could've accessed the camera footage, because she had access to your passwords, and she was here on her own at the time.'

'Yes, but why would she do that?' Arabella looked at us in disbelief. 'You're not suggesting she could have murdered Kelly?'

'She had the opportunity,' I said.

'But no motive, surely? I find it hard to believe that she and the victim would've moved in the same circles. Marissa keeps herself to herself, even among her colleagues.'

'So we've heard,' said Nathan. 'Thank you, you've both been very helpful. I will be passing all of this on to DI Mackintosh in due course. One last thing. Has Marissa been back since the night of the murder?'

'Of course,' said Robbins. 'She's on the night shift. She was here last night and she's due in again tonight, ten o'clock until six tomorrow morning.'

'Okay. Please keep this conversation to yourself for the moment. We may need to talk to her when she comes in.'

We left the manager anxiously going through his desk drawers, presumably looking for something, anything, that would confirm or disprove the possibility that Marissa – or someone else – had found his passwords. I could hear

Arabella chastising him for being so careless with them as we shut the door behind us.

Nathan looked at his watch. 'It's getting on. Sunil, you probably need to go home and look after that lovely wife of yours.'

'Yes, Guv – if you don't mind? I'm happy to stay if you need anything else?'

'No, go home, but take Marissa's file with you and have a read through, see if you can find anything odd.'

'Yes, Guv.' Sunil turned to me with a smile. 'Night, Jodie. I enjoyed your un-wedding. I can honestly say I've never been to one like it before.'

I laughed. 'Nor have I. I'm hoping the next one will actually have a wedding ceremony in it at some point.'

We watched Sunil leave and headed back to the party.

'Right, I can't see what else we can do now.' Nathan grabbed a couple of glasses of champagne from the bar and handed me one. 'Here you go, Almost-Mrs-Withers-Parker. Let's have some fun.'

'I already was,' I said, and Nathan's laugh told me he had been too. We danced our way over to the buffet table, which was looking very sorry for itself by now, but there were still people hanging around it, picking at the leftovers.

'There you are!' cried Tony. 'We've hardly seen you all evening. What you been up to, or shouldn't I ask?' He winked. Carmen rolled her eyes.

'Nothing like *that*,' I said, pretending to be shocked. 'In case you've forgotten, we're not even married. But we have been trying to track down a murderer, which is almost as much fun as the *disgusting* things you were suggesting.' I grinned. 'We've got *those* pencilled in for later…'

'You've been investigating?' Matt was slurring slightly, and I got the impression he and Tony had been matching each other drink for drink, only now they were off the wine and champagne and on the local, extremely strong, cider. Matt turned to Tony. 'What did I tell you? You owe me a tenner.'

'He never took that bet,' said Carmen, 'not with these two, that would be throwing your money away.'

'So,' said Chrissie, who was rather more sober than her boyfriend, 'did you find anything? Mackintosh will be *fuming* if you solve it before her.' I could tell from her grin that she liked the idea of getting one over on Mackintosh just as much as the rest of us.

'Time will tell,' said Nathan. 'But we have some new lines of enquiry.'

'Spill!' said Matt, but Nathan shook his head.

'Nope, not until we know we're on the right track.' He looked around. 'Where are Ben and Danny? I should probably go and talk to them…'

We found them out in the relative quiet of the terrace, Danny attempting to listen in as Ben took a phone call.

'That's brilliant, alright lad, we'll see you in a bit.' Ben disconnected the call and looked up. 'That was good timing. I just heard from Craiggy boy, they're letting him go.'

'They are? Thank God for that,' I said.

'About time,' said Nathan. 'What did he say?'

'Mackintosh has just said he can go, she's got no further

questions for him,' said Ben, shrugging. 'Probably means she's got nowt to prove he did it, because he didn't.'

'Yep.' It was a relief to hear she'd let him go, because although I *knew* he hadn't done it, I hadn't *actually* known he hadn't, not like Nathan and the lads had. 'Is he on his way back? I don't suppose any of you are sober enough to go and get him?' I asked.

'We've just spent the last few hours at a party where there's a free bar,' said Danny. 'Does that answer your question?'

'Yes, perfectly.' I smiled at Nathan. 'I suppose we should really take advantage of the bar ourselves, as we're paying for it…'

Chapter Twenty-One

Two drinks later, having led Nathan onto the dance floor and exhorted the DJ to 'get this party started', I was sitting in the corner of the room yawning my head off, while the dog made herself comfortable on my feet.

'Oh Germaine,' I said, 'I am such a lightweight...'

Debbie danced over to me and tried to persuade me to get back on my feet, but I waved her away. 'I'm knackered,' I said. She shook her head in mock disgust.

'You're nowt but a soft southern shandy drinker,' she said. 'I thought you could handle your liquor.'

'I don't know who told you that, but they were lying.' She laughed and danced backwards onto the dance floor, narrowly avoiding a collision with Jocasta and Mum, who were (to my shame) still having a boogie, albeit not a very energetic one.

Nathan came over and plopped himself down in the chair next to me.

'If you're going to try and persuade me to dance again,' I said, 'don't. I am out of action for the foreseeable future.'

'Don't worry, I need a rest too,' he said. 'Although neither of us has actually drunk that much. People have been handing me drinks all afternoon, but I've been abandoning them after a few sips to follow another lead.'

'What time is it?' I asked. 'Is it too early to go to bed?'

'Well, it is our wedding night, so we've got a good excuse.' He pulled his phone out of his pocket to look at the time. 'Nearly nine o'clock.'

'Marissa will be on duty soon,' I said. 'We could always go and interrogate her. That would wake me up.'

Nathan laughed. 'It would me too, but I think we need a bit more to go on first.' He frowned. 'Hang on, I've got two missed calls, both from Sunil…'

'Bingo,' I said, heaving myself back onto my feet. 'Let's go somewhere quiet and call him back…'

The quietest place turned out to be the honeymoon suite. I lay on the bed while Nathan dialled Sunil, with his phone on speaker so I could hear. I shuffled over and lay my head on his lap, which Germaine (who had come with us) took as a sign that she should do the same in *my* lap. Nathan laughed and stroked my hair, as I stroked Germaine. 'You and that dog,' he said, 'you're kindred spirits.'

'Hello, Guv?' Sunil's voice floated out of the phone.

'Yes, Sunil, sorry I missed your calls but it was a bit noisy here,' said Nathan. 'You're on speakerphone so Jodie can hear you.'

'Hi Sunil,' I said.

'Hi Jodie.'

'Hi Jodie!' Eesha's voice came through the phone too, although quieter than Sunil's. I laughed.

'Aww, this is nice,' I said, 'couples investigating. Makes a change from dinner parties and wife swapping.'

Eesha roared with laughter, but I could almost *hear* Sunil blushing. Nathan looked at me, shaking his head, but he was laughing too.

'Ignore my soon-to-be wife,' he said. 'What have you got for us?'

'I looked through Marissa's HR file, like you asked,' said Sunil. 'Not a lot to go on, though. So I rang the two hotels she said she'd worked for before, and guess what? They've never heard of her.'

I sat up quickly, almost throwing Germaine onto the floor. I grabbed her and hauled her safely back up onto my lap. 'Whoa, I hadn't expected that,' I said. 'But Robbins must've checked her references with them?'

'She gave him the name and number of someone in the hotels' HR departments,' he said. 'I rang them first. Both numbers were disconnected. So I rang the hotels directly and gave them the names of the staff members who had given her a reference, and they don't exist.'

'Blimey,' said Nathan. 'Well, that *is* suspicious.'

'But lots of people lie on their CVs,' said Eesha, in the background. 'I have.' There was a slightly shocked silence, and then I heard Sunil muttering something. 'Oh don't be such an old woman, Sunil. It was only applying for a job in the supermarket when I started university.' Nathan and I grinned at each other.

'Yes, this is a bit more serious than that, though,' said Nathan.

'And that's not all. Marissa had to put her previous address down as part of some background check for the hotel, but Robbins has left a note in her file not to check it because she'd apparently left after her landlord made a pass at her. She turned him down and it got a bit nasty, so she didn't want him to know where she'd moved to. But I looked up that address and it's an Anglican church in Eccleshall.'

'Where on earth is Eccleshall?' I asked.

'Staffordshire.'

'Right…' Nathan looked at me, perplexed. 'What about stuff like next of kin? That must be in her file.'

'She's an orphan,' said Sunil. 'And single. So no next of kin.'

'That's convenient,' I said. 'So Marissa is a bit of a mystery woman. Mysterious to the point of being completely made up, maybe?'

'That's what I was thinking,' said Sunil, and Nathan nodded.

'Yes. I think we'll be having a word with Mysterious Marissa when she turns up for work. If she turns up for work…'

'You might want to ask her about Megan Reynolds,' said Sunil, with the air of someone who had saved the best until last.

The Cornish Castle Murder

'Who the bloody hell is Megan Reynolds?' Nathan sounded exasperated.

'She's a receptionist who worked at one of the hotels Marissa listed, the Clockhouse Hotel in Manchester. I sent the manager the photo on her HR file and he said they knew her as Megan. She started work there three years ago. She was there for about a year, a model employee, very responsible, and then all of a sudden she just left, with no warning.'

'Did she give them a reason?'

'No, but the manager thinks it might have something to do with the thirty-five thousand pounds' worth of jewellery that went missing from the hotel safe the night before she left.'

I felt my jaw drop, and Nathan whistled.

'Oh yeah, I expect that had something to do with it,' he said. 'What about the other hotel? Did they recognise her?'

'The Royal Victoria Hotel in Leamington Spa. No, although the manager there said she did look a bit like Sharon Cooper, only Sharon had red hair. She worked for them nine years ago, so obviously she's changed a bit. Sharon worked there for two years, they never had any problems with her, although there *was* a spate of petty thefts not long after she started. And then just before she left, two of the guests reported money and jewellery missing from the safe in their rooms. That added up to about five thousand pounds.'

'Bloody hell,' I said. 'Maybe she's the phantom loo-roll nicker…'

Eesha laughed in the background. 'She's gone down in the world.'

'More likely the petty stuff is just to test out how rigorous Robbins's security measures are,' said Nathan. 'Or it's a coincidence and someone else is taking it.'

'Do you think she's planning something, then?' I asked.

'Well, she's faked her references and is living under an assumed name, so – yeah,' said Nathan. 'But why would she kill Kelly?'

'Kelly found out about it,' I said.

'How, though? She didn't even work here.'

'Unless Heidi said something,' suggested Sunil, but I could hear Eesha scoff.

'Then why would she kill Kelly and not Heidi?' she asked, reasonably enough I thought. 'Ooh! Maybe Heidi's next!'

'Are you sure you should be thinking about things like this, in your condition?' asked Sunil. *Oof.* The one thing you never say to a pregnant woman is 'Should you be doing such-and-such *in your condition*?' I waited for the explosion, but it was only a minor one.

'Sunil, my grandmother was working on a tea plantation up to the day she gave birth to my mother,' said Eesha, sounding exasperated.

'That's a bit different, *meri jaan*,' said Sunil. 'Your grandfather owned the biggest plantation in Assam. She was only working in the office, not out in the fields picking tea.'

'And I'm only *thinking* about murder,' said Eesha.

'Although if you keep wrapping me up in cotton wool, I might do more than think about it.' Nathan and I exchanged grins. 'Now where's that foot massage you promised me? Working on a Sunday night and you're not even on the case anymore.'

'Sunil, mate, it sounds like you've got your hands full,' said Nathan. 'Eesha, my apologies, you can have your husband back now. Give that bump a little pat from both of us.'

'She's not having puppies, babe,' I said, rolling my eyes.

We said good night to both of them and disconnected the call. We lay back on the bed, rolling onto our sides to look at each other.

'Well,' said Nathan. 'You did say you wanted to go and question her.'

'And you did say we'd need to have a bit more to go on before we did,' I said. 'The only thing is, why *did* she kill Kelly? If that's what we're thinking. Like Eesha said, if Heidi had noticed something wrong at work and mentioned it to Kelly, why didn't she kill Heidi too? And if Kelly did know something, how would Marissa, or Megan or Sharon or whatever her real name is, how would she know that Kelly knew? They didn't know each other.'

'As far as we know,' said Nathan.

'That's a lot of unknowns,' I said.

'I know.'

Germaine gave a little harrumph and leapt off the bed. She trotted to the door and started to paw at it.

'Oh bog off, Germaine, let me rest,' I moaned, but

Germaine didn't bog off (to be fair, I'm not sure how she could've done). I leant over and kissed Nathan, then sat up. 'Okay you furry slave driver, I'm coming…'

'Come on,' said Nathan, 'we'll take her for a walk. It'll wake us both up.'

We wandered down the corridor and got in the lift (Germaine only had little legs and struggled with the stairs), travelling down the two floors to the ground. As we got out we came face to face with Marissa, who was about to enter the lift. She stepped back to let us out.

'Oh – hello,' I said, trying not to sound like we'd just been describing her possible life of crime and deception.

'Good evening,' she said politely, with a strained smile. *She must know that Nathan's a police officer*, I thought. Did she have a guilty conscience? Or more likely, was she wondering what we knew about her?

'Just taking the dog for a walk,' I said, gesturing to Germaine. She smiled.

'Oh, what a sweetheart!' she said, squatting down to make a fuss of her. She straightened up. 'Enjoy your walk.'

'Thank you,' I said, and steered Nathan and the dog out through Reception before I gave the game away by being awkward and weird.

'Just because she likes dogs, it doesn't mean she's not a bad 'un,' said Nathan, as we got outside.

'I know,' I said. 'Dammit, you always know what I'm thinking.' We walked across the car park and onto the golf course, where I let out Germaine's lead as far as it would go, so she could roam almost completely freely. The course was closed now, obviously – it was almost ten o'clock, and it was very dark out there – and I didn't think there would be any pilled-up middle-aged ravers playing golf at this time of night, not after the revelation of where Friday night's missing ball had ended up. Even though we hadn't told them it had probably contributed to Kelly's death, I got the impression they were shocked enough to think twice before playing golf in the pitch black again.

'If Marissa, or whatever her real name is, has been working here for a year already, *and* she worked at those other hotels for quite a while too before anything went missing, she must think it's worth playing the long game,' I said, watching Germaine nosing around a nearby bush before disappearing into the darkness.

'Thousands of pounds' worth of jewellery probably does make it worth it,' said Nathan. 'Although she won't have been able to sell it for that much. You wouldn't normally get market value for stolen goods, would you?'

'No, I suppose not. And of course in the meantime she's been getting paid by the hotel while she waits for an opportunity. Lucky for her that a guest turned up with expensive jewellery.'

'Not really,' said Nathan. 'The Clockhouse is a very expensive hotel, and most of their guests are probably very well-heeled. I haven't heard of the other one, but this place is pretty posh too, isn't it?'

'Yes. I wonder… Have you got your phone on you? I haven't exactly got pockets in this frock so I had to leave mine upstairs and I feel *naked*.' Nathan laughed and handed me his phone. I pulled up the hotel's website and clicked on the 'Events' button. 'I thought so. Here, listen to this. *The Kervoy Castle annual grouse shooting event will run from Monday 11th until Wednesday 13th August, to celebrate the start of the season on 'the glorious twelfth'. Events will include a welcome dinner on the 11th, and culminate in a black-tie gala banquet on the 13th. Guests will be able to participate in a full or half day's shoot on the 12th and 13th, or relax and enjoy the spa facilities, while indulging in delicious food and drink.'* I looked at him. 'Don't you remember? We looked at booking the weekend before that, but they didn't have enough rooms for everybody because some guests were getting here early for this shoot thing.' I scrolled through the photographs taken at previous balls. 'Bloody hell, it looks proper posh. They've got the "rich old white people" demographic covered. They must come from all over the country to this shindig. Look at that woman's necklace! I bet there's more money round her neck than in the whole of Cornwall.'

'I remember,' said Nathan. 'That's only two weeks away now. Maybe that's what she does? Targets hotels that have special events that she knows will attract very rich people with very expensive jewellery.'

'She started working here just over a year ago, didn't she? She probably timed it so she was here for last year's shoot, so she could see how it went down. And then she's spent the whole year in between planning it, worming her way in so Robbins trusts her.' I turned my attention back to the phone and did a bit of Googling. 'Did you know Chanel surprised everyone and chose Manchester to unveil their latest collection a couple of years ago? The city was full of very rich fashionistas, there to see the show.'

'Does that coincide with her working at the Clockhouse?'

'I think so. And even if it doesn't, in a big city like Manchester there must be a ton of fancy events going on that would attract rich people and their jewellery...' I grinned at Nathan. 'I have to admit, I wouldn't cry too many tears over someone losing their valuables if they're booked in here to shoot grouse – I mean, we were only going to do clay-pigeon shooting, and I was still worried it might upset the wildlife. But if Kelly got wind of it somehow, and Marissa killed her...'

'But how?' Nathan sighed. 'We keep coming back to that, don't we?'

I glanced down at the phone in my hand as it vibrated. 'Ooh, you've got a message. Davey's sent you an email, apparently.' I went to open it, and then thought better of it, handing Nathan his phone back. 'Yeah, you should probably read it first...'

'Well, well, well,' said Nathan, reading the email.

'What is it?'

'It's very interesting...'

'Yes, but what does it say? Tell me!' I tried to grab the phone but he laughed and kept hold of it.

'Only if you promise to love, honour and obey me,' he said, and then he shrugged. 'Okay, maybe not *obey*, we did agree to leave that bit out...'

'Yes, yes, I'll love you and honour you, however I'm supposed to do that, I dunno. Now spill it, buster.'

'Okay, okay… So Davey looked into Kelly's family background, specifically her sister Claire. We'd heard Claire was a wrong 'un, yes? Well, she certainly *was* a wrong 'un, because she served two years of a three-year sentence for theft.'

'No! What kind of theft? And how didn't we know that?'

'It wasn't round here, it was in – wait for it – Manchester.'

'No!!'

'Yes. She was part of a gang who used to get all dressed up and sit in the bar of a fancy hotel, targeting lonely but wealthy businessmen staying on their own – usually businessmen wearing expensive watches. They had two ways of hitting them. Get the suckers to take them up to their rooms under the promise of "a good time", where they would wait for them to fall asleep or knock them out with Rohypnol and nick their valuables. Or if the target didn't fall for that, they'd pass their description on to a couple of thuggish male colleagues outside, who would lie in wait and relieve them of their Rolex at knifepoint.'

'Nice,' I said, grimacing.

'Yes. And guess which hotel she got caught at?'

'The Clockhouse.'

'Yes.'

'But Marissa can't have been part of the gang,' I said. 'She worked there.'

'The police thought there must be someone on the staff, passing on the descriptions of the wealthiest, single male guests,' Nathan explained. 'Maybe that was her. But the rest of the gang got caught and sent down, and Marissa, or Megan as she was at the time, carried on working there for another two months, before disappearing at the same time as that thirty-five grand's worth of jewellery.'

'Bloody hell…'

'Claire had been sent down before, a couple of years prior to that, for prostitution and drug offences. She served time in both instances at HMP Drake Hall. Which is in Eccleshall.'

'Isn't that where Marissa's fake previous address was?' I shook my head in amazement. 'Maybe that's where they met?'

'Maybe. Until we know Marissa's real name we won't know if she ever served time, but if she was operating in that part of the country and got caught, she'd probably end up at Drake Hall.'

'That other hotel she put down,' I said, 'that was quite a while ago, wasn't it? Nine or ten years ago. And then there's a gap. Maybe she was in prison during that gap.'

'That would make sense.'

'So – what do we think? Do we think Claire's in on whatever Marissa's planning here, and Kelly found out that way?'

'I don't know,' said Nathan. 'But looking at her recent behaviour, she seems to have gone straight. She never missed an appointment with her parole officer. She's now working full time at the Crowthorne Arms in Morwenstow, and she rents a house with her boyfriend in Stratton.'

'Hmm...' I felt a tug on the lead as Germaine tried to head even deeper onto the dark golf course. 'No, Germaine, come here!' I began to reel the lead in, but Germaine began to bark. I looked at Nathan. 'Why is she barking? She never barks – not like that, anyway – unless it's at that Golden Labrador down the road from us. Or at a person she doesn't know.'

'It's probably a fox or something,' said Nathan, but he could see I was concerned. We quietly followed the sound of Germaine barking until we could see her.

'Nothing there,' said Nathan. I shook my head.

'No, there's someone down there,' I said, pointing towards the river. Not that we could see it, but I knew it was in that direction. 'There's a faint glow, see? Someone's looking at their phone.'

'Stay here with Germaine,' said Nathan. He kissed me and then began to creep away towards the glow, where he was soon lost in the dark. I squatted down next to Germaine – with difficulty, in that dress – and soothed her with a stroke and a scratch around the ears, which she loves.

'Good girl, Germaine,' I said. 'Who's that down there, then?' I shivered, wishing I'd thought to put a cardigan on before we'd left the hotel, but really, what kind of knitwear goes with a long red Chinese-style fitted gown? I was the sort-of bride, I had appearances to keep up.

Nathan arrived back by my side after a couple of

minutes. 'Male, mid-thirties,' he said quietly. 'At least, I think so. I couldn't really see him, but I could hear him talking to someone.'

'Was it someone from the hotel?'

'No idea. He said, "There's someone out here walking their bloody dog—"'

'The cheek!' I put my hands over Germaine's ears. 'Don't listen, baby.'

'"—I'll have to come back later." Or something like that.' Nathan looked thoughtful. 'I don't know what all that was about, but it can't be good.'

'No... maybe we should call it in, get Uniform to come and have a look round?' I said. I yawned. 'I don't know, even with all this excitement I can hardly keep my eyes open.'

Nathan put his arm around me and we started to walk back to the hotel. 'It's been a busy day,' he said. 'I've emailed Davey back and copied in Sunil, and told them to pass all this on to DI Mackintosh. We've done enough of her job, she can take it from here.'

'We've done the donkey work and she'll get all the credit,' I grumbled, and Nathan laughed.

'You must be used to that. I always take the credit when you solve a case for me.'

'Yeah, but I don't mind when it's you.' I sighed. 'I used to think Di was alright when we were at Stockwell, a bit up herself maybe, but I knew what it was like, being a woman in a male-dominated environment. But she's not exactly covered herself in glory with this one, has she? She's followed reasonable lines of enquiry, it's true, and in her shoes I would've looked at Frankie Lewis and at Craig, but... it's like she doesn't want to admit she might be wrong until she's wrung out every possible drop of proof. There's nothing wrong with following multiple leads, is there?'

'She's not been down here long, though, has she?' said Nathan. 'I think she's making the same mistake I would've made, if a certain caterer hadn't pulled me up on it during my first Cornish murder investigation.'

'Which is?'

'As much as it shames me to admit it now, I probably heard the funny accent and thought you were all country bumpkins, and as a big city copper I knew better.'

'*We've* got funny accents?' I asked in mock outrage. 'Have you heard yourself speak?'

He laughed. 'Yeah yeah, I know. But it takes a while to get into the way you do things down here, especially coming from a city, so we should probably cut Mackintosh a bit of slack.'

'Yeah, you're right…'

We were back at the hotel car park by now. As we cut across the gravel Germaine suddenly decided to stop and do a number two. I groaned.

'It's alright, I've got a tissue,' said Nathan, because we are responsible dog owners and don't leave our doggy's doo-doos lying around where someone might tread on them. He bent down to pick it up, cursing the dog. I looked up as I heard a noise at the front entrance of the hotel.

'That's Marissa!' I said. I grabbed Nathan's arm and dragged him and the dog behind a parked car, where all three of us peered out to watch the hotel receptionist's actions.

There were three wide stone steps leading up to the entrance, which was a massive wooden door studded with black iron rivets, propped open to reveal clear glass inner doors. The wood looked mediaeval, but it wasn't; the earliest parts of the 'castle' only dated from the 1800s, with the wings housing the swimming pool and spa and the Art Deco bistro added much later, in the 1920s. On either side of the stone steps stood two massive carved urns, both planted up with a tall spiky plant in the middle, some colourful bedding plants around the edges, and trailing ivy drifting down towards the ground. As we watched, Marissa, silhouetted in the light from the open doorway, placed something in the right-hand urn. She took a phone from her jacket pocket and typed something in, looking around furtively before putting the phone away again. Then she headed inside.

'What the hell...?' I breathed. 'You don't think...?'

Nathan nodded. 'Oh yes,' he said. 'I think Marissa or Megan is up to her old tricks.'

Chapter Twenty-Two

We waited a few minutes before we made our way over to the entrance, to give Marissa time to get back behind the reception desk; we didn't want her knowing that we'd seen her, until we knew exactly what she'd been up to.

Nathan headed over to the urn and rummaged around in it carefully, holding the ivy out of the way with one hand. 'Look at this,' he said.

Tucked under the trailing plants was a plastic ziplock bag. Inside we could see various pieces of jewellery, gold and gemstones sparkling in the soft light coming from the hotel entrance.

'Bloody hell,' I said. 'She must be desperate, stealing from our lot. There ain't going to be thirty-five grand's worth of stuff in there.'

'No,' said Nathan. 'Can you hold this so I can take some photos?' I grimaced as he passed the tissue-wrapped dog poo he'd been holding awkwardly in his other hand to me, then snapped a few pictures of the bag in situ.

'What do we do? Are you leaving it there?' I asked. 'It's evidence. We probably shouldn't move it.'

'No,' said Nathan, 'but I don't want whoever that was on the course coming back and taking it.'

'You think that's who it was?'

'Yes. An accomplice. Someone who's parked out on the road somewhere and walked across the course, so they're not picked up on the CCTV camera on the drive.' He gestured to the CCTV camera above the entrance. 'And unless that camera has a very wide angle of vision, I don't think this urn would be covered by it. So he can walk straight up here in the dark and take whatever she's left, without being picked up by anything.'

'Except Germaine,' I said.

'Yes, except our good girl Germaine.' Germaine wagged her tail, hearing her name mentioned. 'That's why they're using the urn on this side, not the other one, because *that* one probably is covered by the camera.'

'So are we taking it?'

'Yes, we are. We might not have footage of her leaving the bag, but there'll be footage of her going outside, and footage of *us* coming back inside, carrying it.' Nathan grinned and carefully picked up the bag, holding it by the corner so as not to cover up any fingerprints Marissa may have left. 'And with the photos I've just taken, with all the timestamps matching the CCTV footage, not to mention her previous exploits and hopefully a few fingerprints on this, I think we're covered.'

'Hang on,' I said, moving the trailing ivy aside slightly and reaching into the plant pot. I dropped the stinky (and still slightly warm) bundle of tissue into the gap left by the bag of stolen jewellery and grinned at Nathan. 'In case her accomplice pops by. We wouldn't want him to go away empty handed, would we?'

We mounted the stairs to the front door, Nathan looking up at the camera and holding the bag aloft so it could be clearly seen.

'As long as she doesn't see that and delete the footage,' I said, but Nathan shook his head.

'There's no screen to watch the footage from at Reception,' said Nathan. 'And from what Robbins said earlier, she'd have to go into his office to tamper with it anyway. At this time of night there's still another receptionist on, isn't there? She'd have to wait until after midnight, when she's on her own.'

He tucked the bag behind his back as we walked past the desk, smiling and nodding hello to Marissa and her colleague. We headed into the function room, where the crowd had started to thin out a bit; it was still early, for a party, but it was a Sunday night and some people probably had work the next day.

'What now?' I said, taking a seat at an empty table.

'I'll send Mackintosh those photos and tell her she needs to get over here,' said Nathan. He put the bag on the table and covered it with a discarded napkin, then began tapping into his phone. 'I think we need to assume that Marissa has made a move early, stealing stuff from the guests here at the moment, because she's planning to have it away on her toes in the next couple of days.'

'You don't think she'll be tempted to wait for the shooting ball?' I asked. 'It's only a couple of weeks away. That was probably her original plan, and it's more likely to be a big payout for her.'

'She might, but I think if she *was* going to do that she wouldn't risk it all by stealing anything now. Robbins won't be able to ignore theft from his guests, especially after the murder, and the place will be crawling with police after this. And those wealthy guests she was planning to target might even cancel.' Nathan shook his head. 'I think she's worried that we're closing in on Kelly's murderer, so she needs to run now before we tie it to her.'

'And she doesn't want to leave empty-handed,' I said.

'Who's leaving empty-handed?' said Mum, popping up behind us.

'You are,' I said. 'That's if you still want to head home tonight, like you were hinting before? I know you prefer to be in your own bed. Although I forgot to book you a taxi, so it might not be possible.'

'Ooh no, I'm not leaving now,' she said. 'Not after all the excitement. Not now we're investigating.'

'Well, Shirley, we probably won't have any more investigating to do—' started Nathan, but Mum interrupted him.

'Oooh, does that mean you know who it is? Did we solve it?'

'No,' said Nathan. 'It means that now we've gathered some more evidence, we need to step aside and let DI Mackintosh do her job.'

'Pah,' said Mum. 'Not even married yet and you've already got boring.' She looked around. 'This lot are lightweights. Your friend Nina was looking for you, I think she's going home in a minute. Some nonsense about having to go to work tomorrow… Youngsters. Jocasta put her back out while we were dancing and *she's* still up for a good time, and she's in her seventies.'

'And retired, Mother,' I said. 'No work to get up for in the morning.'

Mum sniffed. 'Lightweights,' she said, and weaved across the dance floor to the bar. There weren't that many people still dancing and she really didn't need to weave, but that's what too much free booze will do to you.

Nathan grinned at me. 'I'm not boring already, am I?'

'I'm assuming you won't let me go and rugby tackle Marissa and force her to confess?'

'In that dress? Not a chance.'

'Dammit, you've got a point there. But I could nip upstairs and get changed—' But I didn't get to hear Nathan's thoughts on that plan, because Liz and Roger appeared in the doorway of the function room, looking upset. Roger spotted us and led his wife over.

'Mum! Are you alright? What's happened?' Nathan jumped to his feet and offered Liz his chair.

'Some thieving bastard's been in our room,' said Roger. Nathan and I exchanged looks.

'Oh no,' I said, carefully. 'What have they taken?'

'The necklace Nana left me,' said Liz, looking tearfully at Nathan. 'It's not even worth that much. But it means a lot to me.'

'Where had you left it?' asked Nathan. 'In the safe?'

'No, I just left it on the side in our room. I was going to wear it, but it's too long to go with this dress – it kept getting caught up in the lace.' Liz indicated the lace trim around the neckline of her dress. 'I can't believe someone would steal it.'

'Not just your necklace, either,' said Roger. 'We heard another guest – not one of our lot – telling the woman on Reception that she's been burgled, too.'

'Bugger,' I said, looking at Nathan. 'She must've known people would realise they'd had stuff stolen, but probably not so quickly. We need to stop her leaving.'

'Yeah, we do.' Nathan stood up and reached out a hand to help me get out of my seat – it was difficult to move easily in that dress, gorgeous as it was.

'Nathan? What's going on?' Liz looked at her son, then at me. 'This hasn't got something to do with that poor girl's death, has it?'

'That's what we're about to find out,' said Nathan. 'In the meantime…' He whipped the napkin off the bag of jewellery, like a stage magician revealing a concealed bunny or something. All it was missing was a *Ta da!* Liz gasped.

'There's my necklace!'

'Don't touch it for the moment, Mum,' said Nathan. 'And don't let anyone else know you've got it, either. It's evidence.' He covered the bag back up. 'Just sit here with Dad and wait until I come and get you.'

'Okay, love…' Liz and Roger looked bewildered, but also quite proud of their son. Nathan turned to me.

'Ready?'

'Born ready, babe.'

We headed into the reception area, where Marissa and the other receptionist were in discussion with the aggrieved guest Roger had mentioned.

'I'm so sorry, madam,' said the other receptionist. 'I'll call the police right now.'

'Are you sure it's missing?' asked Marissa. She was standing in front of the phone, and made no attempt to move out of her colleague's way. 'Could you have just misplaced it? If it was left in your room, it should be perfectly safe. Are you sure it hasn't fallen down the back of the dressing table, or something like that? It's easily done. It would be very embarrassing to call the police out and then find it.'

'But that other couple—' The other receptionist was looking at her in disbelief.

'I'm just saying, everyone's had a few drinks, and it's easy to misplace something.' Marissa held her ground. 'How could anyone get into the guest rooms?'

'Yes,' I said, standing next to the protesting guest. 'It's very easy to misplace something after a few drinks. You never know when it could end up in a plastic bag, tucked inside a plant pot, for example. Isn't that right, Marissa?'

'Or is it Megan?' asked Nathan, thoughtfully. 'Or Sharon, was it? I don't know, I doubt any of those is your real name, is it?'

'What are they talking about?' demanded the other receptionist. Marissa glared at me and Nathan.

'I have no idea,' she growled.

'No? Maybe your friend – the one prowling around the golf course, waiting for the signal to come and collect the swag – will be able to tell us your real name,' said Nathan.

'I'm not listening to this rubbish,' said Marissa, rattled. She reached under the desk and I felt Nathan tense – but she was just collecting her bag. She stormed out from the reception desk and headed for the door, but she was halted by the massive form of Davey Trelawney.

'In a hurry to get away, ain't you love?' he said. 'I thought you was on until the morning.'

'I need to leave,' she said, firmly. But her exit was further prevented by DI Mackintosh, who had been somewhat hidden from view by Davey's uniformed bulk.

'Harriet Riley—' she began. Nathan and I exchanged looks.

'Harriet Riley?' I said. Marissa's confidence immediately evaporated. 'Ah, *that's* your real name.' I sniffed. 'You don't look like a Harriet.'

'Harriet Riley,' repeated Mackintosh, ignoring me. 'You're under arrest for theft, identity theft, fraud, and the murder of Kelly Lawson.'

'I dunno about you, but I'd have led with that,' I said to Nathan, who chuckled.

'Anything you say will be taken down…' Mackintosh read Marissa – or Harriet – her rights, then Davey slapped the handcuffs on her and took her outside to a waiting police car. Mackintosh turned to us. 'Where's the stolen jewellery now?'

'My mum's looking after it,' said Nathan, and unexpectedly she laughed.

'Oh my God, you really do do things differently down here,' she said. 'I know all the guests will be keen to get their things back, but I need to take it in as evidence for now.'

'I know, I'll go and get it,' said Nathan, looking slightly surprised at her friendly demeanour. Mackintosh turned to me as he left.

'Nice work, Jodie,' she said. 'Bloody irritating, but nice work. I'd have got here in the end without you, though.'

'I don't doubt it for a minute,' I said, magnanimously. 'We only had a head start over you because we knew it wasn't Craig.'

'We have to pursue all leads,' she said, a tad defensively.

'Absolutely. We just knew it wasn't him.' I turned as Nathan brought the bag of jewellery in.

'Here you go.' He handed it over. 'Sorry, no gloves – didn't think I'd need them dressed in my wedding suit, and Jodie doesn't even have pockets…'

'No, I don't suppose she does,' said Mackintosh. 'Nice dress, by the way.'

'Thank you.' We followed her to the door. 'Can I ask? It's pretty obvious she's been targeting all these different hotels and nicking stuff, and that's what she was planning here, but have you definitively linked her to Kelly?'

Mackintosh smiled. 'You know I don't have to tell you that, don't you?'

'Yeah, but you know you want to. For old times' sake.'

Di Mackintosh laughed. 'You haven't changed. After PC Trelawney and DC Bakshi sent me their findings, we went to speak to Claire Lawson. She told us that she first met Harriet Riley at HMP Drake Hall. They went on to work together on a series of stings at the Clockhouse Hotel in Manchester, which I believe you'd already worked out.'

'Yes,' I said.

'Claire was arrested in connection with that, but Harriet managed to stay out of it. Claire decided after her second prison term that she was going straight, and she's stuck to it. It sounds like Claire was released from prison around the same time as Harriet was deciding where to go next – she needed to get away from Manchester, and Cornwall is a long way away from it. She looked Claire up and tried to persuade her to join in with her next scam, but Claire wanted nothing to do with it. Kelly was there when Harriet turned up at the pub where Claire works, and she witnessed an argument between the two women. Both Claire and Kelly were under the impression that Harriet had moved on somewhere else – they didn't realise she was working here. We think Kelly recognised Harriet when she was here on Friday night, and that's why she arranged to stay with her sister – to warn her that Harriet was still around.'

'So Marissa – I mean, Harriet – killed Kelly, to keep her quiet?' asked Nathan.

'That seems the most likely motive,' said Mackintosh. 'She probably thought that Claire and Kelly would grass her up and get her fired, and of course if she's been working here for a whole year with a plan to rob this fancy gala ball in a couple of weeks, she'd have wasted all that time for nothing.'

'That's what we thought,' I said. 'That she was planning to hit that ball and then disappear.'

'Yes. We'll know more once we've interviewed her, of course,' said Mackintosh. 'Anyway, enjoy the rest of your night. I'll keep you posted, DCI Withers.'

'Nathan.'

'Nathan. And I'm sure you'll keep Jodie posted…'

Chapter Twenty-Three

'And *then* of course she had to admit she was the one who killed Kelly, because we had her bang to rights.'

It was the Wednesday after our un-wedding, and I was standing in the graveyard of St Botolph's church talking to my dad. Mackintosh had been as good as her word and kept Nathan updated (even though he was officially off work for another couple of days), he'd kept *me* updated, and now I was passing it all on to Dad. I liked to think that he was looking down from wherever old coppers go, watching the goings-on on his old patch. I usually sat on the grass next to him, but not today; not in that outfit.

Harriet Riley, aka Marissa, aka Megan, aka who knew how many other names, had initially denied everything, but in the face of a growing mountain of evidence against her, she'd seen sense and come clean. Yes, she had targeted Kervoy Castle because of the shooting season ball, which attracted some very wealthy guests. She'd followed the same MO as before, working at the hotel for a year to gain the manager's trust and see how everything worked. The theft of an expensive watch not long after she'd started had potentially been a disaster, but she'd turned it to her benefit; not wanting the police to start poking around and looking too closely at members of staff in case they realised who she really was, she'd used the master key and gone through the staff lockers, hoping to find the thief herself. And she had. She'd then told Robbins that she'd seen Janette, the light-fingered housekeeper, put the watch in her locker, and persuaded him to confront her himself and smooth things over with the guest rather than call the police, as it wouldn't reflect well on the hotel if word of the theft got out. This had proved to Robbins that she was trustworthy, which made her real job – scoping out the hotel – much easier. She hadn't been behind the petty thefts, but once she'd become aware of them she'd taken advantage and used them to do a few dry runs; they'd allowed her to check out the hotel's security systems, and work out the best way to get the jewellery she was planning to steal off site, using the male accomplice we'd heard in the dark – who so far hadn't been tracked down, although DI Mackintosh was confident he would be. She'd realised that she'd been too quick to resign after her previous heists, which had of course thrown suspicion on her, so she'd needed to work out the most discreet way of relieving guests of their valuables and getting them away from the hotel without too much danger of it coming back to her. It had all been going to plan.

And then Kelly had turned up.

Harriet/Marissa hadn't been on duty when Kelly and her fellow waitresses had arrived, and the first that they'd seen of each other had been when 'Marissa' had come up to the room to tell Nathan and his stags to turn the music down. Harriet hadn't seen her properly; but Kelly had spotted the woman who had turned up at the Crowthorne Arms and had a massive argument with her sister. Claire had told Kelly exactly who she was, and warned her that she was trouble. Both sisters had thought Harriet had left the area after that, as neither of them had seen her again. Until that Friday night.

Already rattled, after the showdown with Frankie Kelly had texted her sister, asking to stay with her. She hadn't mentioned Harriet in the text, because she hadn't wanted to worry her sister until she knew that the receptionist was definitely who she suspected. The three waitresses had all left together, Kelly risking another look; and this time, Harriet had seen *her*, recognising her immediately as the resemblance between the two sisters was strong. No one knew for certain, but Mackintosh had postulated that Kelly had known full well that her 'missing' apron wasn't in Ben's room at all, but she'd made it up as an excuse to go back into the hotel on her own, one last time, to check out Harriet again before leaving.

Harriet had been unsure if Kelly had recognised her, but when the waitress had come back in for that last look, she'd known. And she'd realised that Kelly and Claire could potentially jeopardise her whole plan. Still, Kelly would've lived if Frankie Lewis hadn't been hanging around in the car park.

Harriet had begun her usual sweep of the hotel, deep in thought, and had come across the fire exit propped open. Through it, she'd heard the sound of the couple arguing. She'd watched as Kelly ran off into the night, leaving Frankie glaring after her. He'd shaken his head angrily and then gone back to his car. And Harriet had left the hotel and gone after Kelly.

Harriet Riley swore that she hadn't intended to kill the girl. She'd gone after her with the intention of getting her onside, pleading with her to keep her identity secret and not even tell Claire until after she'd hit the shooting ball and got away with her haul of jewellery. She even promised her a cut of the proceeds in return. But Kelly had refused, and had threatened to tell the police. She'd taken off her torturously high, spiky heels and threatened Harriet with them, telling her to stay away from her and her sister. Harriet had grabbed the heels from her and chased her across the grass, down towards the pond, where their argument had continued. And then suddenly, out of nowhere, Kelly had stopped shouting and staggered, clutching her head, closer and closer to the pond. Harriet had seized her chance and pushed her in, where Kelly had struggled weakly amongst the reeds. Harriet, shocked by her own actions, had clambered down the bank, slipped off her own shoes and waded into the water – but as she started to haul the unresisting girl back out, she stopped. If Kelly died, Harriet's problems went away. No one else knew who she really was. So instead of hauling her back onto the grass, where she might have recovered, Harriet had pushed her further out into the water, hoping that the police would assume she'd had a seizure or something – she hadn't spotted the golf ball, which had rolled down the bank and into the water.

'Don't forget to tell him about the shoes,' said Nathan, arriving next to me and taking my hand.

'Oh yeah, Dad – Harriet took the shoes because she knew her fingerprints would be on them,' I said. 'She went back to the hotel – only the golfers had already been back and shut the fire exit, so she had to go through the front door. She cleaned the fingerprints off the shoes and put them in Heidi's locker, because she knew Heidi never used it and she thought she could leave them there and then get rid of them when things had cooled down a bit.'

'And then she used the hotel washing machine to wash out her uniform trousers,' said Nathan. 'The pond water was filthy. There are spare bits of uniform kept in the staff room, for emergencies, so she borrowed another pair of trousers for the rest of her shift, and then put her clean but still damp ones on again before she left.'

'And she edited the CCTV footage of the front door,' I said. 'As we suspected, she knew where Robbins kept his passwords and she was able to delete those few seconds of herself entering the hotel from the recording.'

'She also used his other passwords to transfer some money from the hotel accounts to her own, just before we stopped her leaving,' said Nathan. 'She was determined not to leave empty-handed, but she knew it was too risky for her to stay until the ball.'

'*And* Di Mackintosh turned out to be alright in the end,' I said. 'She was just suffering from a bout of upcountryitis.'

Nathan laughed. 'Is that what I had when I first got here?'

'*Had?*'

'Cheeky.' He pulled me towards him and kissed me, before turning to my dad's grave. 'Now, I'm sorry Eddie, but your daughter and I have an appointment with the vicar. She's keeping everyone waiting.'

'I'm not late, am I?'

'No. But Craig did send me to say that he can't miss his flight home, and my dad keeps looking at his watch and muttering about our lunch reservation at the Falcon being at three…'

I laughed. 'Fair enough. Bye Dad, I love you.' And then my very-soon-to-be husband led me across the graveyard, to the church where our closest friends and family were waiting to hear us say, 'I do.'

Thanks and Acknowledgements

These get harder to write the longer the series goes on – not because I don't have anyone to thank, but because it's normally the same people every time, and I don't want to make this bit dry and boring. I always try to do something a bit different, so maybe I'll do this one in the form of a wedding speech…

Dear readers, we are gathered here today in the sight of HarperCollins, to celebrate the coming together of this writer and this book. Looking around the room, I recognise a lot of you from book one (thank you for coming!), as well as some new faces. I hope you've had a good time and you all stick around for the next book. You scrub up well, especially you, Carol. I LOVE that hat.

On to the thank yous. First off, thanks to the **Bovey Castle Hotel** for being the inspiration behind the setting for this book. What a beautiful venue. I love what they've done with the table settings. And if you haven't tried the canapés yet, well, too late, I've eaten them all. Stick around for the cake though, it's lush.

Next up, can I have a round of applause for the

bridesmaids, **Jade Bokhari, Carmen Radtke, Nina Kaye, Sandy Barker** and **Andie Newton** – don't they look beautiful? Although I think a couple of them might have had a bit too much to drink – someone get that bottle away from Andie before she starts dancing on the table... Anyway, the writer would like to thank the bridesmaids for always having her back, for being constantly available to chat, bitch, moan, celebrate and basically be the best friends an author could ever have, because without them she wouldn't even have written 'Chapter One', let alone said those two magical words every writer dreams of, 'The End'.

Next up, Maid of Honour **Lina Langlee** deserves a special mention because, without her ever-present gentle guidance and occasional tough agent love, the writer would've ended up at the wrong publisher, writing unconvincing science fiction or something. Thanks also go to the editorial celebrant, **Jennie Rothwell**, and **Arsalan Isa** and all the other altar boys at **One More Chapter**, for officiating and overseeing publication of this book. And of course we can't forget **Lucy Bennett** for dressing all the books so beautifully.

Let's also raise a glass to the writer's son, ring/tea bearer/brainstorming partner **Lucas Leitch**, and last but far from least her husband, **Dominic Leitch**, for sharing some of his golfing knowledge (and now she knows what goes on during his lads' only golfing weekends, she might have to tag along). I know the writer would want me to tell you just how much she loves you both and to thank you for your undying support, even in the light of last minute nerves and plot changes.

So, dear friends, please charge your glasses, coffee mugs or tea cups and join me in a toast to book eight and everyone involved in the making of it. I hope you'll agree it was a match made in Heaven. Or Cornwall, at least.

Jodie's Tried and Tested Recipes #8

The Chocolatiest Fudgiest Chocolate Fudge Cake In the World EVER*

When you think of wedding cakes, you'd normally think of something multi-tiered and elegant, covered in pure white icing and dotted with delicate sugar flowers. Maybe a few edible jewels, a bit of glitter, a few – I dunno – peacock feathers or something if you're having THAT kind of wedding (and why not? Your day, your way). Most bakers would go for a sturdy kind of cake, like a rich fruit cake, or maybe a simple sponge. But I'm not most bakers, or most brides, so of course I wanted a chocolate cake. And again, why not?

This is not, however, one of your simple chocolate sponges, the type many mums have found themselves knocking up half an hour before their child's birthday party because said child's useless father forgot to pick up the Disney Princess cake you'd ordered from Tesco. Or is that just me? Maybe it is. Anyway, THIS cake is rich, chocolatey, gooey, and moist (apologies if you don't like that word but come on, we're all adults and this is a cake we're talking about).

If you're looking for elegance, for a cake that you can decorate with the aforementioned sugar roses etcetera, then maybe skip this one because delicate is not a word to associate with this monster. It's chocolate fudge, for heaven's sake. When you decorate this, you have to go all in with the chocolate theme. Swirls of frosting, chocolate truffles, maybe mini macarons (chocolate-filled raspberry ones would be EPIC with this), Maltesers, M&Ms, shards of mint chocolate, those praline-filled chocolate seashells, segments of Terry's Chocolate Orange. I'm not suggesting that you use every single one of these, although that *would* make this the Liberace of all chocolate cakes. Basically, go big or go home.

*I think so, anyway. Other chocolate fudge cakes are available.

Follow me as I dive head first into chocolate fudge heaven… US measures/ingredients are in italics.

1. Preheat the oven to 180°C/*350°F* (160°C if you're using a fan oven, or gas mark 4) and butter and line the bottom of two 20cm/*8 inch* sandwich tins.

2. Mix together **400g/*2 2/3 cups* plain/*all-purpose* flour, 250g/*1 1/4 cups* caster/*superfine* sugar, 100g/*1/2 cup* light brown muscovado sugar** (you can just use 350g caster sugar, but the muscovado gives it a nice, subtle hint of caramel), **50g/*1/4 cup***

cocoa powder, 2 tsp baking powder, 1 tsp bicarb of soda/*baking soda*, and a pinch of salt in a large bowl.

3. In a separate bowl or jug, whisk together **3 large eggs**, **140ml/*1/2 cup* sour cream** and **1 tbsp vanilla extract**.

4. Melt **175g/*12 tbsp* butter** in a saucepan, let it cool and then beat in **125ml/*1/2 cup* corn/vegetable oil** (any type of vegetable or sunflower oil is fine, but I wouldn't use olive oil as it's got quite a strong taste). Add **300ml/*1 1/4 cups* chilled water** and beat until just combined. You can use an electric stand mixer for this, but equally you can do it by hand and give your arms a good work out!

5. Add the butter, oil and water mix into the dry ingredients and give it a good stir, before adding the egg and sour cream mixture. Beat everything together until blended, then pour into your lined cake tins. Bake in the oven for 50-55 minutes, or until you can stick a skewer into it and it comes out clean. No unbaked goo in the middle! Let the cakes cool in their tins for about 10-15 minutes, then turn them out and let them cool thoroughly on a rack. And now onto the fudge frosting – yum... Try not to eat it straight from the bowl

while you're waiting for the cakes to cool. Or is that just me again? Probably.

6. Melt **175g/*6 ounces* dark/*bittersweet* chocolate** – I know a lot of people don't like really dark chocolate, but it works best for frosting and we'll be adding a fair bit of sugar in a minute. Try to go for around 70% cocoa solids. Don't, however, go for one of the really high cocoa content ones – I tried one of those 100% cocoa chocolate bars recently and I can honestly say it's the only time in my entire life that I had to spit chocolate out. It was more bitter than a bride who's been jilted at the altar after the groom ran off with her best friend AND took her cat with them, AND then plastered photographs of themselves (and the cat) enjoying the honeymoon (planned and paid for by the jilted bride) all over Facebook. And that's pretty bitter. Where was I? Oh yeah, melt the chocolate (you can use the microwave or do it old school over a pan of boiling water) and let it cool slightly (but not harden up again, obvs).

7. In another bowl (you need a lot of bowls for this recipe, or you need to be on top of the washing up/have a willing partner who will do the dishes as you cook), beat **250g/*18 tbsp* butter** until it's soft and creamy, then beat in **275g/*2 3/4 cups* icing/*confectioners'* sugar**. Strictly speaking you

should sieve the icing sugar to avoid lumps in the frosting, but life is short so if you want to be a rebel and skip it, be my guest (I am a rebel and I have skipped it, and it was fine). Anywho, then add the melted chocolate along with **1 tbsp vanilla extract** and mix together until it's as smooth and glossy as the hair in the 'After' picture in a shampoo advert.

8. Sandwich your now-cool chocolate cakes together with the frosting, leaving enough to cover the top and sides. And then dump half a ton of chocolate truffles, berries or your indulgent decoration of choice on top of that. And then pose for a photo in front of it with your beloved (partner, child or pet, it doesn't matter) before tucking in.

Proper job!

Read on for an extract from
The Cornish Campsite Murder.

Chapter One

I've never liked festivals. Don't get me wrong: I love music, and I love going to concerts, but I love going home afterwards even more.

The worst thing about festivals is the weather. Festival weather is predictable only in its unpredictability. It's either scorching hot, turning festivalgoers lobster pink and making them half crazed with dehydration; or the heavens open and the showground turns into a recreation of that bit in *The Never Ending Story* where the pony gets sucked into a bog (a scene that traumatised a generation of young moviegoers), only with Crocs rather than ponies, and mud instead of quicksand.

The other worst thing about festivals is having to listen to a load of bands you have no desire to see, because you only came to watch the headliners and of course they're on so late in the day that it's almost next week. I was persuaded (against my better judgement, but I was young and naive) to go and see Radiohead at Glastonbury in 1997. And of course there was a monsoon and I ended up getting trench foot, but worse was to come. We sought refuge from the downpour in the World Music tent, which was probably a mistake. I discovered that I wasn't really interested in Portuguese folk singing, although I have to admit I *was* fascinated by one song, a traditional ballad sung by the women of a small fishing village on the beautiful Mediterranean coast while their fishermen husbands were out at sea. Entitled 'Meu Marido Continua Olhando Para os Banhistas de Topless (e não se Concentrando nos Peixes)', which roughly translated into 'My Husband Keeps Looking at Topless Sunbathers (and not Concentrating on the Fish)', there was much wailing and gnashing of teeth, and a fair bit of tearing at their hair, but it was at least authentic and strangely catchy. I found myself singing 'Ignore as vadias de seios nus e leve suas sardinhas para casa' ('Ignore the bare-breasted floozies, and bring your sardines home') for a whole week afterwards. It was certainly better than the display of Inuit throat singing, performed by a bohemian-looking woman from Huddersfield, that came on after.

But actually, no, the *worst* worst thing about festivals is being forced to camp in close proximity to other people. Some festivalgoers are determined to wring every last drop of fun out of the experience, and while in theory I think, *Good for them!*, in real life I hate them. *It's 5am, when do you plan on going to sleep? You don't? Okay, then. I'll stay awake all night too. Don't mind me, I'm sure...*

So it was with a feeling of mild surprise and a fair bit of trepidation that I found myself heading to Wave Masters, a music, arts and surfing festival just along the coast from my home town of Penstowan. Wave Masters had started back in the 90s, and had primarily been a surfing contest. It had proved popular enough to grow from a one-day event to two, then three; a market had sprung up, offering the surfers fast food, handcrafted jewellery and clothing. And then buskers had turned up and started playing, even though nobody had asked them to; which had led to stages being erected and bands being invited, until now it was really all about the music, and the surfing was almost a second thought. And once you'd driven through the gates onto the campsite and parked your car, entry wristband fastened on tightly, there was no way out of the maze of vehicles and tents until the end of the festival...

'Cheers, mate.' Nathan thanked the steward on the gate and turned the van in the direction the hi-vis-clad man had indicated. He looked over at me. 'You all right, babe?'

'Yeah,' I said, watching out of the window as we passed the labyrinth of parked cars, bewildered festivalgoers weaving in out of them. If they were bewildered now, wait until later. 'Yeah,' I said. 'Only I was looking forward to this weekend being just you and me, not – LOOK OUT FOR THAT PLONKER ON THE UNICYCLE!'

The plonker on the unicycle, who had veered dangerously in front of the van, steered himself out of our path, where he stopped and glared at me. And then I remembered that I had the window open, and that he'd heard me call him a plonker. I stood by it, though. Germaine, my inherited Pomeranian and quite possibly the cutest dog in the entire universe (although I might be biased), obviously agreed with me, as she barked loudly at him and then snuggled back down on the seat between me and Nathan.

'I saw him,' said Nathan, mildly. 'He's wearing a red and blue jester's hat. I could hardly miss him.'

'It's even got bells on,' I said, unable to contain my disgust, but the jester hat-wearing, unicycling plonker had moved on. That was the *other* worst worst thing about festivals. They were full of people wearing ridiculous trousers, waistcoats (over bare chests) and stupid hats, riding unicycles or walking on stilts, and if you were unwise enough to catch their eye and not look away again in time, chances were they would come and juggle at you.

Nathan laughed and changed gear, easing the van up an incline and parking it in a spot marked by a couple of flags. We got out and stood admiring the view as Germaine, never one to let an opportunity pass her by, relieved herself. We'd certainly got the best spot, perched on top of the hill which looked out across the whole festival site. From here we could see the campsite to the right, and to the left, the field that was normally home to a herd of sheep but now – for this weekend, anyway – housed the main stage, with a couple of other big tents scattered around. And in front of us, down the hill and across the sand dunes, the sea, sparkling turquoise in the sun. I couldn't deny it was beautiful. I sighed. Nathan reached over and pulled me in for a hug.

'Come on, it's not *that* bad,' he said. I snuggled into him.

'I know it's not, it's just that this weekend was supposed to be you and me in Paris, wasn't it? Not you and me running a food truck in a muddy field.' Germaine yapped and I corrected myself. 'All right, you, me and the dog running a food truck in a muddy field.'

'It was you that said yes,' he pointed out, and I couldn't deny that, either. A friend of mine from catering college, Sean, owned the food truck, and he made a good living going around all the festivals in the summer. He'd already booked his spot at Wave Masters, which was one of his best earners, when his daughter had told him she was getting married on a beach in Halkidiki and that she (of course) wanted him there. Sean had offered me the chance to take over the food truck for the weekend, in return for a share of the profits. I got the impression he'd already asked a few other people and was getting desperate. Besides, the extra money would be welcome.

'I know…'

'And it means you can keep an eye on Daisy and her mates,' he said. My almost sixteen-year-old daughter had been pestering me for the last six months about coming to the festival with her friend Jade, and Jade's older cousin Ellie. There was no way on God's green earth I was going to let them come without a responsible adult – Ellie had just turned eighteen and *seemed* sensible, but that was in front of the grown-ups; who knew what shenanigans she would encourage my sweet and innocent daughter to engage in once they were free of the parental shackles? But of course, the last thing any of them wanted was a responsible adult tagging along and cramping their style, plus all the responsible adults I knew could think of much better ways to spend the weekend than in a muddy field with a bunch of teenage girls.

'Yeah,' I said, knowing that he was right and that the weekend would probably be more fun than I was expecting, but slightly unwilling to let my grumpy mood go, 'if I ever manage to find her in amongst all this—'

'There you are!'

I turned to see Daisy standing behind me. Honestly, was *no one* going to let me carry on being moody?

'Where have you been? We got here ages ago.'

'We had to pick up some stock before we left,' I said. 'Where are you camped?'

'Down there,' said Daisy vaguely, waving her arm over at the campsite, which was already starting to resemble a Brazilian favela constructed of brightly coloured but poorly erected tents. A few campers swayed in amongst them, clutching bottles. I narrowed my eyes. There was already someone juggling.

'Rather you than me. We'll be all nice and cosy in the

truck,' I said, although I actually had a few reservations about that.

'You wouldn't catch me dead sleeping in that,' she said firmly.

'What's the matter with it?'

Daisy looked at me like I was a bit simple. 'Mum, it's called Pie Hard. It's got pictures of pies painted all over it.'

'And? We're selling pies, what should it have painted all over it? Noodles? Hot dogs?'

'Now you're just being silly,' said Daisy. 'I'll stick with Jade and Ellie in the tent, thank you very much.'

'All right,' I said. 'But no bringing boys back to the tent.'

Daisy rolled her eyes. 'Not much likelihood of that happening. Ellie prefers girls and Jade's asexual, although her mum reckons she's going through a phase and she'll change her mind when she meets the right bloke. But if you're straight, no one ever says it's just a phase you're going through, do they?' She had a point.

'No, that's true,' I said. 'Anyway, if you do change your mind and you want to sleep here instead, there's room for you – all of you.' Nathan cleared his throat and looked at me with an alarmed expression. I put up a placatory hand. 'Not inside the truck, obviously. But we've got an awning we can put up next to it. If there's heavy rain, or you're just scared…'

'Why would I be scared?'

'You never know. I mean, you can take the dog with you for protection if you like.' Daisy snorted. 'Okay, she's not much of a guard dog. But there are some weird people around...'

'Cooee!' We all whirled round to see my mum standing behind us.

'I see what you mean,' muttered Daisy.

'This is exciting, innit? I never been to a festival before. Not one like this, I mean. I've been to the harvest festival at the church—'

'I think that might be a bit different, Shirley,' said Nathan. 'Did you find your tent?'

'Jocasta says it's a yurt,' said Mum.

'She does, does she?' I said. I wasn't entirely sure I approved of Mum's new friend, who had moved to Penstowan almost a year ago. She was a retired lawyer who had left London to 'find herself', a process which seemed to involve crystals, scarves and metre upon metre of tie-dyed cheesecloth. She'd also found my mum, who had taken her under her wing and introduced her to the regulars at the Wednesday coffee morning (ten till twelve, Penstowan Methodist church hall and community centre, entry fee of £2, which entitled you to one cup of tea or instant coffee and two biscuits). In return Jocasta had introduced Mum to reiki and CBD oil. 'And where is Jocasta? Off scoring some patchouli?' Daisy and Nathan both snorted, but Mum either ignored the jibe or didn't hear it.

'She's setting up her foot massage stall,' she said. I shuddered. Having been in a tent full of fellow trench foot sufferers all those years ago at Glastonbury, the last thing I'd be doing at a festival would be going anywhere near people's toes. Mum noticed my look of disgust. 'Jodie, love, you're so narrow-minded.'

'I am NOT narrow-minded!' I spluttered, mildly outraged.

'Yes you are. You should let Jocasta have a go at your feet. I feel twenty years younger since I let her loose on my bunions,' said Mum. She sighed, and her face took on a dreamy expression. 'I never realised another woman's touch could bring me such relief,' she said. Nathan choked back a laugh, while I snorted like a hysterical pig.

'Is there something you want to tell us, Nana?' asked Daisy, completely straight-faced. 'I promise we won't judge you.'

But my elderly mother missed her chance to come out and was forced to stay in the closet (or the yurt), as we were interrupted by one of the festival marshals coming to check that we were set up okay. Mum tottered off to the glamping area, which was set back from the rest of the festival, away from us workers and plebs. Daisy wandered back to the rather less salubrious tent where Jade and Ellie were waiting, Germaine trotting beside her, sniffing at all the exciting smells coming from all the exciting people, her little doggy nostrils flaring as she passed a group of festivalgoers smoking suspiciously scented cigarettes.

The festival was very proud of its green credentials. There were solar panels and wind turbines all around the site, although with the great British summertime being as unpredictable as it was, I was betting there were probably some back-up generators hidden away under the main stage just in case. Here in the food stall area, a dedicated row of solar panels had been erected, along with a complex array of tubes which piped clean water to each cooking site; a godsend, as it meant we didn't have to keep the engine or a petrol-powered generator running to keep the fridge on, or rely on bottled water. There were three food trucks, including ours, and four or five stalls were also being set up to serve food. It looked like festivalgoers would have plenty of choice. As well as our pies and pasties, one of the trucks would be serving burgers and hotdogs, while the other dished up organic ice cream and homemade fruity ice lollies. I already had my eye on the Cornish clotted cream vanilla and strawberry sundae. It was too early to tell yet what food the stalls would be selling – they were still setting up – but one of them had already started cooking, and the smell of cumin, coriander, onion and garlic wafted across to us. Oh dear. It was still fairly early in the day and I was already feeling hungry. Good job I'd given up diets years ago.

The rest of the morning (not that there was much of it left by now) flew by as we set to work. I was used to working with Nathan, of course, but not in a kitchen; I'd helped him (or 'stuck my nose in', as some people might uncharitably – and more accurately – call it) with several murder investigations since moving back to Cornwall. I'd even been given a trial as an auxiliary detective a year earlier, as I'd served as a sergeant in the Metropolitan Police for almost twenty years, and I wasn't exactly an amateur. That had been a weird but ultimately very useful experience. Weird because Nathan, the love of my life (after Daisy), had been my boss, which was difficult for both of us; and useful, because it had confirmed in my own mind that I had been absolutely right to leave the police force in the first place. Daisy had begged me to quit after a nasty terrorist incident when she was ten, and I'd remembered how I used to worry about my dad when I was her age. Eddie Parker had been Chief Inspector of the police at Penstowan, which in those days had been a pretty sleepy place with very little serious crime. My own daughter had had far more to worry about than I had, so how could I put her through that? She'd been so relieved when I quit, and so angry with me when I'd put myself in harm's way again by rejoining. I'd handed my notice in at the end of the trial period, and I'd kept my word and not done any investigating since. Admittedly it helped that there had only been two suspicious deaths since then, and both guilty parties had done such a lousy job of covering their tracks that they were practically wandering around with flashing neon signs above their heads saying 'I DID IT!' I'd let Nathan handle them on his own.

And now he was helping me in the kitchen, or rather the tiny work area of the truck. We were cooking with gas (literally, rather than motivationally), so after hauling the heavy gas bottle into place I turned on the oven; Sean had pre-made all the pies, which were now residing in the fridge, and all we had to do was cook them.

Available now in paperback, ebook and audio!

Have you read the rest of the
Nosey Parker series?

Still spinning from the hustle and bustle of city life, Jodie 'Nosey' Parker, is glad to be back in the Cornish village she calls home. But with a missing bride on her hands, murder and mayhem lurks around every corner…

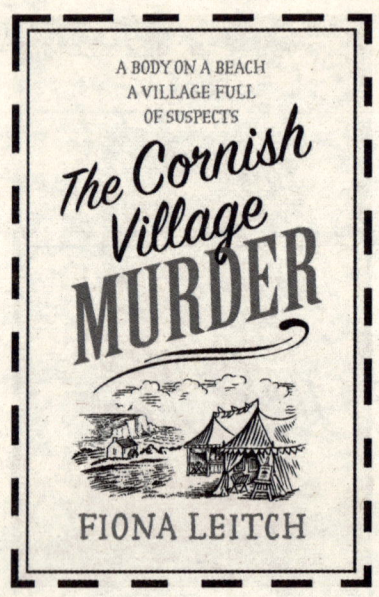

When a body turned up at her last catering gig it certainly put people off the hors d'oeuvres. With a reputation to salvage, Jodie's determined that her next job for the village's festival will go off without a hitch.

But when chaos breaks out, Jodie Parker somehow always finds herself caught up in the picture…

Can she find the killer before the village faces another brush with death?

A film company is coming to the Cornish village of Penstowan, and the whole community turn up to be cast as extras, even Jodie 'Nosey' Parker.

But right on cue, the company's caterer is sabotaged and Jodie must step up. It soon becomes clear that someone is out to spoil the filming… With actors behaving out of character and the house literally being brought down, breaking a leg is the least of their worries.

Can Jodie save the day once again, or will it be their final curtain call?

A PINCH OF PARANOIA

It's three days before Christmas, and detective-turned-chef Jodie 'Nosey' Parker is drafted in to cater an event run by a notorious millionaire at a 13th-century abbey.

A DASH OF DECEPTION

Things get more complicated when a snowstorm descends, stranding them all…

A MURDER UNDER THE MISTLETOE

Secrets mull in every corner – can Jodie solve the crime before the killer strikes again?

When 'The Best of British Baking Roadshow' rolls into town and sets up camp in the grounds of Boskern House, former police officer Jodie 'Nosey' Parker finds herself competing to represent Cornwall in the grand final.

But with a fellow contestant who will stop at nothing to win, Jodie discovers that the roadshow doesn't just have the ingredients for the perfect showstopper cake, but also for the perfect murder…

Can Jodie expose the culprit? Or will the murderer become the real showstopper?

A Siren's call… to murder

While tourists and locals alike are falling under the spell of the annual mermaid festival with its captivating legends of Sirens luring fishermen to their deaths, Jodie and Nathan fear they may have found themselves in the middle of a very real – and very dangerous – turf war.

As the casualties start to stack up, they must face the likelihood that something sinister has been going on under their noses for some time…

A campfire gathering. A circle of suspects.

Just along the coast from Penstowan, the local festival has filled the area. Former Met police officer Jodie 'Nosey' Parker has agreed to step in and help run the Pie Hard food truck, along with her reluctant fiancé, DCI Nathan Withers.

As they prepare for a weekend of camping, Jodie hadn't bargained on witnessing a fight between members of the lead band. But when the body of one of the band members is found not far from the campsite, Jodie finds it hard to believe it was an accident. Especially when the other members had so much to gain…

ONE MORE CHAPTER

YOUR NUMBER ONE STOP FOR PAGETURNING BOOKS

The author and One More Chapter would like to thank everyone who contributed to the publication of this story...

Analytics
James Brackin
Abigail Fryer

Audio
Fionnuala Barrett
Ciara Briggs

Contracts
Laura Amos
Laura Evans

Design
Lucy Bennett
Fiona Greenway
Liane Payne
Dean Russell

Digital Sales
Laura Daley
Lydia Grainge
Hannah Lismore

eCommerce
Laura Carpenter
Madeline ODonovan
Charlotte Stevens
Christina Storey
Jo Surman
Rachel Ward

Editorial
Kara Daniel
Simon Fox
Charlotte Ledger
Ajebowale Roberts
Jennie Rothwell
Caroline Scott-Bowden
Helen Williams

Harper360
Jennifer Dee
Emily Gerbner
Ariana Juarez
Jean Marie Kelly
emma sullivan
Sophia Wilhelm

International Sales
Peter Borcsok
Ruth Burrow
Colleen Simpson
Ben Wright

Inventory
Sarah Callaghan
Kirsty Norman

Marketing & Publicity
Chloe Cummings
Grace Edwards
Emma Petfield

Operations
Melissa Okusanya
Hannah Stamp

Production
Denis Manson
Simon Moore
Francesca Tuzzeo

Rights
Helena Font Brillas
Ashton Mucha
Zoe Shine
Aisling Smyth
Lucy Vanderbilt

Trade Marketing
Ben Hurd
Eleanor Slater

The HarperCollins Distribution Team

The HarperCollins Finance & Royalties Team

The HarperCollins Legal Team

The HarperCollins Technology Team

UK Sales
Isabel Coburn
Jay Cochrane
Sabina Lewis
Holly Martin
Harriet Williams
Leah Woods

And every other essential link in the chain from delivery drivers to booksellers to librarians and beyond!

ONE MORE CHAPTER

YOUR NUMBER ONE STOP FOR PAGETURNING BOOKS

One More Chapter is an award-winning global division of HarperCollins.

Subscribe to our newsletter to get our latest eBook deals and stay up to date with all our new releases!

signup.harpercollins.co.uk/join/signup-omc

Meet the team at
www.onemorechapter.com

Follow us!

 @OneMoreChapter_
 @onemorechapterhc
 @onemorechapterhc
 @onemorechapterhc

Do you write unputdownable fiction?
We love to hear from new voices.
Find out how to submit your novel at
www.onemorechapter.com/submissions